"WHO IS THIS JOHN CHRISTMAS?"

The men looked askance at Pensteven when he asked the question, and Vince Carter spoke up, with a jeering voice: "John Christmas is along at the end of the year. If you wanta find him, you better go there. You might find him quicker than that, if you got the right kind of nose. But your nose don't look none too good to me."

"I don't like that way of speaking," Pensteven answered.

As he spoke, he stepped aside from the furious blow Vince Carter launched at his head, and brought his fist up under Carter's jaw . . .

Carter fell in a heap.

"And now?" said Bob Pensteven, "you were talking about John Christmas?"

Now the town of Markham knew something of Pensteven, though he introduced himself as John Stranger. And if Stranger couldn't find out where Christmas was, maybe Christmas would want to come to him . . .

Warner Books

By Max Brand

Man From Savage Creek
Trouble Trail
Rustlers of Beacon Creek
Flaming Irons
The Gambler
The Guns of Dorking Hollow
The Gentle Gunman
Dan Barry's Daughter
The Stranger
Mystery Ranch
Frontier Feud
The Garden of Eden
Cheyenne Gold
Golden Lightning
Lucky Larribee
Border Guns
Mighty Lobo
Torture Trail
Tamer of the Wild
The Long Chase
Devil Horse
The White Wolf
Drifter's Vengeance
Trailin'
Gunman's Gold
Timbal Gulch Trail
Seventh Man
Speedy

Galloping Broncos
Fire Brain
The Big Trail
The White Cheyenne
Trail Partners
Outlaw Breed
The Smiling Desperado
The Invisible Outlaw
Silvertip's Strike
Silvertip's Chase
Silvertip
The Sheriff Rides
Valley Vultures
Marbleface
The Return of the Rancher
Mountain Riders
Slow Joe
Happy Jack
Brothers on the Trail
The Happy Valley
The King Bird Rides
The Long Chance
Mistral
Smiling Charlie
The Rancher's Revenge
The Dude
Silvertip's Roundup

MAX BRAND

THE INVISIBLE OUTLAW

WARNER BOOKS

A Warner Communications Company

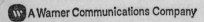

Chapter 1

They were talking about John Christmas in the Elbow Room, which was the best saloon in the town of Markham. It wasn't strange that the talk was about John Christmas, because in those days, wherever three men got together in any part of the West, their talk, almost inevitably, turned on the great bandit and his ways. People afterward remembered that John Christmas was the subject of conversation on this day, when Pensteven first appeared, because everything connected with that first appearance stood out in the minds of beholders as a bright light against darkness.

Someone said: "Christmas shot up Parkerville last Friday."

"Friday or any day is shooting time for him," said the bartender. "He carries his Christmas tree with him, what I mean."

Pensteven spoke for the first time, then. He had been standing very quietly at the end of the bar. He was a big fellow, with a dark, strong face that was spoiled, as it were, by a continual and almost stupid expression of good nature. His eyes were as soft as the eyes of a girl sixteen.

Now he said in his quiet, apologetic way: "I say, who is this John Christmas?"

The men looked askance at him. His accent was not that of the range.

"He says, who is this John Christmas," the bartender repeated to the crowd, without looking at Pensteven.

It appeared, at once, that Pensteven was to be hazed a little, and Vince Carter took the lead in the badgering, for

7

it was he who now spoke up. Vince was a pretty good fellow, but he was so large and powerful that he was always feeling the excess of his own strength, and looking for some means of expending it. When he walked, the bulge of muscles about his shoulders kept his arms swaying well out from his sides. When he turned his head, he turned his body as well, as though the massed and corded strength of his neck bound head and shoulders too stiffly together.

Now Vince Carter spoke up, with a cheering voice: "John Christmas is along at the end of the year. If you wanta find him, you better go there."

Pensteven said nothing in reply. The gentleness in his expression had not varied, but now the others viewed him more and more askance. It was true that Vince Carter's remark had not been downright insulting, but it was the sort of thing that a man of the right spirit follows up. Perhaps the stranger was not quite a man?

Then Vince Carter spoke again, for he felt that the crowd would be with him if he persecuted the tall stranger. Vince often wanted to make trouble, but he seldom found anyone his size. Even though this stranger was not half so formidable in bulk as he, he was fully as tall.

"If you wanta find Christmas, you follow your nose to the end of the year, and there you'll be pretty sure to find him," said Vince. "You might find him quicker than that, if you got the right kind of a nose. But your nose don't look none too good to me."

It was far too much to say. Everyone realized that but, after all, there is a natural feeling against strangers, particularly among uneducated men. There was not a fellow in that barroom who would have failed to give Pensteven a hand on the trail or in any sort of need; but, on the other hand, there was hardly a man of the lot who failed to take pleasure in the present episode.

Pensteven turned about, his face as bland as ever, but he said: "I don't like that way of speaking."

Vince Carter blinked. He could not believe his ears. Then he brushed aside the intervening forms and stood close beside the stranger.

"What's your name?" Carter demanded.

"My name is too good to be thrown away," said Pensteven.

Carter blinked again. Once more he could not believe his eyes, but a wave of joy welled up in him as he made sure that there was nerve in the stranger to stand up to him.

"You mean," said Carter, very carefully, "that you wouldn't be wasting your name on me, eh? I ain't good enough. You wouldn't be casting your pearls before swine, like they say. Is that it?"

Pensteven had a habit, in a crisis, of raising his left hand and running the finger tips delicately down the part in his hair. This he did now and smiled gently on Vince Carter.

"That's exactly what I mean," said he.

"Well," declared Vince Carter with an oath, "I'm gonna change your mind for you."

"Go outside, fellers!" yelled the bartender, determined to have no fracas in the saloon.

Bob Pensteven said: "It's hardly worth while. This won't take long."

As he spoke, he stepped aside from the furious blow that Vince Carter launched at his head—stepped aside and a little back, and brought up his fist under Carter's jaw. It snapped the bulky head back. Under the jaw appeared a dusky streak that looked like red paint, and the crowd gasped.

Pensteven, they noted, did not follow up his advantage. He stood with his right hand resting on the upper rail of the bar, but his expression was no longer so boyishly pleasant. Rather, it was one of grave and detached attention, as though he were looking at a fight fought by other men.

As for Vince Carter, he was totally bewildered. He could not believe that a mere empty hand had done this to him, and he presently gasped out: "He slammed me with something, the thug."

"He slammed you with his five fingers," said a cowpuncher. "There ain't anything crooked, Vince. Go right on in."

Vince was willing enough. As his brain cleared and he realized again the slightness of the stranger, he gathered himself for a final rush, but this time he abandoned attempts to box and pushed in for a wrestling hold.

Bob Pensteven regarded the coming bulk for an instant, then made a half step to meet him. He had used his right before. Now he used his left and the twin brother of the former punch floated up between the big hands of Vince Carter and lodged under the opposite side of his jaw.

Vince walked backward on his heels until his wide, thick shoulders struck the wall. There he paused with an involuntary grunt.

"I don't want to hurt you," said Pensteven. "I just want you to answer a question decently instead of slanging me."

"I'll see you damned sideways and endways," said Vince Carter. "I'm gonna knock your face in on the floor, young feller."

He came in a third time, but more warily. He tried to box, but Pensteven carried a pocketful of thunderbolts, and he exploded a pair of these against the face of Carter. Poor Vince began to stream blood, but he gained through this punishment what he wanted. He came in close enough to get a wrestling hold on the stranger.

The bystanders sighed with relief. It had looked, for the moment, as though their champion was about to be soundly thrashed. However, now that he had the other inside his grasp, the story was bound to be different.

"Don't drip blood all over my coat," they heard Pensteven say.

Then they saw that the head of Vince Carter was not, in fact, dripping its blood upon the clothes of the stranger. Instead, his head was held high and inclining backward, an odd angle for a man who knows how to go about a wrestling bout!

Next, the bystanders discovered that it was an involuntary position for Carter. The stranger, they now saw, had whipped his right hand behind the shoulder of Carter and over that shoulder so that his fingers, like a claw of iron, were hooked over the jawbone of Vince. That leverage worked the head of Vince far back.

He tried to brush the body of the stranger with his thick arms, but he did not succeed. He freed his right hand and used it as a club to smash into the face of Pensteven, but the latter struck the knees of Carter on the inside with his own. Carter fell in a heap.

The stranger rested on one knee beside him. He held the right hand of Vince in both his own hands. The elbow of Carter was upon the floor, and with a slight turning movement Pensteven promised to burst the shoulder joint of the fallen man.

"I was asking about John Christmas," said Pensteven, "and you were saying—"

"Lemme up," said Vince Carter. "I'm gonna break you in two."

"You were saying something about John Christmas?" went on Pensteven.

A groan burst from the lips of Carter.

"You're smashing my shoulder! Stop him, somebody. He's ruining me!"

Tom Randal yelled: "Leave Carter be, stranger! He's down, leave him be!"

Tom Randal came stamping across the floor, but Pensteven looked up to him with gravely considering eyes.

"Don't disturb us, please," was all he said.

But Tom came to a halt. He began to finger a gun in the holster at his right thigh, but he did not draw.

"And now?" said Bob Pensteven, "you were talking about John Christmas?"

He put on more pressure.

"Damn you!" shouted Carter. "Christmas—I dunno where he is. I never seen him. I dunno. Leave go of my hand!"

Pensteven stood up and dusted the knee that had touched the floor; he stood looking down at the blood that had coated his right hand, across the fingers and the palm. Carter, reeling to his feet, reached for a gun, found that he had none and rushed out of the Elbow Room.

Pensteven went to a tap at the corner of the room, washed his hands, dried them with a handkerchief that he pulled out of his shirt breast pocket, and went back to the bar. He had been drinking beer, and now he took a sip from the glass.

"Why did you do that to Carter?" asked the bartender, who was small, Irish, and a tiger.

"Because he wanted to find out what was inside me besides stuffing," said Pensteven. "Also, because I wanted to introduce myself to Markham and the range around it."

11

Chapter 2

Smiles are denials, in a sense. And as Pensteven went on talking, saying more amazing things than ever had been heard before in the Elbow Room, that palace and natural home of wild stories, he continued to smile as he talked, so that one might say that he was simply entertaining the crowd.

The bartender made the leading remarks. "Well, I guess you've showed us that you're a pretty slick fighting man, stranger," he ventured.

"Yes, I know how to fight," said Pensteven gently.

A little thrill ran through the crowd that heard this remark. Good fighting men never boast. Never! That is to say, when they are in possession of their sober senses.

And this fellow was admitting that he was very good, indeed. The eyes of Jerry, the bartender, squinted so hard that they almost disappeared.

"I can't help noticing, stranger," he observed, "that you smile when you say that."

Pensteven sipped his beer and still smiled.

Jerry, incredulous of the boast despite what he had seen, continued: "Take you with your fists, ain't it too bad that you don't go into the prize ring, eh? Lots of easy money to be picked up, one way or another, in the ring!"

"I could make a good deal of money, perhaps," replied Pensteven. "But I'd have to take some thrashings, sooner or later. And I don't like to be hurt. Everyone can't be champion of the world at the same time."

"I thought maybe you was champion of the world," observed Jerry.

"No, you didn't think that," said the amazing Pensteven. "You are simply trying to draw me out and make a fool of me."

Jerry opened his bright, savage little eyes. "It'd be pretty hard to make a fool out of you, wouldn't it, stranger?" said he.

"You're wasting your time when you talk like that," said Pensteven. "I don't want to make trouble and you're heading yourself straight for a fight. Don't do it, bartender."

Still smiling, he spoke, still gently, kindly, considerately.

Jerry shook his head, like a dog coming out of water.

"There's other ways of fighting than with fists," he remarked.

"You mean knives and clubs and guns?" suggested Pensteven.

"Why, for a stranger," said Jerry, sneering, "you're a real mind reader. But maybe you're just as good with a gun as you are with your fists?"

"It depends on what sort of a gun you're speaking of," said Pensteven. "With a rifle I'm only fairly well trained. With a shotgun I'm a good deal better, though I've met a great many duck hunters who could give me cards and spades, really."

"You sure surprise me by saying that," said Jerry sarcastically.

The rest of the crowd listened, mute with interest. This quiet man was listing down his own qualities as though he were a steer, an animal to be sold in a market!

"But with a revolver," concluded the stranger, "I'm an expert."

He sipped his beer, and, while the eyes of Pensteven were down, Jerry rolled his eyes like a wounded bull. He might have been groaning, judging by his expression. His lips were parted, but he made no sound whatsoever.

At last Jerry was able to say: "I guess you're one of the best in the world, eh?"

"Yes," said Pensteven, "I dare say that I am. One of the very best."

"I'm mighty glad to know it," pursued Jerry. "Because I've heard a lot about the dead-shot fellows with a revolver, but I never seen one in all my born days. I mean, the kind of fellows that stick six apples on six barbs of a wire fence; then trot a horse by, twenty-five yards away, and knock the six apples right off the barbs. That's one of the fool stories I've heard. But to a real, great, world expert like you, stranger, I reckon that a thing like that wouldn't be no trouble at all."

"No, not the least," was the answer.

Jerry grasped the edge of the bar with both hands, and pinched it hard. His face was red and swollen. His stertorous breathing was audible up and down the line of curious listeners, all with incredulous smiles frozen on their faces as they heard Pensteven boast.

"Brother, I wouldn't wanta put nothing in your way of showing what you can do with a gun," said Jerry. "Because a feller like you, that's a dead shot, and all of that, it's better to have his talents aired on six apples than on six he-men, ain't it?"

"That's exactly my idea," said Pensteven. "I know that on the range one generally has to fight one's way. If I show that I can take care of myself, I hope that I won't have any serious trouble with other people."

"That's your hope, is it?" asked Jerry, gasping out the words.

"Yes, that's my hope," said the genially smiling Pensteven.

"Stranger," groaned the choking voice of Jerry, "I got six apples here; and there's a barbed-wire fence across the street, and there's a lot of hosses strung up and hitched to the rack, outside of my place. Not that I would wanta bother you none, but just as you say, it might be a considerable saving, if you was to step out and slam them six apples in the eye, while your hoss was moving past. I reckon that we wouldn't insist on the hoss trotting, neither. Just moving along at a walk would be good enough for us. We're modest. We don't do nothing special in the way of shooting. If you want some guns, maybe I could lend you some?"

He reached beneath the bar as he spoke, and there was a red devil in Jerry's eye.

But from beneath the coat of Pensteven appeared two revolvers, the muzzles of which pointed toward Jerry. Then he saw that the stranger did not appear to be looking at him at all, but down at the guns, examining them. Jerry abandoned the unseen weapon which he had snatched up. Instantly the muzzles of the two Colts turned down toward the floor, and it occurred to Jerry that this had not been an accident. He had, in fact, been covered by as lightning a draw as he had ever, in his wildest dreams, dreamed of!

He saw, furthermore, that the sights were filed from the two weapons. He looked closer and saw that the triggers were also gone. These weapons could only be fired by fanning the hammers.

"The guns seem to be in good order," said Pensteven. "If you'll simply put the apples on the fence I'll—"

"Listen," said the bartender, "what did you do to those guns?"

They had suddenly disappeared; Jerry's keen eyes actually had not followed the definite course of their removal.

"That is sleight of hand," said this astonishingly frank fellow. "I worked for years on sleight of hand—all sorts of objects; palming, finger exercises, all that sort of thing, before I began to handle a revolver. A loaded revolver is not entirely safe to play with. I had to make sure before I began. Even now, I always have an empty chamber under the hammer. That gives me only five shots to each gun. However, it's much safer, and you'll agree with me that safety is the important thing. But about the handling of revolvers, of course, one knows that in a gun fight the draw may be the most important feature. So I had to learn to get out the weapons with the greatest possible expedition."

Jerry, staring, now picked six apples out of a half-filled box and, finally silenced, he led the way before the stranger and the rest of the crowd from the cool dimness of the Elbow Room to the brilliant sun and heat of the open.

He crossed the road, and stuck the six apples on six barbs, close together. They were little yellow ones and there was only an inch or so between them. That would make the shooting necessarily much faster.

"You can pick your own hoss," said Jerry hoarsely, and he waved toward the line of animals at the rack.

"I know nothing about horses," said the stranger. "Will you tell me which is the gentlest and steadiest of this lot?"

"You don't konw nothing about hosses?" echoed Jerry. "Well, stranger, I dunno that I could tell you anything

15

about anything. I ain't that bright, but if I was you, I'd try that one-eyed bay gelding yonder. He stands like he didn't need tying."

"All right," said Pensteven. "I'll try the bay gelding. I don't think you're tricking me, bartender."

He looked steadily at Jerry, though he still smiled. In spite of the smile, Jerry stiffened a little, as he said: "If you got any doubts about the bay gelding, take the gray mare alongside, there."

Pensteven nodded, mounted the gray mare, and rode her once or twice up and down the road, first at a walk, then at a trot, then at a rolling canter.

As she was cantering, quite unexpectedly, he dropped the reins, whipped out both guns, and sent a brief burst of bullets at the apples. He fired as rapidly as one could count. When he had ended, only one apple remained, and this, hanging by a shred of skin, now dropped to the ground.

Pensteven brought the mare back and tied her to the hitching rack. He reloaded six bullets, five into one gun, and one into the other.

In the meantime, the entire crowd had flocked to the fence, and was looking down at the broken bits of apple that lay scattered in the grass.

One might have thought that they were bits of gold. Then, very soberly and seriously, they returned to the saloon and found that Pensteven was already there, sipping his unfinished glass of beer.

Jerry marched around behind the bar and confronted the man.

"That's the slickest shooting I ever seen," he admitted.

"Thank you," replied Pensteven. "I was high and to the right with one shot. It was almost a miss. That's my fault—I'm high and to the right very often."

"Well," said Jerry, "lemme tell you this. Don't be high and to the right when you meet Stew Carter. Vince won't bother you none, after he hears about the apples. But as sure as sin, Stew is gonna come and have a chat with you, and he'll bring his guns."

Chapter 3

The crowd remained silent in the saloon until Pensteven left. Then they discussed him in brief phrases. "He ain't a fathead, after all," said Jerry.

"He beats me," admitted another.

"All his cards on the table, face up. That was all," observed another.

"He didn't talk down, none."

"He's got a kind of a half-witted smile."

"What's he doing out here?"

"I dunno."

"We'll find him doing something before long."

"Yeah, his kind don't stay in the wood long enough to get aged."

Presently other townsmen came in. They had heard murmurs; now, as they were informed of the facts, the crowd grew.

After a time, the swinging doors were pushed wide. At the entrance to the saloon stood a man with short, very bowed legs, and he was as much too long above the waist as he was too short below it. He was forty years old; desert labors had starved his face and blackened his skin.

"Is the stranger in here?" he asked. "The one that fought my brother, Vince?"

It was "Stew" Carter. Jerry sang out that the stranger was gone, and Carter went on: "If anybody meets up with him, tell him that I'll be here about this time tomorrow, will you? I'm kinder looking forward to meetin' up with him."

17

He turned and left the saloon, and a murmur grew up out of silence after he had departed.

"That means a gun fight," said everyone. Their eyes gleamed and they nodded. Gun fights were worth watching, when they were between experts.

At the hotel, in the meantime, Pensteven had said to the clerk: "I haven't much money. Will you give me a cheap room?"

"I can fix you for one buck a day," said the clerk.

"Well, I can afford that for a while," replied Pensteven.

"Here's the book. Register?"

"That's a waste of time, isn't it?" said Pensteven.

"All depends," said the diplomatic clerk. "Some mind it, and some don't."

Pensteven picked up the pen and scribbled: "John Stranger."

"That's what I'm called here in Markham," he observed to the clerk, as he laid down the pen.

The clerk looked at the writing, looked up with a smile at the new client.

"That's all right," he said. "This here is one of the most silentest hotels you was ever in, when it comes to askin' questions about where was you from and what was your nickname in the home town."

He took Pensteven up to an attic room. It was a hot little hole in the wall, with the sun beating fiercely down upon the roof. The rafters and the shingles were both visible. "How's this?" said the clerk.

"It's a fine view," said Pensteven, with his smile, and laid down his blanket roll on the bed.

The clerk left, and Pensteven sat beside the window patiently, paying no heed to the furnace heat of the little apartment. He looked out through the narrow aperture of the dormer window and saw the green hills wash down in waves to the desert, where all their greenness was consumed and a dusty, purplish haze stretched away to an unknown horizon. If he leaned forward a little and looked to the right he could see the higher mountains, with the dark pine forests ranked about them, high up to timber line, and, above that, the glistening, savage rocks of the summits, with snowlike chalk marks in the ravines.

Before he was done, he would probably have journeyed

over both the desert on the one hand and the lofty crags on the other.

Where his trail would take him, he could not tell; he only knew that where John Christmas was, there he himself must eventually be.

It had been hard for him to get to this place. He was not at all sure, either, that this was the right town to have come to. He could merely hope that it was somewhere near the central part of the territory over which the great John Christmas rode.

In the meantime, he would have to sit and wait. That was to be his task until he ran across some clew. He had eleven dollars and a few cents in his pocket, and wolfish famine was rooted in the center of his being. It was easy for him, now, to give up his imagination to the construction of a glorious feast. How long would it be before he dared to spend freely for food and stop tightening his belt?

A tap came on his door. He turned toward it and saw a man of fifty or fifty-five, with a careworn face, entering. He removed a hat from a bald head.

"This is a hot devil of a room," said the older man.

"It's my pocketbook that picked it out for me," said Pensteven.

"My name is Charles Wace," said the other. "I'm the sheriff of this county, and I had to come here and call on you, Mr. Stranger."

"Thanks," said Pensteven.

He stood up and shook hands. He offered the one chair to the sheriff, but the latter shook his head and sat down on the bed.

"I gotta talk business with you," he announced.

Pensteven nodded. "What I mean," said the sheriff, "is that you've made a stir and a splash here in Markham, though you been here only a couple of hours. You come in on the last train?"

"Yes."

"Blind baggage?" asked the sheriff cheerfully.

"No. On the cushions. I pay my way. I'm not a tramp, Mr. Wace."

The sheriff waved his hand.

"That's all right, too," said he. "I ain't gonna be too curious."

"Thank you," said Pensteven.

19

"But I wanted to tell you something. About Markham. It's a place that agrees fine with a lot of folks, and it don't agree at all with other folks. I've lived here so long that I can tell at a glance the gents that will flourish and the ones that will fade in this kind of a climate."

"You mean," asked Pensteven, in his frank way, "that you think I should not stay here in town?"

"No," answered the sheriff. "You sure should not. Maybe you ain't heard the last news about yourself."

"Perhaps not," said Pensteven.

"Well, the fact is, that the brother of Vince, Stew Carter, went into the Elbow Room a while back and wanted somebody to look you up and tell you that he'll be there again at the same time tomorrow. He wants to meet you, and that's another way of sayin' that he wants to kill you."

"Does he?" asked the other.

"Yes, Mr. Stranger, or whatever your name might be. He wants your scalp, and the scalps that Stew Carter wants, he always gets 'em. He has a way of always gettin' what he wants.

"That's interesting," said Pensteven. "Can't you tell me some more about him?"

He was born with a gun in one hand and a knife in the other, and he uses 'em every day of his life, practicing."

"So do I," said Pensteven.

"You ever shot a man?" asked the sheriff.

"No," said Pensteven.

"I don't believe you," remarked the sheriff. "But, anyway, shooting apples ain't shooting at a gent like Stew Carter. Apples don't hit back."

"That's true," replied Pensteven.

"So," said the sheriff, "you'd better move along. If you've paid something down on this here room, I'll fix that for you."

Pensteven shook his head.

"I won't move on," he declared. "You think that I'm a tramp, at least. I'm none of those things."

"Oh, ain't you?" asked the sheriff. "Ain't you none of those things. Mr. John Stranger?"

"My name bothers you, does it?" asked Pensteven.

"Not much. Names don't bother me. It's the men that count and not their monikers."

"You know, I think you may believe me when I tell you that I've never done an illegal thing in my life, so far," said Pensteven. "I've never stolen a penny, never hurt any man with more than my fists, and very few even with those."

The sheriff narrowed his eyes. He grew thoughtful.

"I kinder pretty near believe you, son," he remarked. "But if you wanta keep that record, or save your own hide, you'd better move along out of Markham."

"No," said Pensteven, "I have to stay here."

"If you stay," said the sheriff, "you may sleep in jail. I dunno. I ain't made up my mind. But I don't like these here arranged gun fights, and I got an idea that I'll break this one up."

"Then grab Stew Carter and put him in jail. He's the one who made the appointment."

"You want to make a name for yourself by killing him. Is that the idea?"

"I don't want to hurt him," said Pensteven. "But I've never stood in front of a man who wished to kill me. I'm curious about it. I want to see how my nerves bear the strain. That's all."

"It ain't all," said the sheriff. "You got something behind you. You're playing a game, and you're playing it deep. But mind you, son, I'm watching you close. Mind every step you take, or the next one will be behind the bars!"

Chapter 4

Jail was not, however, meted out to young Pensteven. He stayed in his room until the evening, ate a frugal supper, and then went up to bed. That was the cheapest place to stay.

In his room, before he retired for the night, he labored steadily for an hour with his pair of revolvers, practicing the draw, letting himself fall into many twisted positions, and making snapshots, in gestures, as he fell. It was a foolish-seeming employment of time. Nevertheless, he persisted until he was in a profuse perspiration at the end of the hour. Then he undressed, gave himself a cold sponge at the washstand and went to bed.

The mattress was simply a cotton sheathing packed, now, with straw, and a good many sharp edges of the straw had broken through the covering. They cut cruelly at the body of young Pensteven, but he, fixing his attention on the blackness above his face and the one star that glinted through his window, was quickly asleep.

And there he slept, as he had trained himself, until the first gray of the morning light. He had put in seven good hours of repose and he was content. Next, he arose, dashed cold water over his lithe body, dried himself, shaved quickly, dressed, and went down to the street where the dust was still blackened with dew.

He walked back of the town into the pine trees, jogged two miles, at least, up hill and down dale, and finally found a bit of cleared land. There he drew his revolvers and worked hard with them. He selected four marks, went to the center of the clearing, and then acted as though he were dodging bullets from all four directions, and as though enemies were scattered about on the ground at his feet.

Ten bullets left his guns. Then he reloaded and went to examine the targets. He had sunk six of the ten exactly where he wanted them. Two were not bull's-eyes, and two had completely missed the targets!

He was not content. He returned gloomily to his position and tried the trick over again. For an hour he worked in exactly that manner. Ten times he emptied his guns; at the tenth trial, all the bullets had flown straight to the mark.

He was far from content. He had other work to do, such as picking a target, running away from it, turning, firing; or, again, running away from it, hurling himself sidelong to the ground, firing as he fell and after he actually was stretched along the ground.

He chose a target on the side, and fired as he passed it walking, then on the run. He repeated with two targets on a side. Then he picked a target on the right and on the left. That was the most difficult of all the tricks that he attempted—to fire suddenly to one side, then to the other, with any accuracy, while running at speed.

His score was astonishingly high, but it was not so high as he wished to have it. It was so high as it had been before. However, he had learned to take these comparative failures with composure, for in the years during which he had been training himself, he had learned that progress is up and down from day to day, but with each month, one day reached a higher crest than any that had gone before.

It was hard work, bitter work that he had kept himself to these years, but with a Spartan patience he endured the toil until, at last, he felt himself fitted to undertake the adventure that was nearest his heart.

Now he was in the midst of unfamiliar scenes. He was not a cowpuncher, but he had patiently taught himself to ride, to use a rope, and he had read books, in part, and spent some time on the trail as well, learning to read sign.

These things, he well knew, he never had completely mastered. They were only a minor goal to him, the first and foremost being the ability to handle rifle, knife, or revolver, but the revolver most of all. He had reached a skill that might be equalled here and there. It might even be surpassed by some Heaven-endowed genius of eye and hand. But he felt that he was not likely to encounter, in all his life, more than one man who would be able to match him in a gun play. It was when he arrived at that conclusion that he decided to go out on the range and take his chances.

He sat resting for a moment on a stump, thinking the matter over, when something stirred among the branches of a pine. Then a form slipped down from bough to bough and hung from a lower branch—not the wild animal he had at first suspected, but a human being—a youth in ragged overalls. No, hanging in that fashion by the hands, he saw by the slenderness of the shoulders and the curves of the figure, that it was a girl.

She dropped lightly as a cat, falling forward as though to receive some of her weight on her hands, if necessary. But it was not. She stood erect and settled the tattered sombrero lower over her brown face.

"Hello, gunman," she called out.

He let guesses ripple through his mind. She was eighteen; twenty, perhaps; too big a share of jaw and too little of nose to be actually beautiful, but pretty as the devil; saucy, too. The clothes were not all that made her seem boyish.

"Hello," he responded, as he finished cleaning and reloading his guns.

"Shot away enough good powder and lead to feed a family for a whole year, didn't you?" she asked.

"If one could get close enough to shoot deer with a revolver, yes," said he.

"I can," said the girl.

"Ah-ha," exclaimed Pensteven. "Perhaps you can, but, then, you're no more than a feather, you know."

She considered his half-mocking, half good-natured grin.

"Look here," said she, still very critical and aloof, "who d'you want to murder, practicing like that and scaring the squirrels to death, for one thing?"

"I wasn't gunning for you," replied Pensteven. "I didn't know that you were up the tree."

"While you were practicing," she observed, with a nod of the head, "anybody could have come along and blown your head off. Whoever your enemy is, don't let him ever find you in the woods or he'll eat you."

"Will he?" asked Pensteven.

"Yes, he will," she insisted.

"Explain how," said he.

"I'll explain how, all right," answered the girl. "This is the way you walk along."

She started slouching forward, imitating his long-swinging stride; and every footfall crackled upon twigs, or crunched among the pine needles.

Then she turned about.

"Here's the way a woodsman walks," she went on.

She covered exactly the same ground and, though she was looking toward him and not at the places where she stepped, her footfalls made no sound.

"You're a woodsman, all right," said Pensteven. "You've practiced to get that."

"You must have eyes in your feet, like the eyes in a bat's wings," she answered him. "That's what you need for working in the woods. Who are you?"

"John Stranger," he replied.

Stranger?" she slowly repeated. "You're strange, all right. But there's no such name, is there?"

"Yes, because it's the name I wear."

"Well, some people take on and put off names like old hats and new ones," said she. "But you don't look like a crook."

"So far I'm not," said he.

"And now you're just neutral?" she asked.

"More or less."

"I see." She nodded at him. "You've come out West to be free and independent and all that rot."

"Why is it rot?" he asked.

"Because nobody's free, so far as I can see. Nobody except me."

"Everybody's tied down to something, you mean?"

"Of course. Everybody's either a mother, a wife, a daughter, a sister, an aunt, a niece, a cousin, at least. The same with the men. You can't be a human being without duties. It makes me sick to see how much work there is."

"What's your name?" asked Pensteven.

"Barbara Stranger Still," she replied.

"Barbara Still, you mean?" asked Pensteven, grinning.

"You can call me that," she said. "I'm not a crook either, just yet."

25

"But you say that you're the only person in the world that's free, Barbara," said Pensteven.

"That's true," she replied.

"Go on and make that clear, if you don't mind."

"Sure, I don't mind. If you can follow me that fast! This is the idea. When a girl's much younger than I, she's depending on somebody else. And then she gets out of childhood and falls in love, and a girl in love is no freer than a fly stuck in molasses. The fly thinks that it's fine, but it's clogged up and dying of sweetness. And I'm between childhood and falling in love, I have no relations, there's nobody I depend on, and nobody depends on me. I'm the only free person you ever met in your born days."

"You sound free," he observed.

"And I am free, you can bet your bottom dollar," said she.

"Where do you live?"

"Back here in the wood with my stepmother."

"Ah, but there's a relation," said he.

"Some stepmothers are almost relations," said the girl, "but not this one."

Chapter 5

He considered her for a moment. Then he sat down again on the stump he had occupied before he first caught sight of her. He folded his arms and watched as she went behind the trunk of the tree she had climbed and came toward him again with a Winchester slung carelessly under her arm.

Something caught her attention as she was halfway across the clearing, and she paused, rising on tiptoe, the most balanced, easy, and graceful thing that he ever had seen in all his days.

She came on and sat down on a rock near him. She was all rags, with patches on top of patches. But he saw that the overalls were as clean as a recent scrubbing could make them. In fact, much washing had faded the blue out of the jeans and left them a watery-gray, with streaks of the stain remaining here and there.

She was a thing as much subjected to open weather, sun, and wind, as any range steer. The tips of her dark eyelashes were sun-faded, and so were her eyebrows. The hair that thrust out about her head was partly dark, dark brown, and partly the color of dust, for the very same reason. Her skin was all brown, deep brown, even in the small wrinkles about the eyes, that come from peering against strong lights. From the same cause, there was a trace of a frown always coming and going from between her eyes. She sat now like a man, with her knees crossed, and her hand resting upon her knee. She looked young Pensteven fairly between the eyes.

"I know what you mean," said he, "but if you're one

of the unlucky girls who has a bad stepmother—why, how can you call yourself free if you're bullied and badly treated at home?"

"Bullied and badly treated?" exclaimed the girl. "Bullied and badly treated? My eye!"

She laughed a little, then she said:

"I tell you what, Stranger, if she tried to bully me, I'd throw her out the window or roll her out the door, considering the size of her, and keep her out and run the house myself. And she knows it, too. She's not a storybook stepmother. She runs that boarding house because she wants to make a living. But she doesn't run me. She tried it a coupla times, but she always finished last. Nobody would ever put a cent on her chances against me."

"But you live with her, eh?" he asked.

"Why not?" asked the girl. "It's an easy life, and I've got a good right there. Half the house belongs to me from dad's will. So that's all right. I don't have to make beds or sweep and clean, or dust and cook. Sometimes I serve and wait on the table. Sometimes I don't. I do as I please, because I like to be free."

"Maybe that's hard on the stepmother," said Pensteven.

"I supply the fresh meat. I catch the fish, too," said the girl. "It's my fun, and saves the butcher's bill. The boarding house is always full because the fellows like venison and trout. And you can see for yourself that this makes a pretty fair bet for her and for me."

"It sounds fair," he replied, "but speaking of freedom, I don't see that you're a whit more free than a young fellow of your age."

"Give your eyes a rub, and then you will," said she. "It's as plain as day. A young man of my age generally has a father and mother to nag at him and poke at him. If not, he has his career to think about, his cows to ride herd on, his roping to do, his practicing with guns, say, and some enemy or other to get ready for."

She indicated him with a nod and then continued: "As for girls of my age, they're always falling in love. That's the devil of their lives. They're always in and out of love. They're breaking their hearts or getting a thrill. It's sickening. You know the way they are."

"They've never bothered much about me," he admitted.

"But I suppose that you'll never waste time on me, no matter how long you live?"

He was still smiling.

"Oh, I'll be poisoned one of these days," she answered. "I know I can't escape, because it's nature. It's like death and winter. You've got to come to it. Some boiled-in-oil, tool-proof, mean-faced cowpuncher or sourdough will come along one of these days and crook a finger at me, and I'll just roll my blankets and follow him down the trail. But I'm nobody's squaw up to now, and I'm just living from day to day and enjoying things."

"It sounds like a good life," he commented. "I'm surprised that more people don't try it."

"They don't have the same luck, or the same eye for a rifle, or the same layout to live in," she suggested. "There's a lot of reasons why other girls never are free. Sometimes I think that they don't even want freedom, really. They're born tame, like ducks in a barnyard. They never fly north and south, chasing the summer. But that's the life for me. Say, Stranger, I've been doing a lot of talking."

"I'm a professional listener," said he, with a smile. "Don't bother about me. It's as safe with me as though you'd been talking to the squirrels."

"You're one of these old young men, are you?" she asked.

"I don't know," he answered. "I haven't much time to think about myself."

"Duty, eh?" said she. "Is duty the devil that hounds you and runs you up a tree?"

"You can call it duty," he answered.

She nodded at him. Her dark-blue eyes were compassionate and bold, at the same time. "You're a hard one to get at," she observed. "There's something on your mind and, when a fellow has trouble on his mind, it's like looking at him through muddy water. He's hard to make out."

"Is he?" asked Pensteven. "There's no mystery about me. I'm common or garden man."

She shook her head.

"Nobody, common or garden, can sling a gun the way you do, Stranger," said she. "I've seen a lot of good ones, but never anything better."

"I'm glad you liked the work," he replied soberly.

"I didn't like it," she answered tartly. "I don't like murder, and that's a fact." ·

"What does murder have to do with me?" he asked her.

"You're on a blood trail of some sort," she said with conviction. "I can guess that much. And the point is that you may be after one man, and you'll wind up by getting a dozen. You're too good with a Colt not to use it overtime."

"I hope not," he replied.

"You better stop hoping and begin praying," she replied. "It's the fellows like you that wear a rope necklace before they get very old."

"I don't follow you there," said Pensteven.

"I've talked so much that I might as well talk some more," said she.

"I like your lingo," he told her. "You tell me why I'm going to hang so soon."

"Because," said she, "there's no fear in you. When I slid down out of the tree, where I'd climbed to take a look at you, that was enough to give you a scare. But you weren't bothered. Your eye was as still as standing water, when I dropped down and took another look at you."

"That means that I'll do murder because I'm not afraid?" said he.

"It does," she answered. "You're not afraid because you're sure of your hands and the guns that are in 'em. I've seen the same look in the faces of other young fellows. Good fellows, too, a lot of 'em. But I notice that they all die young. I wish you all the luck, Stranger, but you better go and get licked by somebody. There's too much starch in your neck!"

He smiled at her and nodded.

"That may be good advice," he commented.

"I've got to slope," said the girl. "So long, Stranger."

"Which way are you going?"

"Back toward town."

"I'll go along with you."

"That's fine."

He stepped out beside her. She walked like a young deer, alert and keen always and intent upon the things about her. Every shifting shadow, every falling leaf was noticed. Now and then he stumbled as he walked along.

"Take your eyes off me and look where you're going," she advised him sharply. "You haven't the right eyes in your feet, Stranger."

She paused and turned on him, frowning. "Don't go and get foolish," she said, with an increasing and angry disapproval.

She rested a hand on her hip, as she looked him frowningly up and down. "I'm softening a little about you," he admitted, "but I'm not completely foolish, yet."

"I'm going to take another path," said the girl. "What have I done to give you that gone calf look in the eyes? Tell me that!"

"I don't know," he answered. "It's a queer thing."

"How does it feel inside?" she asked with the air of one at once disgusted and very curious.

"It's a queer feeling. Mostly in the stomach," said he.

"Is it?" she remarked. "Yes, it looks that way. Like seasickness, sorter?"

"Yes. Sorter like that."

She nodded, saying: "It must be a mean thing to have."

"It is," he replied. "It's not very bad, yet. I suppose that it'll all wear off by noon. The morning is a happy time anyway. There's still a little sleep in the brain."

"You can talk sense, all right," said the girl. "How long are you going to be around here?"

"I don't know. A day or so, maybe."

She looked toward the tops of the trees. She considered the distance, as though there were a squirrel in it.

"Well, that's a good thing," she said. "It's sorter like a fool kid, though, to get silly just when I wanted to be friends."

"I'm sorry, too," he admitted. "I don't want to be bothered by having a girl on the brain. I've something else to do with myself."

She nodded again, gravely approving.

"That's the way to talk," she declared. "And you'll be out of this in a jiffy."

"Of course, I will," said he.

"I suppose you've had the fool feeling before?" she said.

"Just a trace," he answered. "Men are fools, in a way. It doesn't take much. A smile, a head turning, a voice sounding just in the right way, will walk a girl over the danger line and put her away in a fellow's thoughts for good it seems. But I've never been damaged very much. I've had other things to think about. Women can't be spoiling my life for me."

She held out her hand.

"You're a cut of the right stuff," she said. "You're all right. I like you. I wish I could have a chance of showing it without poisoning you. So long! You take my advice and keep those guns under cover. They'll never talk to other men without getting you into trouble. I know what I'm talking about. I've seen things happen in my day. And I know that a man with blood on his hands is never happy, unless he's a brute. Because you're as strong as a horse, is no reason why you should spend your life hauling heavy loads uphill. Why don't you take the easiest way? Any duty that makes you go hunting a fight is all wrong."

She shook his hand, turned into the trees, turned again and waved, then disappeared behind the intervening branches.

Chapter 6

The rest of the morning, he was nervous and rather uncomfortable. At lunch time, in the dining room of the hotel, he heard the voice of a girl passing down the street, and the sound of it almost made him jump to his feet and rush to the window. He barely restrained himself.

He began to tell himself that he was afraid; that it was fear of his coming encounter with Stew Carter that turned his heart cold and made it sink like a stone. But he knew that he was not thinking about either of the Carters. It was always a forest scene that clung in his mind, with the resinous scent of the pines and the keen, pure tang of the air.

It was of Barbara Still that he was thinking, recalling again in his memory, her voice, her look, her bold, frank, boyish eyes. Somehow, this aspect of her made her appear all the more feminine, in a way that he could not understand, that baffled and irritated him.

But, just as he had told her, it was like seasickness, somewhat, and homesickness combined. It was also a wild happiness that mingled with the sorrow.

He could wish heartily that he never had laid eyes on her face, but he also felt that he would not trade that brief acquaintance with her for any other memory in his life.

He was very glad when he had finished his lunch and could step out into the brilliant and biting rays of the sun. That, he had hoped, would dim all the pictures in his mind, and he was right. Everything burned out of his mind except the white glare of the street. It was a frightfully hot day. Perspiration streamed down his face, but he was glad of that heat, almost. It helped to cure the ache of his heart.

Presently the lump of ice within him was melted. He went up the street, straight to the Elbow Room Saloon, entered, sat at a corner table in the back room and drank a glass of beer very slowly.

Jerry, the bartender, came up and stood by him, giving the top of the table an instinctive swipe with the towel which he generally employed for polishing the bar.

"I'm sorry about yesterday. You were kind of crowded in here," he said. "I made a mistake. It was my fault. I thought you were a damn tenderfoot. Maybe you are, but you're a man, too. I only hope that nothing happens to you or to Stew Carter, neither. He's all right."

"I have nothing against him," said Pensteven. "I'm here simply because he asked me to come."

"You're ahead of time."

Pensteven looked keenly up into the face of Jerry.

"I thought his watch might start to run fast," said he.

Jerry sighed.

"You're the game kind," he said. "If I was in your boots, I'd be steaming and shaking, lemme tell you."

"No you wouldn't if you'd trained yourself as I've trained myself," replied Pensteven. "I'm not an amateur. I'm a professional. I've never fought a man with guns before, but I've had enough training to make myself a professional."

Jerry sighed again.

"I'm sorry I didn't stop things. Instead of that, I started 'em. I'm a fool. I'm a damn little fool!"

He went back toward the barroom, pausing at the door to say: "It's a whole hour before Carter comes. But maybe he'll hear that you're already here and come hopping. He—he's good with both hands, Stranger. I ain't giving anything away, I guess, when I tell you that."

"Thanks," said Pensteven. "I shouldn't have thought of that."

He continued with his beer, until the back door of the room opened and a tall man with a sallow face and pinched shoulders came in.

He glanced aside at Pensteven, went to the door leading to the barroom, whistled to draw the attention of Jerry and closed the door.

As the door closed, Pensteven could hear Jerry sing out, with an oddly respectable note in his voice. "All right, doc. Nobody else'll go in there."

Doc came back and stood before the table where Pensteven was sitting. He had a smile that never left his face, but there was no mirth in it. It was the forced smile that a man may wear when he is suffering. There was a large black wart high up under his left eye.

"I'm Doc Shore," he announced. "I'd like to talk to you, Stranger."

"Sit down," said Bob Pensteven. "Have something?"

"I'll have nothing but a chair and a whack of your time," said Doc Shore, lowering his lean hips into the chair as he spoke. "I've come to talk to you because you're a cool young gent and because you can shoot, and, besides, the clerk at the hotel says that you're about broke, from the way that you talked to him. Is that right?"

"That's right," said Pensteven.

"I can give you a job."

"What sort?"

"Doing what you're told."

"I'm not a very good rider," said Pensteven. "I mean, I couldn't handle a bucking broncho; but I've had a good deal of experience with ordinary horses. I can handle a rope a little. But I don't know anything about ranch work."

"Who said ranch work?"

"I'm no good for the mines, either," said Pensteven. "Perhaps I could learn."

"The town's full of punchers and miners looking for jobs," said Doc Shore. "I want you for another kind of a slant."

"What sort of a slant?"

"Ten dollars a day and expenses."

He looked at Shore, and Shore looked solidly back at him.

"Well?" said Shore.

Pensteven shrugged his shoulders. In a way, this might fit in very well with his plans.

"I don't know," he said. "What's it all about?"

"It's a job where you keep your mouth shut, your eyes open, and do what you're told. There'll be some riding in it. There might be some shooting, too."

"When would you want me to start?"

"Now."

"I've got an engagement here for an hour from this. After that, I'll take your job."

"You take the job now or not at all."

"Then I don't take it at all," said the young man.

Shore shrugged his shoulders. "You want to kill Carter, do you?" he asked.

"No. I don't want to hurt him. But I want to see what it feels like to look at a gun that's looking at me; besides, I've given him my word that I'll be here, or it amounts to that. I can't possibly run away. Not for twenty times ten dollars a day."

Doc Shore considered him with gravity, and the same rather sick smile. "I'll tell you something," he remarked. "Carter is a friend of mine, and I'm a friend of Carter's. If you leave this place, he won't show up at all."

"He won't come at all?" echoed Pensteven, amazed. "But he'll never back down. He has a reputation to support, I hear. Besides I——"

"Carter," said Shore slowly, "would rather have my friendship than all the rest of his reputation."

"We'll both get black eyes for agreeing to quit and not fight it out," said Pensteven, frowning.

"The whole town will know that I've had a hand in it," said Shore. "They'll shift the blame to me. Jerry knows that I'm taking a hand right now."

"And what are you?" asked Pensteven.

"You'll have to find out for yourself."

There was a growing excitement in the heart of Pensteven.

"Unknown man, unknown job, ten dollars a day," he murmured. "Well, I can make up my mind on that. I'll take the job. But if you're fooling me, and Carter does come here looking for me——"

He paused. His jaw thrust out a little.

"I only lie when I have to," said Doc Shore. "He won't come here. Now step along with me, and we'll find you a horse."

36

Chapter 7.

There was a horse dealer at the southern end of the town of Markham and to his corral they went together. There they looked from the fence at all manner of horses herded together; some with plenty of hot blood showing in their long legs and their finely made heads; others, the most common mustangs.

"Whacha want in the way of a horse?" asked Doc Shore.

"How far do I have to go?" asked the young man.

"It's three o'clock," said Shore. "By this time tomorrow, you ought to have a hundred miles behind you. That means traveling along! You'll have to work relays. I mean, what sort of a horse do you want to start with?"

"I don't know horses," said Pensteven. "Get me a horse with long wind and easy gait."

"Well, how about the black, over yonder?"

"I've heard that black horses don't stand the heat so well as lighter colors. Besides, he looks nervous and high strung."

Doc Shore smiled a little more broadly than before.

"You have an eye in your head, even if you don't know horses," he said. "I'll pick out something that oughta stand a rub."

What he picked out was a middle-sized, lump-headed mustang, a roan, with a slightly roached back and a pair of wicked little red-stained eyes. Doc Shore paid for him, and bought a saddle, blankets, and bridle.

He led out the animal and turned it over to Pensteven.

"I'll go to the hotel and load on my blanket roll," said the young man.

"You ride without blankets," said the other. "You can have a slicker. That's all. Every extra pound is out of your chances and ours, on a trip like this!"

He drew out a wallet.

"Here's your month in advance," he said, counting out the greenbacks. "Here's another hundred for ordinary expenses. Here's two hundred more. Because when you pick up new horses along the way, you'll probably have to pay boot. Study this mustang on the way. Notice his points, because when you get your next horse, you'd better try to find another like him. Be careful of his heels, and mind that he don't snap your head off if he gets a chance. He's mean, but he won't buck more than enough to warm himself up."

He paused, cleared his throat, and went on: "Ever hear of San Jacinto, twenty-five miles south on the river?"

"No."

"You'll find no trail," said the other. "But bear due south and you'll come in sight of it at the end of twenty-five miles. When you get to San Jacinto, try to find a man named Juan Oñate. You may not find anyone who answers up to that name. If you don't, try to locate a fellow with a cast in his right eye. A cast out, so that he seems to be trying to look around a corner. When you find him, give him this."

He took from his pocket a transparent quill which contained what looked like a roll of fine paper. Both ends of the quill were sealed.

"He'll give you your next marching orders," said Doc Shore.

"Suppose that he's out of town?"

"He can't be out of town. But if he is, you turn to and find him. Mind you, Stranger, we're paying you seven to ten times what a cowpuncher would get on the range, and we expect you to do things seven to ten times as well. Besides, you have a horse and six hundred dollars in cash, just for a starter. We invest the hard cash in you, and we expect you to pay us back in brain power. You have a pair of guns, I suppose. But have you a rifle with you?"

"No."

"I'll get you one, and be back in a moment. Try out the roan while I'm gone."

Pensteven obediently climbed on and found that he had

38

sat down upon a boiling kettle of trouble. For the roan mustang left the earth like a skyrocket, exploded in mid-air, so to speak, and shook Pensteven down to the ground among other fragments.

He managed to cling to the bridle but, even so, the mustang dragged him yards before he stumbled to his feet and put on the brakes.

He mounted again. Two or three idlers, the horse dealer and his hired man stood about, laughing, enjoying the picture.

This time, Pensteven was treated to an artistic bit of fence-rowing. But he sat it out. He had ridden a good bit before, and knew the value of balance and a strong knee grip. Now he discovered that every buck of a horse would not shake him off.

Suddenly the roan began to bound into the air and land on one forefoot. The second shock flicked Pensteven cleanly out of the saddle once more.

He was sick and dizzy, this time, when he rose and mounted. The sunfishing began promptly, once more, but this time he learned how to ease himself well back, with plenty of weight in the stirrups and a well-studied balance. He stuck out that ordeal.

The roan, understanding perfectly that this device had been mastered, now spun in a circle like a fire wheel, and blurred the landscape before the eyes of Pensteven. In blind anger at the viciousness of the mustang, he suddenly swung his quirt and cut the horse savagely across the shoulder on the far side, and under the flank on the rear.

To his amazement, the roan stopped spinning. He stood shaking his long, mulish ears, and gradually bringing them forward. He nodded up and down to get more rein, and Pensteven let him have it. He was pleased. Off to the side, he saw that the dealer and the loafers were no longer laughing. And the mustang stood just as quietly as a lamb!

He rode the horse up and down. It answered readily, reining over the neck to the slightest touch. So now he had leisure to dust himself thoroughly, and by the time he had finished that, back came Doc Shore, carrying a rifle under his arm. He thrust it into the saddle holster under the right leg of Pensteven.

"How's the horse, Stranger?" asked Shore. "Looks to me like you've warmed him up with a good gallop."

Pensteven looked seriously down into the face of Shore. He thought that there was just a shadow of hidden meaning in the eyes of the other.

"Oh, we were just getting acquainted," he said.

"All right," said Shore, dropping a bag of rifle ammunition into a saddlebag. "Be off with you then, Stranger. Good luck. Remember," he added, walking a few steps beside Pensteven as the latter started off, "remember that every man you meet on the way may be after you. Remember that they'll cut your throat as soon as wink. If you're caught, swallow that quill; if they find it on you, they'll murder you. If they find it on you and let you live, I'll find a way to have you murdered afterward!"

His teeth clicked on the last words. He stood and waved his hand, and young Pensteven cantered out onto the desert trail.

It was not a proper trail at all. Only, close to the town, a way had been worn for a short distance, but the little, individual tracks soon spread out, twisting to right and left, like the hairs at the end of a braid, fanning out into the thinness of air.

He had nothing but the blank palm of the desert's hand extended before him, and no lines on it to read his fortune. It was fiercely hot. The mist which soon surrounded him and shut out all objects on the horizon except the very heads of the northerly mountains, that purplish mist which he now saw between him and the circle of the skyline, was not at all noticeable as a screen against the direct rays of the sun.

These rays cut into him like a volley of white, electric arrows. They burned and they scalded him. He decided that he had been a fool to take his training in a milder, moister land. Out here, the sheer fierceness of the heat was enough to addle the brains.

He had not thought to take a canteen with him; neither had Doc Shore seen fit to warn him. And yet Shore must have seen that this vital necessity was missing.

Pensteven set his teeth. For he began to feel that Shore had known, in the beginning, all about the bucking talents of the roan mustang, just as he knew about the torment of spending even an hour on the desert without water.

Was not Shore testing this man, to see how young Pensteven would win through the fire? Somehow, that appeared the most likely explanation.

But afterward, what burdens would they place upon his shoulders, what dangers, what great things? And who, above all, were "they"? That was the most important point of all, to Pensteven.

In one way or another, by hook or crook, he must put himself eventually in touch with John Christmas; and in his heart of hearts he did not doubt that Doc Shore was one of the adherents, one of the outlying lieutenants of the great bandit.

He knew that plan by which John Christmas was said to have spread his power so far, the system of buying up valuable and active men, keeping them ready for any emergency, the liberal spending of money in order to make money, the training of thieves in the higher intricacies of their art. Through his agents, he struck here and there; a stream of gold flowed in toward him. But John Christmas himself was almost unseen, almost unknown. Every fantastic deed along the border was attributed to him, but he appeared only as the sun among the shining golden clouds, brilliant but obscure.

To John Christmas, young Pensteven wished to cleave his way and then—he set his teeth and drew his breath with a hissing sound.

He was guiding his horse carefully along a straight line to the south; his mouth was parching, his tongue thickening, when he came across some very alkaline water in a drinking hole. Salty and bitter though it might be, it made a welcome drink to Pensteven, and he was kneeling to scoop up another handful, when the dim reflection of an armed man rose up from the mesquite brush behind him!

Chapter 8

There was no place for concealment around the water hole except the tenuous branches of the mesquite. There was no sight of a horse or of any other animal that might have carried a man to this spot. In fact, it was very much as though the apparition had risen out of the dust and rock itself!

Bob Pensteven leaned still lower, dipped his wet right hand inside his coat, and brought it out bearing a long Colt. Then, turning his head suddenly over his shoulder, he actually fired from beneath the pit of his arm.

It was a hard trick, because the head was pretty well out of line with the gun barrel. But he had spent hours practicing it. The clumsiest position in which a man may try to defend himself is, undoubtedly, on hands and knees, and against that clumsiness he had provided himself with the most careful training.

His bullet sliced the right forearm of the stranger from wrist to elbow! His rifle dropped and hung, useless, in the grip of the left hand.

Rising, Pensteven found himself looking at a man as gray as the dust out of which he had risen, with greasy locks of hair falling down around a face on which vice and crime were written. He must have been at least sixty years old.

The fellow was in rags, literally. Upon his feet were Mexican sandals. His skinny brown shanks showed through the tatters of his pants; but he had, in spite of his brownness and his rags, the pale-blue eyes of a white man.

He stood dumbly, watching Pensteven who came up to

him, took the rifle and threw it aside, then washed and bandaged the long, burrow-shaped wound which his bullet had carved.

Neither of them had spoken.

But when the bandaging was finished, some of the old desert rat's own rags having been used for the purpose, Pensteven said: "You'd better get into town as fast as you can, and show this to a doctor. It needs to be cleaned and a good antiseptic dressing applied."

"I reckon that I was a fool," drawled the old man. "I ought to been happy enough just to bust your back. But that wouldn't do for me. I'd heard tell that you had a whole barrel of fancy tricks, and so I thought that I'd better get you through the head and finish things with one pressing of the bell, like you might say. I was a fool. I was trying to make a sure thing surer!"

"Too bad," murmured Pensteven.

"Yeah, in a way, it's kinder too bad for you, too. Because they're sure to stop you. They just sorter used me as first step. Now you've stepped over me, you'll have some real stairs to climb. Doncha ever doubt that!"

"Who are you?" asked Pensteven.

"I'm just an old fool," said the other. "There ain't nothing much to me except time. There ain't no mystery of a misspent youth and a fine family and all that rot. I'm just an old whiskey soak. That's what I am."

But Pensteven saw that the years and the debauchery had not glazed the eyes of the man. Straight and clear, they looked at the young man.

"You say that 'they' are going to stop me. Who are 'they'?" he asked next.

The desert rat grinned and showed some broken remnants of yellow teeth. "They're plenty," he confessed.

"That doesn't tell me anything," pursued Pensteven.

"Don't it? It tells all that you'll get out of me."

"Look here," argued Pensteven. "You owe me some decent answers, I think. A good many fellows would have put a second bullet through the middle of you."

"Yeah," acknowledged the other. "I gotta thank you for my life. I could pay you hard cash for all it is worth, though. Here's a nickel!"

He held it out in the grimy palm of his hand. Pensteven smiled a little. The other went on: "I wouldn't mind talking to you, kid. You look clean enough. You look like you ain't spoiled meat, yet. But if I talked they'd know about it. They wouldn't kill me with bullets, either. They know better ways."

He shrugged his shoulders, as though a cold wind had struck his back.

"You can't say a word that'll help me?" asked Pensteven.

"Not a damn one," said the other. "I've talked too much already, but you looked kinder young."

"How will you get out of here?" asked Pensteven.

"The same way that I came."

"I see. I can't make you talk, but, with that wound still bleeding a good bit, won't you need help to get to a town?"

The other blinked. "Is this the way you mostly treat the gents that try to bump you off?" asked the veteran.

"I never had such an experience before," replied Pensteven.

The other raised his eyebrows. "Yeah, I reckon that you ain't had no experience," he said. "I reckon that that gun trick you done on me was just tenderfoot luck, I'm old and I'm a bust, but I ain't a fool, kid."

Pensteven picked up the fallen rifle, saying:

"I'll take this a quarter of a mile south and drop it in the sand again. You can pick it up there, if you want."

"Thanks," replied the old man. "I take that real kind. That there rifle is my father's house and my quarter-section of plow land, my clothes and boots, my spurs, and horse. It's my friend, my honor, and my life, all in one. I wouldn't be very happy without it!"

Bob Pensteven mounted. "Better luck to you, old-timer," said he.

"Yeah, but I'm older than time, too," muttered the vagabond.

Pensteven rode off again on the southern trail. Some four hundred yards away, he lowered the rifle gently to the ground and went on.

He was full of thought as he went. Whatever the import of this errand on which he was riding, it was already patent that the "they" who opposed him were aware of his going.

Their means of communication must have been as swift as telegraphy. Otherwise, how could they have had that wreck of an old desert rat in wait for him at the water hole?

Was this opposing crowd working against John Christmas or with him? He grew cold with the thought that his time was wasted—worse than wasted; that in working for Doc Shore and the people behind him, he might be going counter to the famous outlaw, divorcing himself from the opportunity he had sought so long.

To get himself into the presence of John Christmas, he had spent those fierce years of preparation. Were they now wasted?

The questions he asked himself were for the present, at least, unanswerable, and he determined to persist in his first course. In the meantime, the hours were slipping behind him and he began to force the roan along.

It did not need much forcing. Its endurance was extraordinary, as might have been expected from the evil temper it had showed at the beginning of the ride. And now, when the going was at all possible, it broke into a rolling lope; where the sand was deep, it trotted patiently ahead. It seemed to know its own strength and to be willing to give everything to the bottom of the cup.

Now, to the right and far ahead, he saw the sun glinting on glass a few strange sparks of light that presently grew into the outlines of a town, and he rejoiced that he had been able to hold his way so steadily and so truly to a destination twenty-five miles from the start.

Those twenty-five miles had left him thoroughly shaken, with a slight blur before his eyes and an ache in the back of his head—and seventy-five still left to do before his twenty-four hours ran out!

He dared not think about the trail which still remained uncompleted. He had to limit himself to what he already had accomplished, and so confined his thoughts to the present moment that brought him into San Jacinto.

He could bless his knowledge of Spanish now. He might have to bless his knowledge of guns, as well, before he was through with the place.

If a water hole in the desert could produce armed men rising from the sands, then what might not a crowded little town like San Jacinto offer this morning?

So he rode with an eye to either side of the way and, though he seemed to be looking only straight before him,

45

it was as a prizefighter stares straight on, ready, however, for a blow from any direction.

He went on into the central piazza of the little, huddled, whitewashed town, and there he dismounted before a cantina and entered.

There were only the proprietor and one greasy-faced, smoky-eyed patron, who sat at a corner table, looking out upon the desert spaces of life and communing with a hollow soul.

Pensteven took beer and sat down to sip it slowly. It was the worst stuff he had ever tasted, acrid and sharp, with an after flavor as of wood ashes against the back of the throat. But he controlled his expression and managed to keep his lip from curling with displeasure. As he paid the proprietor, he said:

"I'm looking for a gentleman named Juan Oñate. Do you know such a man, señor?"

The proprietor was arranging packages of cigarettes upon a shelf and his hand paused as he heard the question.

Without turning his head, he replied: "I have never heard such a name in San Jacinto."

He went on arranging the packages. From one of them a thin stream of tobacco dust fell slowly on the air; it had been crushed in his fingers.

Chapter 9

Pensteven communed with himself. The name of Juan Oñate had been electric in its effect on the proprietor. That was clear. But it is hard to make people speak of names which are so fraught with significance. In that instant, he gave up all thought of reaching his goal by mere questioning. Doc Shore, in fact, had intimated that questions asked in San Jacinto might lead to nothing.

He must search for the man, therefore, but where? Through the cantinas, and under the trees on the bank of the river; up and down the streets and alleys, examining every face closely. He had not thought to ask for a fuller description. In fact, he was, he felt, an absolute fool. He did not know whether Juan Oñate was long or short, thin or fat, young or old. He did not know whether to look for a beggar or a gentleman. He could only stare at every man and watch for a cast in the right eye!

He got up to leave the place. As he reached the front door, he turned and nodded goodby to the owner. The man stood with a fixed eye and a stony face. He seemed rigid with the apprehension of disaster.

"That rascal knows something," said Pensteven to himself. "Something that's burning the palms of his hands. But how the devil shall I find Mr. Juan Oñate?"

He walked on slowly, but he was examining his problem, rather than staring into faces to find the one that might solve his difficulties.

He saw that he could not search San Jacinto effectively. It was verging toward the middle of the day; it was almost torrid noon, and Mexicans begin to take their luncheons

47

at that hour. Afterward they compose themselves for the long siesta which will carry them through the worst hours of fire later in the day.

He could not go through the town breaking into private homes. He would soon have more knives stuck into his skin than there are barbs in the back of the porcupine. He sighed as he considered this.

There was only one possible clew that presented itself to him, and that was the cantina. The owner knew something, and his knowledge was very definite, so definite that he had stood in icy suspense as his guest departed.

Why had he been in such suspense, his eyes starting from his head? Obviously, when the gringo patron departed, he would rush to bear tidings of the question asked by him. He would rush to Oñate himself, perhaps, and warn him that he was being asked for through the town!

"I should have stayed near and watched the back of the house. I'm only a half-wit!" said he to himself.

Presently he turned back. He could not afford to waste any time. He must follow up his only clew. He must explain to the proprietor of that cantina that he, Pensteven, had no hostile motive in inquiring for Oñate. On the contrary, he was the bearer of a message which probably contained important news for the man!

A little money might help to persuade the owner of the cantina. He had got this far in his thoughts, when he came opposite to the cantina and saw that it was closed and the shutters pulled across the big windows of the front.

He looked at his watch. It was still lacking ten minutes of twelve, and certainly the cantina would not ordinarily be closed before that hour.

No, it was tolerably clear that his simple question had closed the drinking place!

Now he did not pause for further thought. He could not get through that closed front entrance, but he could try the rear one. At all hazards he must attempt it; he must do it by force, if necessary. Though he shivered a little, when he thought of the tigerish speed of a Mexican's hand and its readiness to wield a knife handle, yet he comforted himself by recollecting that he had expected dangers like this; yes, and far worse.

If only, he thought, the thing could be in the open, like that adventure by the water hole in the desert! Death inside the walls of a darkened house is like a snake in the middle of the night!

He marked the house with care, so from the shape of its roof he might be able to tell the back of it from its neighbors. Then he walked around the next corner, down the winding alley, and finally came to what he wanted. It was a blank wall without a single window. There was only a door, less than six feet in height. Proud men would have to bow when they stepped over that threshold.

As he stood before it, he wondered what he should do. To break in suddenly seemed the best way, taking his chances, hoping to thrust in upon the inhabitants before they were prepared. But old instincts mastered him. Instead, he knocked lightly, politely.

Instantly he heard a whistle, behind him, across the street and, spinning about, he was vaguely aware of a shadow disappearing from a doorway that still yawned black and wide. A warning had been sent to the keeper of the cantina, so it would appear!

Furious impatience swelled up in the heart of Pensteven. He gripped the handle of the door. It was locked! He saw that it swung inward and suddenly threw the full force of his weight against it.

There was a slight sound of wood rending and the door giving way. Then he pitched forward his full length into the semidarkness and coolness of a narrow hall.

A knife stroke flashed over his head as he fell forward. He heard the grunt of the wielder, the swish of his hand and arm. Bending his head to keep it from the impact, Pensteven tackled the Mexican hard and low.

The man came down with a bang on top of him, muttering, groaning, cursing in rapid fire.

Pensteven took hold on a slippered foot and, with a most cruel hold, kept the enemy face down. He himself stood up and looked down the passageway.

Feet were scuffling somewhere. Muffled beyond thick walls, a woman's voice was crying out: "Juan! Juan!" Juan Oñate, perhaps?

He raced down the passage to a door nearly at the end of it, and on the right.

It was locked, but again the weight of his shoulder was sufficient, and he lunged forward into a dimly lighted room in which there were three men and a woman.

The latter was crouching at the feet of the fellow with the greasy face and the abstracted eyes whom Pensteven had seen a little earlier in the cantina itself.

The other two men, crouching like cats prepared to spring, stood on the right of Pensteven. One had a revolver ready in his hand; the other had a long knife from which the light seemed to drip like running water.

But they were not the chief forms in the mind of young Pensteven. As he stared at the seated man, who seemed as impassive as ever, he saw that one reason for the odd abstraction in the face of the other was that he had a cast in his right eye. An outward cast!

"Why, I'm only a fool!" exclaimed Pensteven. "You are Oñate!" and he added: "Tell your men to be quiet, will you? I have them covered. Oñate, I'm not here to do you any harm. I've simply brought you a message."

"From whom?" asked Oñate, making a sign with his hand to his two manhunters in the corner of the room.

"From a man who calls himself Doc Shore, in the town of Markham."

"I know the man," said the fat man.

He raised a forefinger, while his hand rested on his knee.

"How did you get through the door?"

"With my shoulder rammed hard against it," answered Pensteven.

"You hear?" said the Mexican calmly to the woman.

"Ah, yes, Senor Oñate," said she. "I hear. *Por Dios,* forgive me. I'll have Pedro kill the dog of a carpenter who made that door with rotten wood!"

"Let it be," said Oñate. "Now you have spoken my name. You are intelligent. You have the brains of a newborn calf. Leave me. Never come into my sight again."

She got to her feet with a sort of screaming sob and ran out of the room. Yet Oñate had not raised his voice.

Down the hall came a hurried, limping footfall and rapid curses.

"Keep out of the room," said Oñate.

The footfall ceased.

"Close the door behind you," came the next command, though gently spoken, to Pensteven. And Pensteven obeyed. His blood was turning cold. To him, the dim light of the room was like a coffin, and half his life seemed already gone.

"How did you dispose of the man at the door?" asked Oñate.

"My shoulders hit him below the knees as I fell into the hall."

"You were lucky," said Oñate.

"Yes," said Pensteven.

"Luck is better than brains and skill," said the Mexican. "What message do you bring me?"

"A twist of paper in a small quill."

"Give it to me. Amigos, cover him with your guns as he comes near."

"If they pull a gun or move a gun, I start shooting," said Pensteven.

Oñate leaned a little forward. A breathless silence entered the room like a ghost.

Chapter 10

One thing at least was certain—the two men in the corner, even with the eye of their master upon them, made no move. This fellow who had broken into the house had too much authority in his manner and actions. Finally, the massive head of Oñate nodded.

"That was foolish," he said. "But you have luck. If one of those two had been another, he would have started gun play and then—" He made a slow gesture that seemed to dismiss the life of Pensteven into uttermost darkness.

Then he resumed: "Now, amigo, come and give me the quill. We shall be as friendly as possible."

Pensteven crossed the room carefully, turning a little toward the two manhunters. He put away one gun; with his left hand he found the quill and gave it to Oñate.

The latter broke it open, simply crushing it between thumb and forefinger. Then he drew out a delicate film of paper, covered with writing almost equally fine.

As he studied this document in a ray of light that broke through the shuttered window, his thick, pale-purple lips moved slowly, forming words.

He started, lowered the slip of paper, stared at Pensteven, and resumed the reading.

Now, however, his complacent manner was disturbed. Twice again, as his hand jerked down, he glared at Pensteven. At last, rising from his chair, he began to pace up and down the room. He was very fat. His stomach wabbled in spite of the broad, dark sash which was tied around his waist.

He came to a pause before Pensteven, raised his right

hand almost to his chin, with the first three fingers peculiarly placed, and slowly lowered the hand again. Pensteven stared at the odd gesture.

"You don't understand?" asked the Mexican.

"No," replied Pensteven.

"Then what devil made them send you to me?"

"That I really don't know. I know nothing at all," confessed Pensteven.

"How did you manage to get here? How, if you know nothing?"

"There was no trouble. Only an old fellow at a water hole out on the desert."

"I know that old fellow. All in rags?"

"Yes."

"And you managed to pass him?"

"He was a little hurt, not very badly," said Pensteven.

Oñate breathed heavily for a moment. He was greatly excited.

"What do you expect to do?" he asked.

"Ride seventy-five miles by three tomorrow afternoon."

"Ah? And where?"

"Where you send me!"

"I send you to the devil!" exclaimed Oñate.

He went back and flung himself into his chair, which groaned and creaked under his sudden weight. Slouched far down, his legs sprawling out before him, he stared evilly at Pensteven.

"I send you to the devil," he repeated. "Why don't you go?"

Pensteven had wit enough to say nothing. He could feel that the yoke of a great power, a power far stronger than Oñate, was being laid upon the man, and he was struggling against the dictates of that power, struggling sullenly, but in vain.

Suddenly the Mexican said to his two men: "Get out of the room!"

They went with slinking, catlike steps to the door, and silently out into the hall.

Oñate pointed: "You are lucky," he said, "or you would be lying dead now, there by the door, with blood around you. Do you know that?"

"No," said Pensteven. "I was not lucky. I was not very much afraid of you all."

"There were three," said Oñate.

"I knew that nothing would happen," said Pensteven.

"How did you know?"

"I knew that you would be afraid for that big paunch of yours. Even a child could not miss such a target."

Oñate leaned forward in his chair, and Pensteven expected a tyrannical outburst of rage. Instead, the fat man began to laugh. His laughter shook his whole body and brought a tuneless complaint from the chair.

"Well," he said at last, "Señor Shore may not know books, but he knows men. He sent me a man. He always sends me men. I hope that you will last longer than the rest. Wait here!"

He left the room by a second door, which Pensteven had not seen before.

The latter sat down in a corner chair, and waited not more than five silent minutes, wondering if he would actually leave that grim chamber alive. But finally Oñate returned. He carried with him a small canvas saddlebag, which he weighed with his hand, and then gave to Pensteven.

There might be a burden of five or six pounds in it and a considerable bulk.

"Do you know what's in here?" asked Oñate.

"No."

"You may as well look now as later."

"I don't care what's in it," replied Pensteven.

"You are lucky," declared Oñate, "but don't be a fool and trust everything to luck. There is enough in there to get ten better men than you murdered!"

"I'm glad to know that," answered Pensteven. "You're to tell me now where I take this."

"Yes, it's seventy-five miles," said Oñate. "You leave San Jacinto and head for the mountains; the Tolliver Trail."

"Where is that?"

"Damn!" exploded the Mexican, in English, delivered with unction. He stamped his flat foot on the floor.

"Well," he went on, after a pause, "you leave San Jacinto and look to the northwest and you see four high mountain peaks, standing close together. The Tolliver Trail runs right through all four of them—through the center."

"I understand," said Pensteven.

54

"When you get to the first pines, or a little after, you'll find a stream running across the trail. It ought to have some water in it at this time of the year. Turn up the stream. Turn to your right and ride up the bank. If you are wise, perhaps you will walk and lead your horse, and carry a gun in your hand."

"Yes," said Pensteven, nodding his head.

"If you get that far, you come to the wreck of an old 'dobe house in about a mile, a big house. There you ought to find people. You tell them that you have been sent by Oñate. And you ask for Señor Al Speaker. If any of the others want to see what is in the saddlebag, don't let them. Fight them off. But give the bag to Señor Speaker. You understand?"

"Yes," replied Pensteven dubiously. "Are these other fellows, if they're on hand, very likely to want to see what's in the saddlebag?"

"So likely," answered the Mexican, with a contented, fat grin, "that they'll probably cut you to bits in order to get at it."

"Well," said Bob Pensteven. "It ought to be a pleasant ride at least. Tell me how I'm to know Al Speaker?"

"He is small and light, he has a great big forehead and no chin. He never did have much chin, and part of what he had was shot away. He looks like only half a face. He is the easiest man in the world to know when you see him. If you have a fight, also, don't have the fight with Señor Speaker. He always wins, and he always keeps on fighting until he has killed the other man. Rattlesnakes, also, are not large. But they kill rats and frogs, and such things. Take the bag, señor. Adios. Take care that the devil I send you to doesn't get you before you find Señor Speaker. He will tell you the rest of your way. Adios, adios!"

He waved his fat hand impatiently. But Pensteven lingered to inquire: "Where can I find an honest horse dealer and get a good horse in San Jacinto?"

"You can't find an honest horse dealer anywhere," said Oñate. "And the good horses in San Jacinto are not for sale. Adios. Hurry, my friend. Beware of the devil, because he specially loves the Tolliver Trail!"

So Pensteven left the darkened room, went down the hallway, and stepped out into the blinding sun. He started, that is; for at his right, pressed close against the wall, was the guard who had been at the first door and tried to knife cut.

The face of the man was distorted with malice and hatred. His eyes glittered. His mouth worked.

Pensteven walked past that face like a thing in a bad nightmare, and so down to the central piazza, where he had left his mustang tethered.

He asked of a boy where he could find a horse dealer, and the fellow eagerly conducted him to a pasture on the bank of the muddy river, where he found an ancient Mexican, with the face of a saint and the smile of a fiend.

Among the horses in that pasture, Pensteven made his selection as well as he could—not one of the prettiest, but a gray with good big bones and capable muscles in the shoulders.

In the exchange, he paid fifty dollars to boot for that nag and cursed it every inch of the forty miles that he sat on its back.

Nevertheless, no matter what its gait, it could travel, and travel it did, while the body, the very soul of Pensteven was racked by the indescribable trot of the beast. Even its walk was a torture, for it seemed to rise high in the hips with every step, while a wave of movement followed, and swayed the rider toward the withers of the horse.

Now, however, Pensteven was crossing the desert with a full canteen.

Chapter 11

There was nothing to that journey—nothing to write down except, simply, forty miles. The forty miles were desert, chiefly. Some of it was shifty blowsand. Some of it was good, hard gravel, from which the shocks of a steady trot were transmitted as if by electricity to the brain of the rider. After that came what seemed an endless stretch of glassy volcanic stone, sometimes flat and polished, sometimes in great heaps that looked like cinder dumps. Its crystals blew into his eyes and tormented him, and the rays of the sun's light and its reflected heat burned and seared him.

Then the mountains, which had danced crazily before his eyes during the heat of the afternoon, turned from blue to brown, and out of the brown grew the shadows of the pine trees, turning at last green. Finally he was riding under that green, with his head and eyes turned upward, drinking it in.

To his tired, blistered eyes, the welcome color was as water to a parched and soiled body. He exulted and reveled in it. At sunset time he came, at last, from under the pine trees, to the stream of which Oñate had spoken.

It meant, if the first calculation of Doc Shore had been correct, that only thirty-five miles of his journey remained!

"Only thirty-five miles? Thirty-five hells!"

He had no sensation from the hips down; and, from the hips up along the course of the spine, he felt as though hammers had been beating upon the nerves. Yet he survived.

When he came to the creek, he found, as Oñate had

expected, that there was water running in the course. He turned down its bank and found a pool, red and gold with sunset lights. The sight was too much for him. He dismounted, peeled off his clothes, shook the dust out of them, and threw them on the grass to "cool," to use the word that was in his mind. Then he dived off a rock into the water, swam and dived.

His muscles were so sore that he could hardly make the strokes, at first, but by degrees he grew more at ease. The strains upon them were from different angles. Sometimes a change of labor is the greatest rest; the blood flows through new channels, as it were, and refreshes the entire body.

And young Pensteven came up refreshed and easy, at the end of ten minutes of this sport.

He whipped off the water. A warm evening breeze helped to dry him, and then he pulled on his clothes.

He was still dressing when a voice hailed him from the brush. "Hello!"

"Hello, yourself," said Pensteven.

He drew his coat closer on the rock where he was sitting. Then he glanced at the mustang, grazing near by, with hobbled front legs. That saddlebag!

A man pushed his horse out through the shrubbery and came into a view with the look, also, of premature years about him.

He was well-mounted, and he was armed to the teeth with revolvers and a rifle in the saddle holster and a bulging look about his clothes, as though they might conceal still more weapons. From his wrist dangled a silver-mounted quirt. His sombrero was glistening about the band with gold work. The trimming on his chaps was plainly solid silver and fancy-work silver, at that. But the clothes themselves were ragged. They were badly in need of mending.

Two things were clear—he had plenty of means to buy clothes, and it had been a long time since any woman's needle had worked for him.

Pensteven, even if he were something of a tenderfoot, was able to put two and two together. This man lived outside the law. He put down the age of the other as between twenty-three and four years, not much more than his own age, in fact.

"Having a little swim, eh?" asked the rider.

"Yeah. Scaring the fish," said Pensteven.

He stood up, having pulled on his boots, and in the operation of getting into his coat, which he made clumsy and longer than necessary, he managed to fit the slings over his shoulders, together with the spring holsters that held his revolvers. He felt more at ease when this had been accomplished. He felt surer of himself with such servants in their accustomed positions.

"First trip up this way?" asked the newcomer.

"First trip," said Pensteven.

"Bound some place?" went on the questioner.

Pensteven smiled his open, rather foolish smile. There was so much thoughtless good nature behind the expression.

"Yeah. I'm bound some place," he replied. "I'm looking for a fellow by the name of Al Speaker around here. Know him?"

"Speaker? What does he look like?" repeated the man of the red hair.

"A lot of forehead and nose and not much chin. Smallish fellow," answered Pensteven. "Know him?"

"He wouldn't thank you for that kind of a description of him," said the other. "Known this Al Speaker for a long time, you?"

"Never saw him. Only had a description."

Pensteven was beginning to grow tired of the catechizing.

"Well," said the other, "it seems to me that I've seen him. Kind of a queer fellow, though. Lives mostly to himself and don't see anybody hardly at all."

"I was sent to him by a friend of his," answered young Pensteven.

The round-faced, red-headed man nodded thoughtfully.

"What might your name be?" he asked.

"John Stranger."

"Alias John Jones?"

"John Stranger is what I said," answered Pensteven. "What's your name?"

"John Redhead," answered the other. "Like the name?"

"I never liked red," said Pensteven, with equal coldness.

"You don't like red, eh?" queried the man on the horse,

sitting a little straighter in the saddle. "And I don't like strangers. And there you are."

"There you are," said Pensteven a little childishly. "It means nothing to me."

"Oh, don't it?"

"No, not a damn bit."

The man on the horse considered.

"You got mountain sickness, I guess," said he. "Breathing this high air, it makes you feel good and strong."

"Makes me feel strong enough," declared Pensteven with well maintained impertinence. "It's not the air that makes me so tired."

"What makes you so tired?" asked the redhead incautiously.

"Your line of chatter," answered Pensteven patly.

The other threw his leg over the horn of the saddle and slid to the ground.

"You want a dish of trouble," he declared.

"It's what I live on," said Pensteven. "I was raised on trouble. How about you?"

"I'm the gent," said Redhead, "that cooks trouble for fools to eat."

He was bigger off a horse, so to speak, than in the saddle. He had big, rounded, smoothly padded shoulders, and the padding was not fat. That much was clear. He walked with his head thrust out a little before him, and his jaw was blunt and big.

"Cook's roustabout, is what you look to me," said Pensteven. And his supple body became taut through all its nerves and sinews. A glory of excitement flushed him.

"I got a mind to show you," said the redhead, "that a roustabout can bring in and dish up more trouble than you can eat."

Pensteven smiled. "I was raised where men grow," he replied. "But I've heard kids talk before today."

"How's this for talk, though?" said the other.

And he smote at the spot which Pensteven's head occupied in the air.

The head was not there, however, to receive the blow. It had ducked to a lower and safer level.

Then it rose again, and at the same time a short left uppercut sprang up under the chin of Redhead and knocked him back on his heels.

"You better go home and grow a while, son," advised Pensteven.

"That's a good trick," answered Redhead with perfect calm. "But here's one that's worth two of it."

He feinted with his left for the head and then drove a mighty righthander for the heart.

Pensteven swayed his body a fraction of an inch out of the line of that blow, and clipped the chin with the same uppercut on the same spot. But it was harder this time.

Redhead sat down with violence.

"That's a good play," remarked Redhead. "But I'd rather be sitting than standing for some kinds of work and here—"

He half pulled a gun from a holster, but found the flash of the other's gun already completely out in the sunlight and covering him.

Redhead, with a sigh, shoved his own weapon back into its holster, then stood up.

"You can box pretty good," he declared. "You been in the ring, ain't you?"

"It's just a trick punch," replied Bob Pensteven, very untruthfully. "There's nothing to it once you get onto the idea."

"It came out of nowhere, so far as I'm concerned," said Redhead. "Who are you, bo?"

"John Stranger is my name."

"You're strange, all right. I dunno that I ever seen a stranger. But what bozo sent you up here to Al Speaker?"

"I didn't get your name," said Pensteven.

"My name is all right, and red is part of it," replied the other. "Who sent you up here?"

"You show me Speaker, and I'll tell him," remarked Pensteven.

His companion grinned.

"Hard-boiled, eh?" said he. "Well, I ain't no three-minute egg myself. I'll take and show you to Al Speaker, if you wanta see him so bad. But there's them that like Al better going than coming. Climb on your hoss and come along."

Chapter 12

It was as strange a companionship as ever two knight-errants could have formed in the days of armor and foolish adventures, when men fought themselves into an acquaintance exactly like youngsters in a modern school yard.

They still regarded one another askance, but with a sort of budding good fellowship, the redhead because he had been fairly knocked down, to say nothing of the little incident of the faster draw, and Pensteven because a certain punch had glanced off his ribs and his side was still sore; also, because he rather admired in his new friend, a certain readiness for fist fighting or maybe murder.

They spoke noncommittally until they were in sight of the house.

"I suppose," said Bob Pensteven, "that I just met you down the road and asked my way."

The other felt his chin. "How does it look?" he asked.

Pensteven regarded the reddened swelling on the chin bone.

"A branch jumped up and back from the pony's head when you were riding through the brush," he suggested, "and it cracked you under the chin."

The redhead grinned.

"You're all right, brother," said he. "My name is Dan Turner. Mostly called Red. Now, what's yours?"

"John Stranger," persisted Pensteven.

He was wondering at the wealth of good-being that he felt since the swim and the fight. Most of the aches of his long ride seemed to have disappeared, though he knew many of them would return before long.

"Oh, yeah," said Dan Turner, "you're hard-boiled, but that's all right. Stick your nag in the corral. There's plenty of feed been forked in already. Want to grain him?"

"I don't know," said Pensteven. "Never rode him or owned him before today."

"Don't risk any grain on him, then," said Turner. "Partly because all this oats and barley is packed up here on muleback and such. And partly because a mustang is liable to die real young of happiness and surprise if it gets a good look at a feed of grain. Peel off your fixings and come on into the shack."

So they unsaddled the horses, and Pensteven, carrying the accouterments of the mustang, followed Turner into the house.

As they came through the doorway, he saw a pair of older men playing cards in the dim light beneath a window at the back of the room. On a stove in a corner, food was steaming in various pots. One of the card players had on a dirty cloth girded around his waist in lieu of an apron. And now, on second viewing of them, Pensteven came to the conclusion that they were not so old in years, after all, not so very much older than he was, but he could tell at a glance that they had been through experiences which never had come within his ken. He felt decidedly immature, and the players seemed to realize this.

For one of them said: "Hello, Red! Who's the child, friend?"

"Just come up from No Place Camp, over on the Somewhere Range," replied "Red." "By name of John Stranger."

"Alias what?" asked the player who wore a long unshaven set of whiskers.

"Alias What-the-hell-d'you-wanta-know-for," answered Red. "If you are hungry, Stranger, we'll eat pretty quick. What are we waiting for, Clare?"

"Ice cream," said the man with the apron sourly. "What would we be waiting for except Al? But, say, who did you bring home?"

He turned from the cards and examined Pensteven, who never had been received in this fashion before and stood a little uneasily in a corner of the room.

"Hang up your things, Stranger," said Red.

Pensteven obeyed. Both the card players, suspending their game, considered him from head to foot.

"This'll make a big hit with Al," announced the one with the black beard.

"All right, Chuck," said Red. "I'm waiting to see Al, too. Let him worry when he gets here. I've worried already."

"Have you?"

"Yeah, plenty."

"What door did he knock on to get in?" asked the cook of the day.

"My chin," said Red, surprising Pensteven by this frankness.

"Yeah? With what, Red?" asked black-beard.

"The son of a triphammer, crossed on a lightning flash," said Red as calmly as ever. "But he's modest and he calls it a left uppercut. It's so long that it kills flies on the ceiling of the church, it's so fast that it lands before it starts, and it's all decorated with shooting stars and midnight."

"Did he sock you, son?" said black-beard, rising suddenly to the majesty of six feet and three inches of seasoned rawhide.

"Don't do that, Chuck," protested Red. "I've got mud on my pants already and why should you get splinters?"

"Chuck" laughed a little, but his eye was thoughtful.

"Whacha want here, Stranger?" he asked.

"I'm calling on your wife's uncle's second cousin," said Pensteven, soberly delighted by the atmosphere of this place.

"He wants Al," said Red, grunting as he finished pulling off the second riding boot. "Shut up and wait till Al gumshoes in."

"Al is gonna be right pleased," said Chuck, sitting down slowly.

"Is he?" said a voice from the door, and Al Speaker stepped into the room.

He had been aptly described by Oñate, but not well enough. He was like a death's-head that has lost the lower jaw—a death's-head fleshed over, with two great, dark, meaningless eyes set under such a brow as Pensteven had never seen before. To make his face more horrible, it was marble-white and picked out with great freckles as red as rust.

He came in carrying his saddle, which he dropped onto the floor. Pensteven was really not surprised when black-beard arose, picked up the saddle and hung it on a hook.

Al Speaker walked up to the stranger. His face was not pleasant at a distance, but it was horrible close at hand. For when he spoke, the scarred lower lip quivered and stretched awkwardly, in the wrong direction, marring his speech, so that after he had spoken, one had to pause for a moment to make out what he had said. He seemed to be speaking from a distance, yet close at hand, like the sounds one hears when passing under an anaesthetic. The wound which had almost destroyed the lower part of his face had so drawn the lower lip that speech was not quite safe for him. He had to have a handkerchief in his left hand, al-ways ready to press to his distorted mouth. He held the handkerchief, like a woman, under the last two fingers of the hand, pressed against the palm.

He was very small and delicately made. But the most extraordinary feature of his face was the pair of expres-sionless, flat, black eyes. If there was any depth in them, there was no meaning.

"Who are you, and what do you want?" he asked of Pensteven.

As may have been seen before, Pensteven was not one to respond to such treatment. Opposition reacted in him like flame under dried timber, and curtness was a signal for war.

"Red can tell you who I am, and I don't want a damn thing from you," said he.

The little man eyed him without emotion. He dabbed the handkerchief, which was of the whitest, cleanest, soft-est linen, against his lip. Still looking at Pensteven, he said: "Red, what about him? And why did you bring him in here?"

"His name is John Stranger," replied Red, "and he wants to see you."

"He knocked you down, and so you brought him, you fool?" asked Speaker.

Red glanced up sharply. His lips tightened.

"Don't call me a fool," he came back.

"You are a fool," said Speaker, "unless you tell me why you thought that you could bring him here."

"I'll tell you," said Red. "He's a sick man, and the disease that he's got is called gun-speed. You're the best doctor in the world, bar one, for that kind of sickness."

Speaker smiled. It was a most horrible grimace. Only from the wrinkles around the eyes could one tell what it was intended to be.

"That gets me nowhere," he told Pensteven. "What brought you up here?"

"Doc Shore and Juan Oñate," said Pensteven. "Know 'em?"

The little man dropped his head, so that he could look up under his finely drawn brows.

After a moment he said: "Yeah, maybe I know them. They sent you, did they?"

"Shore sent me to Oñate, and Oñate sent me to you."

"For what?"

"For ten dollars a day," said Pensteven.

Speaker raised a slender hand, the left hand, with the flawless handkerchief held under the two fingers.

"You're a bright fellow," he observed. "But don't be rough. I'm trying to help you out by asking questions. You're young, too young to be rough with me."

A slight tingle went down the spine of Pensteven. For the first time since he had mastered guns, he felt something akin to fear.

"I'm not rough," he replied. "I'm telling you the facts. I'm the only one who's talking. Oñate gave me a saddlebag to bring to you."

The brows of the other were elevated.

"Did he? Then get me the saddlebag."

"It's over there on the horn of that saddle," said Pensteven. "You can help yourself."

He pointed, and little Al Speaker, after first considering the newcomer with care, dabbed the handerchief to his lips once more and kept it pressed there as he crossed the room.

Chapter 13

Whatever else he had accomplished, certainly Pensteven had fixed attention upon himself. Red, Chuck, and Clare, all three, constantly watched him, then turned their gaze for an expectant flash toward their leader, Al Speaker. But Al gave no further sign of emotion, no indication that he had been badgered so keenly by Stranger.

He merely took down the saddlebag, opened it, and rummaged around among the contents.

"All the fuss about that?" he muttered. "Well, that's all right."

And he hung the bag again on the horn of the saddle. The curious glances with which he had been followed now fell away.

"Hey, there's a damn bat in the room!" called out Red.

The flickering little rag of a thing was darting vaguely about the rafters and the ceiling of the place. And Red, drawing a revolver, put in three rapid shots.

Then he shook his head.

"You try, Chuck," he said.

And black-beard emptied his gun in vain.

Streaks and stains of powder smoke were in the air; the roof was being thoroughly ruined by this hail of bullets, but the half-faced man, Al Speaker, oblivious of all around him, sat down cross-legged in a corner, since the table was occupied by dishes, and began to compose a letter, writing with care and much thought, his handkerchief femininely pressed against his mouth.

Clare stood up, a stalwart man with a great throat and chest, and an imperial manner of holding his head.

"I'm gonna plaster that bat," he said.

He did not try shooting from the hip. Instead, he tried to draw a bead, and deliberately, one by one, sent six shots at the invader.

He did not touch it!

"All right, John Stranger," he called. "You're the baby. You take the next whack. Lemme see what you can do?"

Pensteven studied the flight of the bat for a moment. There is neither bird nor insect whose flying compares with the bat's. It has wonderful speed; it can fly great distances, also, like any swallow that follows summer across the seas; but, above all, it drifts and slides and dodges. It seems to drop backward and spin about on a pin point. As Pensteven watched, it seemed to him that the strange creature was striving to baffle his thought and his eye, making itself invisible by sudden shifts.

Actual aiming, at such a distance, would never get the target within the sights and, if it were, the bat would swerve out of the line before the trigger was pulled, even before the hammer could fall. He must go for it, if he tried at all, rather by sense of touch, as it were.

He drew a gun, therefore, and suddenly from just above the height of his hip, he fanned a rattling succession of five shots at the mark. They were so rapid that one seemed stumbling upon the heels of the other. At the last one, the bat dipped suddenly down until it skimmed the floor. Up it rose again, wavering, uncertain.

"He hit it!" shouted Red. "He's packing something more than a left uppercut around with him. He's packing luck! He nicked it, or I'm a liar."

"He nicked it all right," muttered the other two.

They did not look at Pensteven, but at the bat, now swerving and dodging through the air almost with as much speed as before.

He reloaded his gun. He had done enough, he felt.

Then he saw little Al Speaker look up from his writing, and heard the oddly blurred voice say from behind the handkerchief: "You fellows are making a whole lot of noise. I can't think, even!"

And there was a gun in his hand, picked out of the air, at it were. For a moment, his wavering, swerving glance followed the movements of the bat. Then he fired.

The bat disappeared. A little tatter of something fell on

the floor and made a splotch of blood. "Throw that outside, Red, will you?" said Al Speaker gently. And he went on with his writing. But the heart of Pensteven had given one great bound, and then stood almost still. For he realized that there had been something more than luck in his own hit; there was something more than luck, also, in the dead center which Speaker had achieved in his very first venture.

His blood was running cold. The three men looked at the splotch on the floor. Then Red threw the rag of a thing outdoors.

Pensteven found his voice.

"That's the greatest shot I ever saw," he declared, rather hoarsely. "That's the greatest shot I ever heard of!"

"I had a little luck, Stranger," said the muffled voice of Al Speaker, and resumed his composition.

But Chuck commented: "Yeah, Al can shoot a little. Next to Jack Christmas, he can shoot a little."

"You mean that Christmas can beat that?" asked Pensteven calmly.

"You know," said Chuck, "a fellow feels like a fool, talking about the way Christmas can shoot." He paused to laugh.

Pensteven nodded.

"How about a little chow?" asked Clare.

"Yeah, let's eat, Al," said Red. "How about a little chow?"

The little man stood up with a sigh and went to the table. There they sat down, Pensteven with them. He noticed that no one looked at Speaker while he was at the table. He sat at one corner of it, at a sharp angle away from the rest of them, and turned his head still farther away when he raised food to his mouth. Horror and pity mingled in the heart of Pensteven.

There was little talk. They ate rapidly, heartily. Al Speaker, satisfied long before the rest, went back to his laborious writing in the corner. He had not uttered a word since the killing of the bat.

"Another little dash of that coffee wouldn't do us any harm," said Chuck. "That's what old Tom Pensteven used to say always. I was only a kid then. I always remember him saying that, though. He was a funny old bird."

"Yeah, you used to talk a lot about him," murmured

Clare Wilde. "He was the one with the consumption and the Bible."

The heart of Bob Pensteven had stopped again. He drained his cup of coffee and made a cigarette, frowning over his work.

"Yeah, he had a Bible and he had the consumption, too," pursued Chuck. "But he was hearty, all the same. He knew he was dying, but he was hearty. He used to say: 'Take another slice of this roast, boys. You may live only a short time, so you'd better live well.' He used to say: 'If I pray at night, boys, it's not to keep you awake, but because I have accounts to make up.' He'd been around the world and lived a pretty rough life, I think. And the things he had done, they used to bother him a good deal, maybe."

"Who was he?" asked Pensteven, mastering his voice finally, and making his glance only mildly curious. "Who was this Tom Pensteven, anyway?"

"Him?" said Chuck. "Oh, he was an old codger, a good many years back, that come out here with consumption and a Bible, like I said, and he said that he was gonna strike gold, because he had to strike it. He said that he'd wasted all his life except the fag end of the candle, but that that was gonna throw enough light for him to strike it rich for his family."

"People with a family take it easier than that sometimes," said Pensteven.

He drew out a handkerchief, mopped his forehead, and said: "It's mighty hot, this close to the stove."

Then he pushed his chair back until his face was more securely in the shadow.

"Yeah, some take it pretty easy," said Clare Wilde.

"But Tom Pensteven didn't," replied Chuck. "And you know the funny thing? He done what he said. He found the gold, all right."

"Did he?" murmured Pensteven. And he yawned deliberately.

"Yeah, he found a ton of it," said Chuck. "And that was where his bad luck came in. He found so much that Jack Christmas found out about it. He come down and jumped the claim. Tom Pensteven, he fought like a devil. I fought a little, too, till I got a bullet inside the shoulder that gave me a game arm. But old Tom, he fought till he

70

dropped. He was about all corked. I crawled over and held his head for him. He was groaning a good deal.

" 'There was something like this in the Bible,' says he.

"It kinder brought the tears to my eyes to hear him. I mean, I was only a kid then.

" 'You're gonna pull through this, Mr. Pensteven,' says I.

"He took and looked up and smiled at me. He says: 'No, no, my son! I'm dead. I feel the ice next to my heart. I'm a dead man. And other people will die because of me. I have a son at home who must know how I've been murdered. I would have made him and his poor mother rich. Chuck, write to him, and tell him how I died, and who killed me. That's all. Tell him that I died thinking of him and blessing his mother's sweet face.' That was what he was saying when he died. And I give his dead hand a grip by way of promise.

"Afterward, big Jack Christmas comes and stands over me, big and handsome and smiling, like he is. He says: 'Look here, kid. You're game. I could use you. I'm Christmas.'

"I was scared, all right, but I said: 'You could be New Year's, too, for all of me. I gotta write to Pensteven's son and tell him that you killed his old man. I promised a dead man that I'd write.'

" 'Why,' says Jack Christmas, 'go ahead and write to him, of course. That's all right. Only I wouldn't like to do any more harm to that family. The old fool had to fight. There was nothing else for it except to drop him.'

"That was how I came to join Christmas. And that was how I happened to write back to Pensteven's son. And I got a letter back, in a kid's handwriting. Well, I was still only a kid myself. And the letter says: 'You tell John Christmas that I'm going to make myself a fighting man, and that some day I'll kill him, just as he killed my daddy.' "

Chuck ended.

"It's a funny thing," he moralized, "what you bump into, now and then. But, of course, the kid, he never turned up."

"Maybe he's still training himself to be a fighting man?" said Clare.

Pensteven had been breathing hard and deep, but now

71

he mastered himself and commented. "No, fighting men are born, not made, I suppose. When do we turn in?"

"Any time, brother," said Chuck. "There's a bunk over there you can use."

Al Speaker spoke for the first time in many minutes.

"You don't sleep tonight, Stranger," said he.

Chapter 14

He stood by the door and now he added: "Bring your saddle and all your things and come along with me."

Young Pensteven frowned. "The way I understand it from Doc Shore, I'd have only about a hundred miles to ride. I've done sixty-five. There's only about thirty-five miles left, and I have till three o'clock tomorrow to make that distance."

"You have thirty-five by air line," replied Al Speaker. "But the way you'll hoof it, you have twice that far. You'll probably not make it, anyway. You have to go over the Tolliver Range to get back to Markham."

"Hey!" yelled Red. "Whacha talking about, Al? Nobody can get over the Tolliver Range this season of the year. It's iced like nobody's business."

"On this kind of a job," said Al Speaker, "a man can do anything that he's told to do."

And he beckoned to Pensteven.

At the thought of new labors, a wave of aching sleep passed through the body and the brain of the latter, but he rose with a groan and, picking his saddle and the rest of his outfit off the peg on the wall, he waved to the trio in farewell.

"Come back soon, old son," said Red. "I wanta find out something more about the left uppercut. I wanta find out where the wings grow on it for one thing!"

Pensteven went out into the night. There he found Al Speaker before him, carrying a lantern; the shadows of Speaker's legs as he walked, brushed gigantically across the nearest pine trees. He led the way to a corral.

"Get that mule," he said to Pensteven. "Not the big one, but the little one. That's a mule that can walk along the edge of a knife. You want that kind of footing under you. Now look where I'm pointing."

Pensteven looked. "You see the two highest mountains?" asked Speaker.

"Yes, I see them."

"Your way goes between 'em. You can see something shimmer toward the top. That's snow and ice. And here's a hatchet and an ice pick to take along. You'll have to let the mule go at the place where the ice begins. You'll have to cut out steps for yourself and go over the top. If a storm comes up when you're pretty high above timber line, you'll probably freeze to death. But that's Oñate's business. He can make up for you and what's lost besides you. He knew what I'd have to do when the saddlebag came this way to me. Tell me, what did you do to Oñate that made him think you could fly around like a bird?"

Pensteven hardly heard the last words, he was so diligently studying the difficulties that lay before him. And the cold breath of the night wind came down and touched him to the bone. He shuddered.

"I don't know," said he. "I don't know what it's all about."

Speaker laughed. The sound came out in an odd way, hardly framed by the lips.

"You're still John Stranger, eh?" said he. "Well, that's all right. But it was a pretty good dodge, Stranger, hanging up a hundred and eighty thousand dollars in that saddlebag as though there was nothing but barley in it!"

He laughed again, and his laughter made a hissing sound. He broke off, coughing, while Pensteven digested the idea. There was nearly two hundred thousand dollars in that saddlebag! Death, in fact, had been what he was carrying with him. No wonder that Oñate had warned him that many dangers might accompany him on his trail.

"What do you think?" went on Al Speaker. "Imagine that other people may know what you have and where you're going with it?"

"I don't know."

"Well, you have guns, and you know how to use them," said Speaker philosophically. "Where do you go on the

74

other side of the range, before you get to Markham. Know that?"

"No."

"I wish you'd talk out," said Speaker, with irritation. "I know that you're a good man. I'd talk, if you'd open up a little. Will you?"

"I'm talking all I can," replied Pensteven. "But I'd better be making a start, if you'll tell me where to go."

"All right," said Speaker. "You know your own way about, and I suppose that you know your own business, too. You go over there between the roots of those mountains, and down the far side, about a mile by trail below timberline. There you'll find a dead old mining town, a regular ghost town, it's been dead so long. You'll find somebody there, if you hunt long enough. Ask for Cracken, and give the saddlebag to him with everything that's in it. Give him this letter, too. Don't let anybody but Cracken have the saddlebag. It's up to you to keep the others away from it. That's all I can tell you."

"How'll I tell Cracken when I see him?"

"He's one of the old-fashioned make. Wears a saber-toothed mustache on each side of his mouth and sags under the eyes. Always looks tired, and never needs sleep. Lives on cactus and sawdust. You'll know Cracken when you see him. He's about forty years old. Pigskin and raw-hide, well seasoned. You'll recognize Cracken easily enough."

Pensteven was girding the saddle on the back of the mule. It grunted under the strength of his pull on the girth and kicked out viciously. It turned its head around and snapped like an angry dog.

"Goodby," said Al Speaker.

Pensteven drew a breath.

Then he said: "Speaker, you're a wonderful hand with a gun."

"That was luck," replied Speaker.

"People will die that take chances with your luck," said Pensteven.

And he saw Speaker nod.

"Nobody can take chances against my luck," he answered, with the calmness that has no vanity in it. "Not even you, Stranger."

75

"I was a fool," said Pensteven. "I thought that I had to fight my way."

"You did," said Speaker. "But don't fight me. And don't fight Jack Christmas."

"Isn't Christmas nine-tenths reputation?" asked Pensteven.

The other tilted his head to one side. He was still thinking and considering when he asked: "What d'you mean by that?" He raised the handkerchief to his lips while he waited for the answer.

"I mean," said the young man, "that's he's probably been talked about until he's been magnified into a legend, while he's still alive."

"You use big words, Stranger," replied Speaker. "You can talk exactly like a book, and that's a habit you want to get over in this part of the world. It'll keep you fighting with men who don't like to have you talk down to them."

"I'm not trying to talk down," said Pensteven. "But I'll remember what you've said. I'm a Westerner at heart. My blood is Western, too."

"I'll sure believe that," said Al Speaker. "But tell me something. Do you really think that Christmas is a fake?"

"Not that, but hasn't he been blown bigger by talk than he really is?"

Speaker considered again. It was plain that he found the proper words hard to find.

Then he said: "I'll tell you this: Christmas is a simple man. Simple men never seem much at the first glance. But in the pinches they do the great things. Christmas ought to run a nation or an army. He hasn't got that sort of a start, so he's simply the greatest crook in the world. He can do everything better than everybody else. He's like one of the knights in the old stories. He rides better, shoots better. He schemes better. He can tell the truth better, and he can mix up the lies better than anybody else in the world. And he's always simple. That's why people talk so much about him. Because there's so much to explain about him. Nobody knows him as well as I do, but he's still a stranger to me!"

He held out his hand.

"Good luck, Stranger," said he.

"Thanks," said the young man. "I hope I'll see you again."

He heard the strange laughter of the little man.

"It's the first time in a good many months that you've said that, I suppose," said he. And he turned away toward the house.

Chapter 15

From the very first the way was hard. It pitched up through great pines and it crossed streams, dropping down or rushing through the wilderness.

A wind rose. It was not violent, but it carried before it hurricane clouds. The moon rose behind them, and showed the sky covered with great cavalcades of mist. A dozen times he had to pause and, from a clearing or a higher place, study the horizon until, through a partial clearing of the clouds, he saw the twin peaks and the blink of the ice upon them.

He left the denser forest, climbing up among lodge pole pines, and so came to the timber line, where trees crawled upon the ground in serpent shapes, writhing like hatred and fear.

The wind found him now. It had been nothing, with the trees to fend off its force. But now it cut him to the quick and beat him with whips. He rode on over steep, terribly dark moorlands. From the brow of a cliff, he looked down, in a glimpse of moonshine, upon a deep tarn below him. And he shivered; it was like coming under the eye of a merciless enemy, filled with dark thoughts.

Then he reached the edge of the snow and ice. He dismounted, pulled the saddle blanket from under the saddle, tied it about his shoulders, and turned the mule loose. It went off at a trot, slipping and sliding, but apparently rejoiced to be on its way home.

Far below, as he tied the hatchet and ice pick together and slung them over his shoulder, he heard the enormous bray of the mule. It was like the blast of a horn, with crowding echoes, announcing disasters to him.

But now he forged steadily ahead. He angled up snowy slopes. He reached icy cliffs which he had to avoid. There were others where the slope was very nearly perpendicular, but where he picked or chopped out hand and footholds, one by one, mounting by inches, literally. For he did not know the lay of the land, and the glimpses which he had from the light of the moon were merely enough to give him a confused idea of his goal, rather than accurate information about the terrain in between.

He reached cloud line. Heavy masses of mists swept over him. Numb from brittle cold and fatigue, he was like one in a dream, and had to trust to his instinct for direction. But he toiled on.

Youth was running in his blood, and behind him there was a sense of accomplishment, like rungs on a ladder. He had mounted on it so high that he felt he must go on to the top.

Besides, the thought of going back down some of those precipices was far more horrible than the climbing of new ones before him.

A man will fight when there is no sense or strength left in him, except the will to battle. Men totally unconscious remain on their feet in the prize ring, instinctively warding off blows and delivering them. So it was with Pensteven.

Now and then flashes of reason came to him, as he labored through that sweeping mist that stifled him with blindness and the wind that beat and tore at him. That reason told him that he was climbing on to his death.

Even the weight of the saddlebag was a profound burden to his shoulders, back, and legs.

But those flashes were short, fortunately for him. If sometimes he felt that he was climbing merely to find a lofty grave, he would reject the thought at once, leaving only the grim, dogged, brutal determination to go on.

As for cold, it was his companion. It was in him. It was part of the breath he drew, and the blood that pulsed in flurries like the wind through his veins.

Then, above him, he saw the hurtling mists turn to cream, and again to a milky white, only streaked with darkness. He thought that reason had deserted him. He

79

would die, but in a happy madness. Still the sweeping clouds grew bright until he climbed above the level of the clouds and saw himself between the two mountains which were his goal.

Instinct had been a true guide!

Now, above him, the moon stood in a crystal clear sky, and beneath him there was no world, but only the strange and terrible sea of the clouds that drove against the sides of the mountains and washed like waves high up the icy, gleaming cliffs.

He could see clearly now, but it was only to make the surety of death more certain.

There had been a storm before, but now the wind seemed to possess the whole upper universe. The stars trembled with its force and still it increased with every step that he made.

He could remember, now, what Al Speaker had told him. If a storm overtook him on the heights, he would die. Well, the storm had overtaken him and, when the August sun at last made these heights passable, Al Speaker would climb up here, alone, to find the bones of the messenger and the rotting canvas bag that held a hundred and eighty thousand dollars!

He took shelter behind a rock. But the moment he ceased from movement the cold sank into him like daggers of ice; a fatal drowsiness overwhelmed his brain, and the shriek of the wind was a dirge that exulted in his death.

He got up and left the sheltering rock. The hurricane caught him as a grown man might cuff a child with the flat of the hand and knocked him flat, sending him skidding on the ice. The point of the ice pick sank into his thigh and, like a spur, the pain reacted to raise him to his feet.

He got up and went on, sliding, skipping, falling again and again. What made the falls worse was the necessity of keeping his hands sheltered, whenever possible, beneath the saddle blankets about his shoulders.

Still the wind grew in force. Now it began to gather up the snow that had lain long in the gullies along the sides of the mountains. Its velocity had so increased that it tore off the upper crust of the snow and blew away the soft flakes beneath. It was as though a hundred million feather beds had been ripped open and their contents given to the wind. On the heights, the moon pierced through those crystal flakes, lighting them with a wonderful brilliance. Strange effects appeared and disappeared. Shadows were flung across the ice at his feet, spinning like the shadows cast by a whirling wheel.

Now, in the bitter dryness of that upper air, he saw the effects of electricity. It could not have been another thing, he thought, except the end of the world, high up there above the rolling sea of clouds.

For a glimmering of white, blue, and yellow fire formed on the points of jutting rocks, and he saw, as he reached the heights of the pass, a huge blue ball rolling like a wheel up the ridge of a summit.

Then an electric shock stuck him. It dropped him to his knees. It convulsed him and froze him to stone, with mouth twitching to the side and with limbs distorted.

It passed. But it left him choked, gasping for breath, on hands and knees, and, even so, barely able to support his weight.

He would have cast from him, then, the weight of the saddlebag that streamed out from him as straight as a silken flag in a wind. But he had not wit enough left to think of that. He could only rise, when his strength permitted and flounder on.

He took, perhaps, a hundred steps, and then the wave of numbness struck him again, though with less violence. And all about him, for an instant, the crags flamed.

The very moon grew dim now, and he told himself that his senses were failing, just as his muscles had failed, and allowed his legs to slip and slide.

Still the moon grew fainter and fainter, until it was hardly more than a wisp of cloud.

At last the back of the highest ridge was behind him, the screaming of the wind was less; it was possible to breathe to the depths of the lungs without the fear of freezing them; and for a moment he lingered, leaning an elbow against a rock, gasping like one out of water.

It was while he remained there that he looked out from his swollen eyes and realized that the dimness of the moon had been one effect of the coming of the dawn. For the grand circle of the horizon was now rimmed about with rose and gold; and it was a promise to him that he might not die, after all, but live through the great struggle. Hope is a cordial of exceeding potency, and with renewed strength, he stepped forward.

He was very far spent now, and he found that the sun, for which he had prayed in darkness and bitterness of spirit, was more a torment than a blessing, for the ice fields reflected the light, blinding his weary, swollen eyes.

Once he shot down a grassy slope for a hundred yards and was saved only because he fell into a deep pocket of snow. But he climbed out of this feathery smother to find himself close to the edge of timber line.

The worst part of his trial was ended. The storm was gone and had left the world refreshed and the sky new burnished; and the hot sun, climbing halfway toward the zenith, thawed his frozen muscles.

That thawing made him, at the same time, sensible of immense fatigues; of a thousand aches and pains. He walked in a trance, and then found that he was climbing again. In his nightmare of effort, he had actually turned and was again scaling the terrible heights!

Chapter 16

No medicine could avail him then, as he well knew, except sleep, and sleep he must have. The fright he had sustained in finding himself turned back in the wrong direction acted as a sufficient stimulus to keep him marching in the correct direction until he came among trees.

Then he used the blunted ax to strike down some shrubs, heaped them in a mass, laid over them a number of logs, and set fire to the mass.

He lay down. Sleep rushed over him as he closed his eyes. When he awoke, it was in a hell of fire, as the other hell had been one of ice.

His whole body was exposed to the fierce strength of a sun that was now almost at noon, and the embers of the crumbling fire had reached almost to his side as the mass of the pyre consumed and crumbled away.

He got up, gasping and parched. For a moment he staggered, regaining breath, recovering his wits.

He had slept perhaps two hours. And that sleep appeared to be more of a drug than a blessing. But by slow degrees his mind and his body began to function.

The saddlebag was still at his back, and the money must be in it. Yes, the contents were intact. He did not need to rummage among them to make sure of that. He had only to find the trail and then the ghost town and Cracken, then finally, home to Markham.

It seemed like home now, no longer a wild frontier town, but a place of infinite peace and rest. There he would find Barbara Still. His lips relaxed in a faint smile at the thought.

He was only half conscious perhaps at this time. But he had wit enough to know that he was going into danger. He used three shots out of each revolver, struck his mark each time, reloaded, and went on, more sure of himself.

He found the trail, turned down it and, almost at once, he found himself in the ghost town. That was the only name for it. Long ago abandoned, the forest had been creeping in. He saw houses dimly, half lost behind a dense upspringing of second-growth pines. He saw a tree rising to a considerable height straight through the roof of an old shack. He saw a growth of shrubbery that had taken possession of what had been the main street.

Through this shrubbery he was plodding when he glimpsed the form of a man before him and drew a gun.

He would have taken a life as quickly as he would have picked a thorn out of his hand.

"Stand fast!" ordered Pensteven.

The other turned quickly about.

"Now who the devil—" he began.

Then he saw the gun and gaped.

"Who are you?" he asked.

"Find Cracken for me. Take me to him," said Pensteven.

"Who are you?" repeated the other.

"The devil," said Pensteven, with ungainly humor. "And I'll send you to my house before me, unless I get some action out of you. Take me to Cracken!"

"I'll show you where he oughta be," replied the other, in a muttering voice. "I dunno that he's there!"

He turned, still staring over his shoulder toward Pensteven. He was dressed like a regular cowpuncher, this man of the ghost town, wearing wide-flaring leather chaps, which were useful in walking through the thorns of the brush. Afterward, all that Pensteven could remember of him was the startled look on his face.

Pensteven put up his gun. The other man, at the same time, stopped before a house which had been patched both on the sides and on the roof. The shrubbery on the street had been cleared away; a Dutch oven was in operation in the midst of the clearing, and around this there were three or four men seated. Another man, tall, brown, with a pleasantly smiling face, came and stood at the entrance of the house.

Pensteven's guide hooked a thumb over his shoulder toward the latter.

"Here's a bird I picked up," he announced. "He's covered with guns and says that he wants to see Cracken. Wants to murder him, for all I know. You take him, Jack."

The tall man from the doorway said: "Who are you?"

"John Stranger is my name," said Pensteven.

"It's a strange name," said the other, with his gentle smile.

Through the dream of his weariness, Pensteven stared and thought that he had seen the face or heard the voice before. Doubt and anxiety possessed him.

"I want to find Cracken," he said. "He's a fellow about forty, with saber-shaped mustaches and a sag beneath his eyes."

"Who sent you?" asked the man in the doorway.

"Al Speaker."

"Did anybody send you to Al Speaker?"

"Juan Oñate."

"Ah?"

There was a general murmur. One of the men beside the fire stood up and looked at the young fellow with interest.

The man in the doorway went on: "Anybody sent you to Oñate?"

"Doc Shore."

"More and more of it," muttered one of the bystanders. "This gent needs a bullet through the head or a cup of coffee."

"Give him the coffee," said the man in the doorway.

Someone brought a cup. Pensteven backed away, a gun in either hand.

"I want Cracken," he said.

"Jack ain't good enough for you, eh?" asked the fellow who was carrying the coffee, grinning.

"I want Cracken," repeated the hoarse voice of Pensteven monotonously.

"Polly wants a cracker," mocked someone.

"Be quiet, will you?" said the man of the smile, more

85

gently than ever. "What have you for Cracken? A message?"

"I have something for Cracken," repeated Pensteven. "Nobody else gets anything but lead."

A rider on a small, wiry mule came twisting through the shrubbery in the street.

"Who wants me?" he asked.

He was about forty, he sagged beneath the eyes, he had saber-shaped mustaches. And he spoke with a drawl.

"This gent is locoed," said someone. "Maybe you swiped his watch and chain, Crack. Look out for him, he's full of guns and foolishness."

The newcomer dismounted, with a shrug of his high, narrow shoulders, and came forward with the stilted step of a horseman.

His heels were four inches high! His spurs were still longer and plated with gold.

"You want me, brother?" said he.

"You're Cracken," said Pensteven, nodding. "Al Speaker sends this."

He unslung the saddlebag from his shoulder and presented it.

"And this," he added, and took from his pocket the letter.

Cracken, with a scowl, looked into the contents of the saddlebag. Then he jumped.

"Great Caesar's ghost!" he exclaimed.

He turned to the man of the smile and ran forward, with a short, hobbling step, holding out both letter and saddlebag.

"This is for you, Jack," he said. "Speaker didn't think you'd be here. This is—Great Scott! This is for—"

He finished, muttering undecipherable sounds at the ear of the other; and the latter, with a smile and a nod, took both the saddlebag and the letter.

Pensteven said dully: "I brought you the saddlebag and the letter. You gave 'em away, but that's not my business."

Cracken came back and slapped him on the shoulder.

"You brought them through all right," said he. "I don't know how you did it. Why, it was only supposed to be yesterday that—look here, Jack, he would've had to come over the pass last night to get here by this time!"

"Don't be a fool," said another man. "How could he come through that wind?"

"That's the blister of the sun reflected off ice," said the tall man of the smile, holding the saddlebag and the letter without looking at either. "He came over the pass through the storm and down the slope on this side in the morning. No wonder he's groggy."

"The camp is all yours, brother," Cracken. "Sammy, open up a bottle. What'll you have, eh?"

"A horse," said Pensteven. "I've got to be going now. I'm late."

"A horse?" muttered Cracken. "Not stopping off here? But you're dead. Your feet are bleeding through your shoes. You can't."

"I want a horse, not talk," said Pensteven.

He staggered a little.

Then he put his hand against the trunk of a sapling to steady himself.

"For a horse, I'll pay—" he began.

"Your money's no good in this camp," replied Cracken. "You want a horse? You can take the best one in my string!"

"No," said the man of the smile. "Give him that black chestnut mare of mine, will you?"

"Hey, hold on," said Cracken. "Are you giving him Dainty?"

"Give him the mare. Saddle her for him," said the man of the smile. "Don't ask him any questions. Let him go. He knows his own business better than we do. A fellow who can cross that through the storm has a mind of his own."

As he spoke, he pointed, and Pensteven, following the direction of the hand, saw above him, the rigid, steep sides, the glittering ice and snow of the frozen, rocky hell through which he had passed.

He felt as though he must have left his old soul behind him; he stood here with a new one.

Chapter 17

When he woke up in bed in Markham afterward, he remembered things rather patchily. As he sat in the saddle, he could recall he had asked the way to Markham and the answer had been repeated to him many times.

Then he was riding down a trail with his hands clasped over the horn of his saddle. He had to keep them gripped against the pommel to avoid falling to the ground, such agonies of weariness and of sleep assailed him. Before him rode another man, leading his horse on a rope.

Then, coming out from the trees, he saw a sweep of green, rolling ground, and more trees, and then the far-off glitter of the sun on the windows of a town.

"That's Markham, and here's the trail. I don't dare to go no farther. It ain't chicken stealing that they want me for," announced his conductor.

He could not remember anything else except that the ground rose and fell beneath him like waves of a sea. He could not realize that it was the swift movement of the mare as she loped gently over the swelling land. A gait other than hers would have jolted him from the saddle and left him sprawled on the ground, instantly asleep.

And so he came into the main street of Markham, and the houses sprang up on either side like magic to his startled eyes.

People called out his name—John Stranger. Someone came and walked beside his horse, and asked if he were sick.

"Get me to the Elbow Room," he said.

That was the last place where he had seen Doc Shore.

So this fellow and another got him to the Elbow Room Saloon, and then he was standing, leaning against the edge of the bar and saying to Jerry, the bartender: "What time is it?"

"Two forty, Stranger," said Jerry. "And what the devil you been doing to yourself?"

"Get Doc Shore for me, quick," said Pensteven.

"Sit down there while I fetch him. I'll get him here in a jiffy."

"I won't sit down. I'd go to sleep. Run like hell. I'm dead," said Pensteven.

And Jerry ran. The door of the saloon swished, followed by a heavy footfall.

"Is this the gent?" asked a heavy, snarling man. "I'm Stew Carter. I'm looking for you, Stranger."

"I don't know you," said Pensteven, looking drearily straight before him.

"Is he drunk?" asked Stew Carter.

"No. There's no smell of booze about him. He's tuckered out. That's all. Look at him. He's shaking all over."

"I wish he was himself," said Stew. "It's my damn luck, but some of you boys tell him that I'm gonna see him later on, when he's slept himself out!"

A voice, then, sounded small and far away at the shoulder of Pensteven. It was the voice of Doc Shore saying, with a ring of wonder in it: "It's five minutes to three. Did you make the round?"

"I made the round," said Pensteven. "I rode the desert twice, and the mountains. I saw Juan Oñate—"

"Never mind, never mind!" said Doc Shore hastily. "Hell, I guessed right, when I guessed you! Here, lean on me."

"I've got some expense money left," said Pensteven, feeling that the job must be completed before he fell unconscious. "I spent only fifty dollars."

"Don't be a fool," said Doc Shore. "The rest is yours, and a lot more, besides. More'n you guess, just now. You're made, is what you are. Come on with me. I'll get you into bed at the hotel. In twenty-four hours you done it! Twenty-four hours!"

Again, it was of the mountains that he spoke and that they could not be passed.

Pensteven could remember having said many times:

"You think that I'm here, but I'm not. It's only my body. The rest of me is dead, somewhere there above timber line. I turned back toward the ice and began to climb again. You think I'm here, but I'm not. I'm up there above timber line, somewhere, dead."

"That's all right," Doc Shore had said, as often as Pensteven insisted that he was a ghost. "I understand. Of course you're dead. Come along with me. Lean on me. Of course you're dead and everything's all right!"

That was the last that Pensteven remembered as he lay awake in his bed, with the cool sheets caressing his body.

He felt empty and light. A strange radiance played over the ceiling of the room; the pure fragrance of the pines breathing in the wind.

"I've slept till sunset," he said to himself.

Then he realized that it could not have been so short a time. There must have been many long hours of utter repose flowing through his body and through his mind like a great river through a desert land.

There was no noise from the town, no voices rose to him from the street, no sounds of playing children, such as would be filling that hour. Suddenly he realized, more by the delicious freshness of the air than anything else, that it was sunrise!

He got up.

His muscles were sore and stiff, so he practiced a trick which he had learned long before, taking a dry towel, with which he thoroughly whipped and massaged himself. Then he scrubbed in icy cold water that he found on the washstand in a huge earthenware pitcher. It was a chilling business, but afterward the blood sprang up to the surface.

He shook out his clothes, and then dressed to the boots. But these, as he saw, were of no use. The crags of rock and the knife edges of the ice above timber line had cut the leather to ribbons. His feet, of course, were covered with cuts. Slippers would have to do him for some days. Boots could follow later on.

He put on an old pair of carpet slippers, therefore, and, since the town was well awake by this time and the hotel filled with the bustle of the beginning day, he was about to go down and find a breakfast such as would have

90

satisfied a whole tribe of wolves, when there was a knock at his door and Doc Shore came in.

His skin was yellower than ever, the wart on his face bigger and blacker. He paused inside of the door and surveyed Pensteven.

"Here you be, up and at it, eh?"

"Here I am," agreed Pensteven.

"And looking fit! I thought it would be a week in hospital for you, Stranger."

"My feet are a bit worn, that's all."

"You ought to have no feet at all. Any frostbite?"

"A nip, here and there."

"You'll feel everything a lot more the next day," suggested Shore sourly. "What you up to now?"

"Breakfast."

"Come down and eat on me, will you? I owe you a couple meals. I owe you something more too. You'll get half of it now."

He went to the center table and counted out ten hundred-dollar bills.

"That's a little bonus," said he.

"I took my job on salary and expenses," said Pensteven. "I didn't count on bonuses, and I don't ask for them."

It seemed strange to him that for his work he should be offered money!

Doc Shore frowned at him, but afterward nodded.

"I know," he said. "I know how you feel. You sweated your doggone soul out. The hard cash can't pay for it. But I ain't paying you a cent out of my pocket. They pay for it!"

"Who are they?" asked Pensteven. "Oñate and Al Speaker and Cracken?"

"Humph," said Shore. "Let's go down and feed. I'm hungry myself."

They went down to the breakfast room and passed from peaches and cream through porridge, bacon, fried eggs, potatoes, and beefsteak. Shore, like many starved-looking men, had the appetite of a horse; but Pensteven took double orders of everything. And he polished his plate. He had just finished the beefsteak when the proprietor came in with a great, steaming slab of fried meat. He leaned over the table.

"Venison, gents," said he in a whisper.

And passed out of the room again, grinning complacently over his shoulder.

"And me already full to the nozzle!" groaned Shore. "Why couldn't he've sprung that one trick earlier? They take and favor you, in this here town, brother. They kinder treat you like the long lost son. What you gone and done for them? It was Vince Carter, I guess. He's always been too free with himself. He ain't a bad kid, but there's too much of him. He's always gone and stepped on the toes of other folks, which ain't popular, any way that you look at it."

"No, I suppose not," said Pensteven vaguely.

He was deeper in venison, for the moment, than anything else.

Then came a last cup of bitter coffee.

"Look at the way the waitress looks at you, Stranger," said Shore. "Like you were her first cousin and a gold mine, crossed. You fell on your feet when you socked young Carter. The whole town likes you, now."

"Mostly," said Pensteven, "because you're paying attention to me. What makes you so strong in this town, Shore? Do they love big crooks better than anything else?"

Shore puckered his brows and waited for a long moment.

Then he said: "I see how it is. You've gone and had a college education since the day before yesterday. You've seen Oñate, and Al Speaker. And you've gone and got yourself Dainty. Since you seen John Christmas, you got a real idea of what a big crook is!"

Chapter 18

It was the turn of Pensteven to stare, and he did so with a vengeance. It was that name which most haunted him, the name of the man to accomplish whose death he had spent so many painful years of preparation.

"Christmas?" he gasped.

Shore was impatient.

"You've got Dainty, haven't you?" said he.

"Well, what of that?"

"And isn't she one of the favorite horses of Christmas?"

Pensteven closed his eyes, remembering the tall man of the brown face and the smile, with the gentle, soothing voice.

It was Jack Christmas, of course! Had he not been described in almost these words by the men of Al Speaker?

Yes, it was Christmas.

He said aloud slowly, hardly opening his eyes: "That reminds me of something."

"Of what, son?" said Shore.

"A yarn in the 'Third Reader,' about the kids that started out to find the wishing gate."

"I don't remember ever having heard about that."

"They ran like the devil, all day, high and low, and after a while they were dead beat. They came to an old battered gate and dropped down exhausted. And they put their backs to it and rested. They felt that they were lost and they were scared. All they could wish for was to be home. Suddenly they found themselves at the door of their house. The old battered gate, d'you see, was the wishing gate. They'd worked like the devil and when they got to the right spot, they didn't recognize it."

"What's that yarn got to do with you?" asked Doc Shore.

"Oh, nothing," murmured Pensteven.

He began to frown, looking out through the window.

Yes, the man had called the tall fellow "Jack," but he, with his half-numbed mind and body, had been unable to recognize anything, or to put two and two together.

"You wanted to see Christmas, did you?" said Shore. "Well, all the good things come to him that waits, they say. And now that Christmas knows a part of what you can do, you'll see him again. Be sure of that. He ain't the kind that misses any tricks! How much did Oñate send up?"

"A hundred and eighty thousand dollars, he told me," murmured Pensteven.

"A hundred and eighty thousand dollars—"

Shore had risen from his chair.

"You mean that he sent that much cash by you?"

"Yes."

"Great guns!"

"It was a lot," said Pensteven. "I didn't know how much was in the bag, or what was in it, till Speaker told me. Speaker's the greatest shot in the world!"

"You didn't know? You didn't look on the way?" asked Shore scornfully.

Pensteven lifted his head.

"No, I didn't know," said he.

"Don't go looking for a fight every minute," growled Shore. "You're eating breakfast, not raw meat. I asked you a question. You're one of these honorable crooks, are you?"

"Who called me a crook?" asked Pensteven fiercely.

"Then what in hell are you? What are you doing with me? Who are you working for? What are Oñate and the rest? Say, whacha think you are, son?"

"A fool, likely," said Pensteven.

"Yeah, maybe a fool. But don't try to run out on me with any bluffs like that," murmured Shore. "Make me kinder hot, you do. Who called you a crook? I call you a crook or a half-wit. Maybe you think I paid you three hundred advance and three hundred expenses down for milking cows. Is that it? Maybe that bonus is for clipping

94

sheep. Is that the idea? Big money for sitting still and crossing your hands, brother. Is that what you want to say?"

Pensteven sighed.

"All right," he said. "I let myself in for this."

"Let yourself out again," muttered Shore. "It's all right, though. You're a good fellow, only you don't know what you're talking about, I guess."

Gradually his heat subsided.

"You said that Speaker was a good hand with a gun," he suggested. "Yeah. Sure he is. Christmas taught him."

"Christmas taught him?"

"Sure. Who could be that slick with a gun except he come out of the school of Christmas? Speaker's the only man that he ever taught."

The young man sighed again. His eyes looked far away, and he saw no solution of his problem. He knew that to slay Christmas, he must use a gun. And even against such skill as Speaker possessed, he would be quite helpless. But Christmas? He was the master from whom Speaker had gained such knowledge of the craft as he possessed! He, Pensteven, was helpless!

He reverted to Speaker. "Tell me about Speaker," he asked.

"That's easy," said Shore. "Once he had a chin. Now he ain't. That's all."

"What happened?"

"To him? He was a young bohunk, full of himself. His father had a good ranch. He was a fine-looking kid. I seen a picture of him the way he was in those days. The nicest girl on the range falls in love with him, and will she marry him? You bet she will, and that pleased! Then along comes the day when he gets into a gun scrap with a gent in a saloon that he's dropped into for some ginger ale, because he was a soft-drink artist in those days. And the gent takes and shoots his chin off for him, and little Speaker, nothing but game, crawls through his own blood and puts a knife in the other fellow. Kills him, I mean.

"Then he goes to the hospital for a few months. When he comes out, the girl gives him one look and changes her mind. And I don't blame her. Speaker runs amok. He makes such a stir that Jack Christmas hears about him and gathers him into the fold. Speaker, he'd as soon kill you as

95

ask your pardon. He's that way. There ain't any humanity in him. None at all, except that he hates to be bothered pulling a gun."

Pensteven could remember the calm, expectant glances of the three men in the shack. He understood now. They had simply been waiting for the little half-faced man to kill the big, insolent intruder.

"That means something to me," he remarked aloud, adding:

"You think that Christmas may get interested in me?"

"You ain't a crook," replied Shore, "and what does he want with an honest fellow like you?"

"Drop that," said Pensteven.

"All right," answered Shore, "only, you rile me, sorter. That mare's a beauty, ain't she?"

"I don't remember her very well," said Pensteven truthfully.

"You don't remember Dainty?"

"No, not very well."

"Well, you were corked, all right," said the other. "I gotta admit that. But anybody that can see the sun could see Dainty, I'd say. Old Christmas, he must have taken a shine to you, to give you that mare—hundred and eighty thousand or not. He don't give away his pet horses so cheap as all of that! A fast horse means life or death to him, too often. That's the funny part with him. He's always taking chances."

"He looked rather quiet, and gentle," murmured Pensteven.

"He's that way, too. He's every way. And a devil at the bottom of the well. You finished?"

"Yes."

"Then let's go out and look at that dark diamond, that Dainty!"

They went out and found a crowd gathered around the pasture at the back of the hotel. There were a dozen horses in it, but only one of the lot commanded real attention, and that was Dainty.

To Pensteven she was one flash of glorious beauty. He could not criticize her. He did not want to. She seemed perfect, and suddenly near the heart.

He leaned for a long time upon a fence post, staring at her, studying her. Every line was drawn by a master's hand, every movement filled with lightness and grace. If she turned and looked, many voices murmured foolish and affectionate words.

Pensteven became aware that many people were grouped along the fence, also staring, but their interest was not as undivided as his own, for they were looking first at the mare and then at himself! In their eyes the same expression as of looking at something wonderful, removed, aloof.

Then a voice sounded behind Shore and Pensteven. It was the voice of Sheriff Charles Wace, saying:

"You gone and gathered in that fellow, did you, doc? Well, I can't hang anything on you yet, but I know you, doc. And I know the boss that you work for. He's had luck and you've had luck. But I'll find you, and I'll get you, sooner or later. You can depend on that!"

"Oh, shut up, Charley," said Shore, slowly turning his head.

"You rat," continued the sheriff, through his teeth. "You sneaking, poisonous rat! I'll have you one of these days. This fellow might've gone straight, except that you found him when he was on his uppers. You turned him crooked. I know what he's done. He's joined Christmas. I know what the rest of this here gang of fools knows—that mare was once rode by Christmas and now she calls this fellow boss. I know that you laugh up your sleeve at me, too. But I'll make the score even before I'm through! Trust me for that."

As he finished, he turned, and from the corner of his eye, Pensteven saw the sheriff walk away.

"I trust you for one thing, and that's for being an old fool," said Doc Shore.

But he spoke not overloud, a fact which Pensteven noted with much interest. As for himself, he saw that he had bargained with the devil and that the facts were known.

Chapter 19

Pensteven packed his old blanket roll and rode to the house of Mrs. Still. He found it well out from the edge of town, posted like an ancient fortress on a peninsula with a creek curving about three sides of it, and filling the air with a cool rushing of water through the hottest summer days. The fourth side of the house was overhung by great trees; a table was built under them, apparently for use in the middle of summer.

Pensteven walked around to the back of the house, for the front was deserted. There was only a narrow footway remaining. The creek had worn away the rest, and over the edge he looked down on a shallow mat of soil and tangled roots, and then past the cleanly chiseled face of rock to the water, thirty or forty feet below.

On the opposite bank of the stream the great woods began, and above the heads of the trees the mountains lifted suddenly. It was a wild place; a good setting, he thought, for Barbara Still, so calmly self-reliant and matter of fact.

He went up the steps, now, to the back porch and knocked at a screen door.

"Who's there?" asked a woman's voice, turned away from him.

"Somebody looking for board and room," said he.

She came to the door, and through the screen he saw a round, brown, good-natured face; she was a big woman, and now she was wiping her hands on her clean apron.

"I don't take in roomers any more," she said. "We've got one already and he's enough. My girl don't want any more roomers. We need the house for ourselves." She added: "Barbara has such a pile of cats and dogs and things."

Pensteven sighed with regret.

"You know how it is," he said, "when a fellow has to sleep in a hotel room with the noise off the street."

"Oh, I know," said she. "It's a terrible racket, and it never lets up, day or night."

"There's always a child squawling, or a horse squealing, or men wrangling, or dogs barking, or something like that. A fellow can't sleep."

"You sound like you have nerves," remarked the woman.

"Markham is pretty hard on 'em," lied Pensteven.

She opened the door and came out to him with a friendly smile.

"Yeah," she said, "nerves are terrible things to have."

"You have a rather sensitive look yourself, Mrs. Still," said he.

She smiled broadly; her eyes almost disappeared behind wrinkles of pleasure.

"What makes you think that?" she asked.

"Well," he said, "I don't know how one tells exactly. It's rather a feeling than a knowing, I'd say. A look about your eyes, I think."

Mrs. Still also sighed. Her great bosom rose and fell like a wave.

"That's where I always look in others," she said. "Sleeplessness leaves ghosts in the eyes, I've always said."

"That's wonderfully well put, and it's true," declared Pensteven. "I can see them in your own eyes. You must have done some writing, Mrs. Still, to have expressions like that so pat. Or did you hear someone else say it?"

"About the ghosts in the eyes? No, it's my own idea. I used to write, though, when I was a slip of a thing. You wouldn't think to look at me now that I was ever that. But I was, and I used to write poetry. Rhyme was just nothing to me. In school, when we passed notes, I always wrote mine in rhyme. It wasn't any trouble; it just came."

"That's a wonderful gift," said Pensteven, looking at her with solemn eyes.

"That's what my mother used to say," replied Mrs. Still. "But father said that he didn't want any authoress in the family. And somehow time went on, and the thing slipped. Out of hand, out of mind. You know how it is. I can see that you've suffered, too, poor young man. Such a look as you have around the eyes!"

"You're a strange person, Mrs. Still," said he. "You seem able to look straight into a man's heart."

"It's sort of a gift I have," she replied. "It's not much of a comfort to me, but it's a comfort to others. Poor dear Mr. Still, he used to say that I knew his thoughts before he spoke them. I'm sorry about the hotel."

"So am I," said Bob Pensteven, "especially after I've seen you. I could board here at least, couldn't I?"

"Of course you could," said she. "And I wish that Barbara weren't so set—"

"Any corner would do for me," said Pensteven. "I'm used to rough going. It's only the noise of the town that I can't stand."

"How long would you be staying?" she asked, tilting her big head to one side.

He looked sardonically into the future, a blind and shifting mist before his eyes.

"Until I die, perhaps," said he.

She beamed on him suddenly.

"You really do like the place, don't you?" said she.

"I love it," said Pensteven. "Besides, it isn't entirely the house and the trees and the mountains, and the quiet. You know, it isn't so easy to find an understanding person.

"You come right in and sit down," said Mrs. Still. "I'll go and see if the other room is tidy, and then I'll show you up. If it pleases you, I should think that we could persuade Barbara. She is so headstrong, that child."

She made him sit down in a kitchen chair, and there he remained with a broad grin of duplicity and content on his face, while she hurried away, the stairs creaking under her weight as she slowly mounted them.

The kitchen was a big room, with a range on one side of it worthy of a hotel. Burnished pots and pans decorated the wall. The woodwork was painted white. The pattern had been scrubbed off the linoleum on the floor.

If the kitchen is the heart of a home, he was pleased with what he saw of this one.

A light step came up the back steps and in walked

100

Barbara, one hand loaded down with three large jackrabbits, the other with a rifle.

She gave him a steady glance; he stood up to greet her, but, instead of speaking, she went over to the sink, laid the rabbits on the drainboards, turned on a tap, and began to wash her hands.

As she did so, she turned her brown face and spoke to him.

"Hello, Mr. R. B. Stranger," said she.

"My name is John, not R. B.," said he.

"Mr. Robber Bandit," she enlarged.

"Who says that I'm that?" he asked.

"Who in Markham thinks that you're anything else?" she asked him. "They've all seen Dainty by this time. You must have wanted to advertise your fine, clean profession!"

If the horse was really as well known as this, he began to wonder if John Christmas might have had some ulterior motive in making him a present of her.

"I haven't stolen a penny," he protested.

"Nothing but bank notes, securities, jewelry, and such trifles, I suppose," she said sternly.

"Not a bank note, not a security, not any jewelry, either," he replied.

"I'm not going to call you a liar," she said. "I'm just going to believe that Jack Christmas gives away his favorite horse for nothing."

"If all you people know him so well and hate him so much," suggested Pensteven, "why don't you band together and catch him some day?"

"Why don't we catch lightning in our bare hands?" she replied scoffingly. "Besides, he never does the town any harm. He spends money like water here; and it's his home town besides. Everybody helps to cover up his tracks when he comes here. What brought you to my house, John Stranger, as you call yourself?"

She turned around and began to dry her hands on a roller towel. "I followed my nose and it brought me here," he replied.

"Stuff," said Barbara Still.

"It was Fate, perhaps, that led me here," said he.

"You better smile when you say that," remarked the girl.

He grinned broadly.

"That's better," she said. "Now, you tell me what brought you to this place. What do you want?"

"Room and board."

"You can't have either."

"That's hard," said he.

"It's the way I am. Hard as nails. You get, Mr. John R. B. Stranger."

He went obediently to the door, his head down. She said: "Did you see mother?"

He turned about.

"I saw her," said he.

"You don't need to stop," said Barbara Still. "You can talk while you keep on going."

He backed by slow inches toward the door again.

"Your mother and I found that we have a good deal in common. We both suffer from insomnia. The traffic roar of the streets of Markham is what drove me out here to try to find peace."

"You scalawag," said she severely. "You came here for peace, did you? You go and climb your horse, and get out of here!"

A heavy step came. Mrs. Still burst in panting.

"You might like the room, anyway," she said. "It's rather small, but just come this way and look at it. The Virginia creeper is sweet, hanging all over the window. Oh, hello, Barbara!"

"Humph!" said Barbara, and, giving her stepmother a severe glance, she stalked from the room, slamming the screen door behind her.

Chapter 20

Mrs. Still was evidently upset. She laid a hand over her heart and exclaimed in nervous tones: "Great goodness!"

"I'd better go," said Pensteven. "She doesn't want me here, it seems."

"She doesn't seem to," argued Mrs. Still. "But if she felt as keenly about it as all that, she would have said so. She is really a great one for speaking her mind. Now, I don't know what to say. She would have spoken out, though. She says that Dave Bell is enough roomer to have. She's finally made him give us his leaving date, which is next month. She's a dreadful girl, when she makes up her mind. I don't know what to say!"

"If I move in," said Pensteven, "I can always move out again the moment you say the word."

"Would you?" said Mrs. Still."

"Of course I would," said he.

"Well, then, come and look at the room."

"I don't need to look at it," he told her. "Just to be under this roof is enough for me. I'd sooner make down my blankets on the floor of your hallway than sleep in a double bed in the hotel."

"Would you, now?" she said, blooming and smiling under the praise. "Well, you go and get your things. I'm going to give the room a few more touches."

He went down the back steps and, turning around the farther corner of the house, he saw Barbara seated on a chopping block between him and the corral. She was swaying the splitting ax in one slender, strong, brown hand.

"Going or coming?" she asked.

He took off his hat.

"Coming, if you please," he replied.

"Humph," said Barbara.

She frowned and narrowed her eyes.

"You wheedle old women, do you?" she inquired.

"You're wrong about me, Barbara," said he. "I'm not going to be as bad as you expect."

"Bad about what?" she asked.

"About you," said Pensteven.

"If you start playing calf," said the girl, "off with you that minute!"

"I won't be such a fool as all that."

"I want to believe you," she answered.

He sat down on a log close by.

"I wanted to be near you if I could," he said, "but I'll be as dumb as a horse if you wish."

"I don't know," she said. "I've cured some of the boys before this. Made 'em hate me, in fact. I'm the most unpopular girl in Markham. The boys would rather dance with a barbed-wire tangle than with me."

"I believe you," he said heartily.

At this, she smiled a little.

"You had to join Christmas, did you? You had to go and do that? What does he look like?"

"I thought you knew him?"

"I do. All about him, mostly. But I've never really laid eyes on him. He doesn't lead parades when he comes to town."

"He's magnificent," said Pensteven. "He's an inch or so taller than I am and made like a statue. Very brown and very handsome. Got a remarkable smile and a very gentle voice. His men worship him. Every woman falls in love with him at first sight."

"Stuff!" said she.

But she leaned her chin on her hand and looked curiously at the speaker. "You can imagine how magnificent he is," said Pensteven, "when he gave me Dainty the first time I saw him."

"What had you done for him?"

"Oh, nothing; just made a little trip."

"That's why you're wearing slippers. That's why you came back fainting to Markham the other day?"

"I have corns," said Pensteven. "And the other day I

had had too much to drink. I'm sorry, but liquor is a dreadful weakness of mine."

"You've got a worse one," she remarked.

"What's that?"

"Lying," said she. "After what you've said, I wouldn't believe a word you say."

"You shouldn't ask foolish questions, then," said Pensteven. "You ought to let me talk to you of the thing that I can't help speaking the truth about."

"Such as what?" said she.

"You," said Pensteven.

"I know that lingo," she said. "It doesn't do any good. You like me. There's a sort of something about me. Something about my voice and my eyes that stays in your mind, and wakes you up in the middle of the night. I'm no beauty, but I've got enough face to make the boys tell their story, and I'm sick of it."

She struck the ax into the ground up to the handle.

"You're like every spoiled kid," he said. "You think that everybody wants you for your pretty face. It isn't so pretty, at that. You're too minus nose and plus jaw."

"That sounds like sense," she said. "You and my mirror say the same things. Go on, Mr. Portrait Painter. If it isn't my face, it's the beautiful soul that shines out of my eyes, I suppose. That's what's knocked you silly?"

"I'm not so silly about you, either," said Pensteven. "I'm more curious. Why do people want to ride bucking horses? They're no better looking, or more intelligent, horses. But they ask for riding, and people will keep on trying to give them what they ask for."

"I need a master, do I?" said she, lowering her head a little and looking up dangerously at him.

"Don't you?" he asked.

"Well," she said, "you're different, anyway. You don't give me such a pain. You're almost interesting. How would you go about mastering me?"

"You don't give a final examination to a student just beginning a course," said Pensteven. "I don't know enough about you yet. I've only read the title of the book."

"What's the title, then?" said she.

"It's a romance called 'Spoiled and Proud, or All for Herself'!"

"Going to waste your time on a book like that?"

105

"I might. But I know those stories. They always end the same way. The heroine kicks the poor man in the face for forty-two chapters and in the forty-third she suddenly realizes that her soul is starved for him, and she makes a great self-sacrifice, such as spreading an umbrella over him in the rain or letting him kiss her lily hand or some such business as that."

Barbara Still threw back her head and laughed.

"You're all right, John R. B. Stranger," she declared. "Maybe you wouldn't be such a nuisance around the house. Hello, Dave!"

A small man, with dark, bright eyes and the bearing of one who wished to command more respect than his inches called for, came around the corner of the house, slapping a quirt against his chaps.

"Hello, Barbara," said he.

"Here's a little playmate for you, Dave," announced the girl. "He's the new roomer at our house. John Stranger is the way he calls himself in today's paper."

She added :"This is Dave Bell, the mining expert. He's stopping with us between mines, so to speak."

They shook hands, and the bright eyes of Dave Bell fastened on the face of Pensteven.

"You kick me out and take him in, Barbara," he said to the girl. "What's the matter? He ain't as pretty as a collar ad, at that. Or is it pounds that you're looking for?"

"He has a new lingo," said the girl. "He talks like a lion tamer."

"Well," said Dave Bell, "you know I stopped talking sloppy a month ago. I'm cured of you, Bobbie, but I like your ma's cooking. You oughta be a good little girl and let me stay. I oughta have a chance to see you open his eyes wide, like you done to mine."

He spoke half sourly, half smilingly, then he turned to Pensteven.

"I saw Dainty out in front," said he. "She's a bird, all right."

"Is she out in front?" exclaimed the girl. "Let's go look at her."

They went together and found Dainty hanging her head as though asleep. She raised it quickly, her eyes brightened and her ears pricked up at the sight of them—which is the way a horse has of smiling.

"She's a dear," said the girl.

"There's sixteen hands of that dear," said Dave Bell. "And she's all hammered iron. Look at those legs! She could carry a ton a mile a minute. Shes' so sure-footed that she walks up cliffs that make the hawks dizzy, and then she runs on top of the clouds."

"Don't chatter, Dave," said the girl. "I want to look at Dainty. May I try her, John?"

"I'll give you a leg up," said Pensteven.

"Thanks," she answered, and whipped lightly up into the saddle.

At a walk, at a trot, at a canter, at a racing gallop, she let Dainty fly away among the trees; the sound of the hoofbeats was deadened in the distance.

"Nothing like her!" murmured Dave Bell.

"No," said Pensteven, "she's a good mare, it seems to me."

Bell turned his head with a quick, birdlike movement.

"Oh, all right," said he. And turning his back on Pensteven, he walked into the house.

Chapter 21

The room of Pensteven was in the top story just under the eaves of the old house. When he leaned out through the curtain made by the leaves of the Virginia creeper, he could see the window of Bell's room, to his left and not far away. But Bell's chamber was larger and far more commodious. He had been shown the inside of it by his landlady.

The outside of the building, as he noticed when he leaned through the window, staring at the rushing, white-streaked water of the creek, was strengthened with two or three big upright beams, and several crosspieces, a proof that the frame of the old house was none too strong and had needed this buttressing. Even so, when the wind blew with sudden strength, the old building groaned from head to heel.

It was a long, still, warm day. Pensteven spent a large part of it resting in his bed, lying face down. He had also spent considerable time in tightening the bandages upon his feet, for he had to get them into shape for the wearing of riding boots before long. He believed what Doc Shore had said to him, that John Christmas would send for him soon.

In fact, the gift of the mare had been, it seemed, the way of Christmas in proclaiming to the world that this man was his.

What would he, Pensteven, do, if he found himself asked to the camp of the outlaw? He had come to kill John Christmas. For that purpose he had trained himself, but now he knew that he was a child and that the other was a master. The problem was one that he could not solve. He determined, like a wise fellow, to wait until events forced him by their own weight to a conclusion.

In the evening, he went out and found Dave Bell helping Barbara to clean and stretch a deerskin. When the larger man joined them, Bell went at once into the house.

"Why am I poison to your old chum?" asked Pensteven.

"It isn't you," she repiled. "He was poisonous from the time he grew up and found himself minus about eight inches of where he wanted to be. He's the runt of a big family. That's why he's so chesty. He's always daring the world to damn him; and he's always damning the world because it doesn't dare. He's that kind of poison. But he's all right; he's no fool. I like him pretty well."

She went over to the woodpile and began to chop wood.

"Let me do that," said Pensteven.

"Can you do it any better?" she asked, between strokes.

"I can get the work done," said he.

"You never handled an ax in your life," said she.

"How d'you know that?"

"We shook hands once, and your palm is too soft for honest work. That's why you have to be a crook, I suppose. But now you stand off and watch my style. It's good for the stomach muscles to swing an ax."

She made the big-bladed ax flash in wide circles, cleaving a block at every stroke. When she came to a knot, she cut through it with rapid, fierce blows. And she was never missing the line.

"How's that?" she asked finally, stepping back and gesturing toward the completed pile.

"That shows you off pretty well," said Pensteven. "Any Indian would know enough to appreciate a girl who can work like that. Can you make moccasins, too, and do beadwork?"

"Go on and carry in that wood to the kitchen," said Barbara Still. "You make me tired."

But she smiled as she spoke.

Dinner was a cheerful affair that night, and it was crowned by a huge deep-dish apple pie, served with quantities of yellow cream. Pensteven ate in eloquent silence.

After the pie, they sat about the table, resting their elbows on it. It was the best time of the day, Mrs. Still declared. She now talked somewhat of her nerves and of her youthful leaning toward the Muse. She sipped black coffee as she spoke and shook her big head in sorrow for her wasted talents.

"Quit it, mother, will you?" Barbara protested. "This Stranger, here, has just been kidding you along a little. He doesn't give a rap about your rhymes and, the first thing you know, you'll be quoting them!"

Mrs. Still blinked.

"I'm surprised, Mrs. Still. I'm really surprised. I don't know what to say," said Pensteven.

And he looked across the table with a sad dignity toward Barbara.

His hostess regained courage and her wind.

"A girl of her age," she said, "wants all the attention. She thinks that the older generation ought to confine itself to the kitchen. But I can tell you that I have time for my own thoughts, whether I'm doing dishes or cooking, little Miss Minx!"

Pensteven, shortly after, went up to bed, still smiling to himself. He was well satisfied with his lodging house. It was a place of rest, indeed. His only puzzle was whether or not he could maintain his attitude toward Barbara Still, and whether it would be at all possible to soften her a little in the long run.

With that problem, he fell into a sleep that thronged with dreams of Oñate's pale and greasy face, of Al Speaker, with the handkerchief pressed against his mouth, and of the tall man of the smile and the gentle voice.

He awoke to find the first gray of morning sifting through the window; and on the floor, gradually approaching him, was a creaking noise.

A revolver was under his pillow. He slipped it noiselessly into his hand.

Then, looming through that early dusk, he saw the outline of a head and shoulders, stooping beside the bed; a slight rustling followed, the figure arose, stood motionless for a moment, then turned and left the room with equal stealth.

There was no sound from the hall following this, but in the next room he heard something like the noise of a boot, put down carefully.

Mr. Dave Bell had visited him, and for what purpose?

He waited another five or ten minutes, then he got up, felt under the bed, and drew out a heavy little canvas sack.

There was not enough light for the examination of the contents, but when he raised it close to his face, he heard the ticking not of one, but of many watches.

When he got to the window, partly by touch, partly by sight, he was able to recognize paper money, stickpins with jewels in their heads, and other jewelry.

Light began to sweep over the mind of Pensteven.

He leaned from his window. Well below the sill there was a big beam, a crosspiece that made a narrow ledge, a dangerous but possible place for walking, if a man moved with his face close to the wall, brushing through the leaves of the Virginia creeper and clinging to the powerful stems of the vine as they gripped the boards.

So he retied the mouth of the sack, made a loop of the string that closed it, and, with this securely over his shoulder, he slid down from his window.

Would Dave Bell be asleep? Much hinged on that, unless a breeze should rise to make sufficient noise to cover the movements of Pensteven.

And the wind was there, and coming stronger every moment! It threshed the leaves and the slender sprouting stems of the Virginia creeper about. So he moved with more confidence, tiptoeing along the crossbeam until he came to the window of Dave Bell's room.

There he found what he had expected and what he wanted, a denser growth of the climbing vine, where the stems had been put to the side to give air and light access to the window. As into a natural pocket, he thrust the canvas bag among the greenery. Then, with equal care and caution, he moved back to his room, climbed in, and lay down in his bed.

He was excited, but he was also amused. Trouble was coming, from exactly what direction he could not say, but certainly Dave Bell meant to remove this new rival from the house. The arm of the law, it appeared, was what Dave favored to do the work for him.

Presently, he thought that he heard the hoofbeats of horses in the distance, but the sound was vague. Afterwards it died out completely, on the soft ground beneath the trees, perhaps?

Still later, footfalls came up the stairs, many of them, making the woodwork groan deeply; but even in that noise

111

there was a stealthiness. They came down the hallway. They paused outside his door.

He thought he heard a sharp, hysterical whisper, such as would come from a woman. Then the door of his room was thrown open, and half a dozen men rushed in.

He sat up in bed.

"Good morning, fellows," he said cheerfully.

The sheriff was in the lead.

"Get the irons on him," he directed.

Handcuffs were snapped over the wrists of Pensteven.

He could hear the panting of the posse that gathered about him; the men were exhausted by the excitement of the danger which they had expected to face in charging into this room.

There was still not enough morning light.

A lantern was brought by Mrs. Still, her eyes great with amazement and fear, like the whites of the eyes of a Negro.

"Oh, poor Mr. Stranger!" she whimpered. "Why, why, why did you do it?"

"Do what, please?" asked Pensteven.

"You robbed the stage at—"

"Never mind, Mrs. Still," broke in the sheriff sharply. "No more talk, if you'll be so kind. I'll ask all the questions that need to be asked. I promised you this, Stranger, and now you've got it! There's gonna be about fourteen or fifteen years in this here for you. You had to show your hoss like a fool, didn't you? You didn't think that the gents here could see that good by starlight or moonshine, did you?"

He sneered and triumphed.

"There's nothing here," said one of the posse. "Nothing but his clothes."

Then Barbara Still came into the room, with Dave Bell behind her.

Chapter 22

Barbara had on a man's dressing gown, a faded old woolen thing much too large for her. The sleeves were folded far up the arms and the skirt of the robe reached to the floor and wrinkled against it. With a frown on her forehead, her hands in the front pockets of the gown, her feet braced well apart, she looked like a boy, a child of fourteen of fifteen.

Pensteven smiled at her.

"What's all this rot, Mr. Wace?" she asked.

"It's highway robbery, Bobbie," said the sheriff. "That's what it is. I'm a tolerable old man, but I ain't so old that I can't put two and two together in a case as plain as this. The Markham-Justis stage was stuck up in the Justis Hills tonight by a gent riding on a hoss that's a dead ringer for Dainty, that your new roomer has been sporting around on lately. We come here and take a chance on finding the thug. We look in the barn and there's Dainty, and dripping wet. There's the saddle behind her and the saddle blanket soaked with sweat. Now, we've got the man and when we get the loot, we'll have the cleanest case that I ever seen in my life."

"Was there much on the stage?" said the girl.

"Couple or three thousand dollars, maybe, in stickpins, watches, and a little money, besides."

She came closer to Pensteven, who sat up in the bed with the clothes gathered about him. She stared into his face.

"You didn't do that job," said she. "You're not such a tinhorn cheap skate as that."

113

"No," said he. "I wouldn't take a chance on prison for a couple of thousand dollars. I wouldn't show on a horse that everybody on the range knows by sight. If I did, I wouldn't leave her sweating in the barn, and I wouldn't leave her wet saddle on the peg behind her. I'm not such a complete fool."

"You're wrong, sheriff," put in Dave Bell. "He wouldn't do that. I ain't seen much of him, but I know that he's not such a fool. You got up last night and went and just took a gallop, didn't you? Didn't I hear you getting up a couple or three hours back, Stranger?"

Pensteven looked at the little man with an odd mixture of interest and disgust. The voice and the manner were perfectly friendly.

"I didn't get up and take a ride," replied Pensteven. "I've spent the night in bed. That's about all I know of the case."

The sheriff broke in: "Come on, man, come on. We've got the cold case ag'in you. Here, Joe, speak up, and say what you seen!"

"I know Dainty," said a man with a short, square beard. "The reason I know her is I bred her. How she come to the hands of Jack Christmas, and then to this kid, I dunno. She was bred and raised a respectable filly. But tonight I seen the masked crook that held up the stage when I was in it. And I seen clear and fine, by the moonlight, Dainty herself. There couldn't be no other. I'd know her head in a million. I'd know her quarters, too, and her outline. 'It's Dainty,' I says to myself. 'And the crook is that kid that calls himself John Stranger and has been fighting and raising hell around Markham. He must be drunk, showin' the hoss around like this, on this kind of a business,' is what I said to myself. Didn't I, Pete?"

"You did," said Pete. "You said that, and you said more. Sheriff, we got him, and so let's take him along."

"Where's the loot, young feller?" demanded the sheriff. "You know how it is—a quick confession, with the goods returned is about nine points in your favor. Maybe you'll get no more'n three or four years, taking the fact of a first offense into consideration, if it is a first one. Maybe it won't be no more than a good lesson to you, that'll help straighten out the rest of your life for you and show you the right way to go!"

"I've no idea where the stolen stuff is," said Pensteven untruthfully. But from his heart he added: "I didn't do the trick."

It began to occur to him, uncomfortably, that though the loot was outside of Bell's window, there was no way for him to suggest that fact to the others. Barbara Still broke in again: "Sheriff, if you take him, you'll be burning your hands. Mind you, I know what I'm talking about."

"What d'you know, Barbara?" asked the sheriff impatiently.

"I know that he's too big a piece of cloth to cut himself up into patterns as small as this little job. He wouldn't spoil himself with this sort of work," she replied.

"He was broke in this here town a couple of days ago," said the sheriff, unconvinced. "He hadn't enough money to eat a full meal, or to get a good room. That's the fact of the matter, and I know it! Bobbie, go out of the room. We gotta have him dress. Stranger, don't be careless. We're watching you, even with your hands fastened."

"I tell you, Mr. Wace, you're all wrong!" cried the girl.

"Go along now, Bobbie," said he. "You're a good girl and a bright girl, but don't you go telling me my business. I know a case when I see one. If he didn't do it, who else would have?"

"He's not the only man in the house," said the girl.

She turned suddenly on Dave Bell: "Here's the little rat that would just fit that hole!" she exclaimed. "And he hates Stranger. He'd do the dirty trick and lay the blame on Stranger in a minute."

The heart of Pensteven beat more freely, and his breathing was suddenly easier. Keenly he watched the face of Dave Bell. And he saw in it nothing but outraged innocence. His respect for Bell mounted, if not as an honest man, at any rate as a man!

"I'm sorry to hear you talk like this, Bobbie," said Dave Bell. "I know that you've gone and got yourself dizzy about Stranger, and all that. But that's no reason you should try to hang a job like this onto me."

"We'll go and have a look in Mr. Bell's room, too," said the sheriff.

"Perfectly welcome to look at far as you please," said Dave Bell.

His manner was pleasant, his voice that of one innocently at ease, and again Pensteven admired him.

The girl, Mrs. Still, the sheriff, and one of the men went to hunt through the room of Bell. He himself remained in the chamber of Pensteven as the latter, with his manacled hands and some help, dressed himself.

"I'm sorry for you, Stranger," said Bell. "It's a mistake, that's all. I don't think that you'd do a trick like this—a low, cheap trick! I don't think so, and I don't feel so. I'm sorry for myself a little bit, too. I mean, the way that Barbara Still turned around and socked me. She's always been pretty friendly before."

Pensteven said nothing. He felt that this was a lesson and demonstration in perfect hypocrisy. He was dressed by this time.

One of the posse had his wallet. Two others each carried one of his guns and one of the spring holsters by which they were usually suspended under the pits of his arms.

"Nobody but a murderer at heart," said the man called "Joe," "would practice to handle his guns like this here! It's gonna be a good thing to get him behind the bars. I hope that he dies and rots there. I say it to your face, you!"

He shook his burly fist under the chin of Pensteven.

"Mr. Honest Man," said Pensteven, "you're talking loud. You see my hands are tied."

A voice cried out in the next room, the voice of the girl. Then rapid voices of men jangled.

"Something's happened," said Joe. "Come on, fellers, and let's see what it is."

They crowded into the room of Dave Bell. The girl was holding the canvas sack in her hands. Bell himself, nervous and shaking, but with a resolute jaw thrust out, stood stiffly in the center of the room, his hands gripped at his sides.

"It's a plant," he was saying. "You look out the window, sheriff, and you'll see where a gent could tiptoe along that crossbeam and get from his room to mine, dead easy."

"That's true," said the sheriff, unwilling to give up his first theory of the case.

"Would he be fool enough to hide it outside your window where you'd be sure to find it in the morning?" asked the girl of Bell.

"You're against me, Bobbie," said he. "I dunno why, but

116

you are. I wouldn't be looking out my window to find money bags. And the leaves would've covered it over pretty good. You got sharp eyes. The rest of us looked there and didn't find anything."

Suddenly the sheriff said: "I'll take 'em both to jail. Then we'll see what we see. Bell, you come along with us. Get him into his clothes."

Pensteven looked upon Joe.

"Do you feel so well now, Mr. Honest Man?" he said with a smile.

And Joe scowled down at the floor, much perturbed.

They took Pensteven down into the cold light of the early morning. Mrs. Still was quite won over by this time. She was declaring it an outrage that an innocent fellow should be torn from her house in the middle of the night.

But the sheriff grimly went ahead.

"You're afraid to let him go," Barbara Still taunted him. "You're afraid that he'd make you a sick sheriff, if you don't put him in jail. Why don't you confess that you're afraid?"

"Be still, Bobbie," commanded the sheriff. "Here, lead the mare over here. Look at the sweat still drying on her. Now give him a hand up. He can ride his own hoss to jail!"

They helped Pensteven into the saddle and fitted his feet into the stirrups. Then there was a general exclamation, for the stirrups were too short and raised the knees of Pensteven very high. It was as though he had been sitting in an English pad saddle.

"That bright Dave Bell," said the girl, "remembered everything but that. He forgot to lengthen the stirrups after he'd sneaked the mare back into the stable."

The sheriff looked on with a black face and, when his voice returned, it creaked like a groaning hinge.

"Turn Stranger loose," said he.

Chapter 23

When Dave Bell arrived on the scene, more than half triumphant, the case had clearly gone against him. To perfect it, they got him astraddle of Dainty and found that his length of leg agreed perfectly, for Western riding, with the length to which the stirrups had been shortened. It might not have seemed an important point to a jury of Easterners; to those men who stood there half by lantern light, half by the light of the dawn, it seemed more than sufficient. They dragged Dave Bell from the saddle and tied him on a mustang, his feet lashed together beneath the belly of the half wild brute.

Someone suggested that he should be turned loose, so that he could take his chances on the back of the horse, either rubbed off against a rock, or smashed to bits against the trunk or bough of a tree, as the animal raced through the forest.

For they felt bitter, those Westerners.

A man may commit a crime for blood, gold, or fun, in the West and still be acquitted of malice. But the dastardly act of trying to load one's sins upon the shoulders of another was too much for the men of Markham. They cursed little Dave Bell, and they would have struck him in the face, except for his size.

Even the sheriff, a hard man, was moved. He went to young Pensteven and said: "I misjudged you, son. I surmise that you're one of the John Christmas rotten gang. But, if I had a son and had to choose between having him like you or like Dave Bell, I'd maybe want to see him like you and living. But I'd rather see him rotting in hell fire than like Dave Bell. Tomorrow I may feel different. But just now, I'd like to shake hands with you. There's my paw."

Pensteven looked at his face and then at his hand.

"You're a sentimental old fool," said he roughly.

It was a great affront for the sheriff, because he had no answer for it. It reproved him and touched upon his most sensitive side. So he looked down at his own hand as if he were seeing it for the first time, then he lowered it and went off with his prisoner.

But the rest of Markham remembered that remark almost as well as the wounded sheriff.

"John Stranger was a hard man," the town decided, with one voice.

They decided, at the same time, to respect him for the qualities of valor, physical strength, and straight shooting. They also decided to remain aloof from him, for the West judges a man, one third by all his other virtues, and two thirds by his largeness of heart.

Pensteven, for his part, went back to bed and stayed there all day.

Twice they rapped on his door and offered him food, but like a healthy animal, still unrecovered from his fatigue of the long ride and crossing the mountains, he recouped his faded strength by one long debauch of sleeping.

The next day he sat about, ate largely, and yawned prodigiously. Also, he went into town and bought a pair of beautiful riding boots, of the softest leather, exactly a size larger than he would have required when his feet were in ordinary condition, but they still needed to be wrapped in a soft layer of bandages.

He rode Dainty into the town on that trip and saw men, women, and children gather in groups and knots, here and there, to look at him as he went past. He was aware that there were awe, suspicion, and open admiration in their glances, and he knew the reasons for all of these things. He was not offended. The awe and admiration for him offset the other thing, for he was very young.

He dropped in at the Elbow Room before he left town, and there chatted kindly with Jerry the bartender. Jerry was liberal with proffers of drink; young Pensteven drank beer, sipping it, as always, slowly.

"Why don't you have a man's drink?" asked Jerry, pushing forward a bottle of whiskey, and peeling the paper label off the cork at the same time to prove that it was real.

"You know, Jerry," said Pensteven, "that I'd like to be regular. But I can't afford to do it. If I'm regular this afternoon, I'm dead this evening."

"Well," agreed Jerry, "some people are born with sense, and some of 'em have it forced on 'em."

What young Pensteven had said passed around the town inside of an hour, as such *mots* are likely to. Men agreed that whatever he was, he was old for his years.

He was still in the Elbow Room when the important news came in. Dave Bell had actually broken out of the town jail in the middle of the day!

Someone had conveyed a good little pair of saws to him, perhaps upon the very day of his capture, and with them he had cut through five supposedly tool-proof bars of steel and he had climbed through three windows, broken a lock, and got away on foot.

Afterwards, a farmer near the town missed a horse and a bridle. There was no doubt that Dave Bell had used his wits and helped himself to the speed of four borrowed feet to elude pursuit, for the posse made nothing of the business.

This news came to the Elbow Room, and Pensteven heard it. Then he went back to the boarding house of Mrs. Still and looked up Barbara.

She was back of the barn, finishing off the building of an additional shed. The uprights already had been sunk in the ground, and the rafters had been fixed in place. Now she was nailing boards to the uprights, grooving them together. She had a carpenter's hammer in her hand, and her mouth was full of long nails. Her lips bristled with them.

Pensteven sat down on a stump near by, and said. "Listen to me, Bobbie my dear, if you don't mind my using a nickname? Did that little poisonous rat of a Dave Bell really love you?"

She dropped the nails out of her mouth into her hand and glared over her shoulder at him. "Now what the devil do you mean by that?" she demanded.

"I mean," said he, "that Dave has just broke out of jail."

"I knew he would," said she. "That's why I didn't cry when he was taken away the other morning. You can't keep a greased snake in a barred cage."

"You sound pretty bright to me this evening," said he. "But what about it? Was he really in love with you?"

"What makes you want to know?" she asked.

"Two reasons," he answered. "The first one, which is enough, is that I want to know how many reasons he has for wanting me dead?"

She considered.

"Well, he was fond of me," she admitted.

"How do you know that? Always asking you to marry him?"

"No. You're wrong. He wasn't always asking me, and that's how I knew. That, and because he raised the devil as soon as you came over the hill."

"Say that again," urged Pensteven.

"You heard what I said. He knew, the first minute, that I took you more seriously than I ever had taken him. Because there's more avoirdupois about you. That's the only reason," she added.

"Oh, that's all right," he answered. "I know that I'm a heap of tomato cans, as far as you're concerned," said Pensteven.

Then he went on: "You think that you're the cause of his wanting to poison me?"

"Yes, I'm the cause," said she calmly. "Me with the minus nose and the plus jaw."

"Quit it, Bobbie, will you?" he pleaded.

"Why are you so serious?"

"Partly because I'm afraid of him. I'm always afraid of a little man. Partly because I would really like to know where you stood with him. Did you ever take him seriously?"

"What d'you mean by that, John?"

"I mean exactly what I say. Did you ever encourage this fellow, Dave Bell?"

"No more than I encourage mushrooms," she answered.

"You're conceited," he told her. "That's what's wrong with you. You've had too much admiration, and all of that. You're out of your head, that's all."

She looked at him, put the nails back in her mouth, picked up a board, and prepared to fix it in place. He rose from the stump and laid hold upon the other end of the board.

She turned fiercely upon him, and mumbled around the

121

mouthful of nails. She dropped the nails out of her mouth into her hand and repeated with vigor: "I'm working. Don't bother me with your foolishness."

Pensteven yawned with an unaffected weariness.

"Don't be a fool," he replied. "You know that I'm going to marry you one of these days. So why don't you try to help me now? It'll count for you when you ask for alimony."

Her anger suddenly made her cheeks red.

"I wish you'd get out of my sight," she said. "I'm working. I told you that before."

"You know that I'm going to marry you, Bobbie," said he. "Times are hard, and you've gotten down to runts like Dave Bell. You've given the rest of the boys more lip than they'll stand. Now I ask you to tell me the truth. Did you ever encourage him?"

"What right have you to ask?" she inquired, with a sudden and wonderful calm.

"Because," he replied, "if you ever so much as smiled at him, he'll never rest now until he's murdered me. Poison, or guns, or a knife in the back."

She considered this, looked up to the top of the trees, and nodded. "No, I didn't encourage him, and I never liked him. I told him so. But he liked me. Men come that way. He'll kill you if he can, if that's what you want to know."

"That's partly it," he admitted. "The other part is: why can't you be friendly, Bobbie?"

"Why should I be?"

"Because you like me and I like you, pretty well. I know that you need a thrashing, but I don't mind that. If I have to be a wife-beater, I'll be one to make her happy."

Then she threw the nails into the grass and faced him squarely.

"I don't give a rap about you," she retorted.

"You're a liar," he answered. "I don't mean," he corrected, "that you care a rap about me in the way that I care about you. You're too young a fish for that. But I mean that you couldn't have helped me out the other night the way you did, unless you had cared a good bit. I'm simple, but I'm not a fool, Bobbie. And what do you want, anyway? A man that will sock you on the chin and drag you away like a cave man?"

"I'd like to see that man," said the girl calmly.

"You'd see him quick enough," said he, "if I'd made up my mind that that was what you were waiting for."

"Quit it, Mr. Stranger," said the girl.

He sighed and regarded her with a sort of calm despair. Then he went on and said: "Listen to me, I'm swift and I'm bitter. I've made up my mind that I'm going to marry you. I'd have you hypnotized right now and take you off to a clergyman, except that I only have about one chance in ten of pulling through the next month. No use to make you a widow as soon as you're a wife; I'm not that rich. But sooner or later, if I live, I'm going to marry you. Understand that, Bobbie, and act accordingly."

She stared at him.

"I think you're almost serious," said she. "What about not living six weeks?"

"I'm up against a game that can't be beaten," said he. "And I know it. You stand by and watch. You think I'm a crook, but I'm not. I'm playing a part because I have to. I've inherited the necessity for playing a part. I'm asking you to play the game with me, and I'll sweat in hell to make you happy."

"Will you tell me what's your game?" she asked.

"Not a word," said he. "I'm young, but not young enough to tell a woman what I'm interested in."

"Then help me to pick up the nails I threw away," said she. "I thought for a minute that I was interested in you. I see that I'm wrong."

Chapter 24

He was up the next morning, bathed, shaved, dressed, and comforting his sore feet with carpet slippers, when Barbara Still came and knocked at his door.

"Hello?" he called out.

"Hello, yourself," she replied. "That loafer, Doc Shore, is downstairs, saying that he's got to see you. Let me go back and tell him that you're busy having breakfast with somebody else."

He opened the door and stood before her.

"That's very kind of you, Bobbie," he declared. "But why shouldn't I talk to Doc Shore?"

She carefully looked him up and down.

"Partly," she said, "because he's a ruffian and a rascal and never was any good, and partly because your feet are too sore to wear riding boots." After a pause, she asked: "Is it true that you walked over the pass the other day in the storm?"

He looked hastily around the room and then back at her.

"That creek makes so much noise," he said at last, "that I can't hear you. Go back and tell Doc that I'll be down in a minute."

She came closer to him and put out her jaw, saying:

"If you see him, I never want to see you again."

And he, looking back at her with apparent contempt that was not contempt at all, remarked: "What you think makes no real difference. I love you, Bobbie, but I love my job a devil of a lot more than I love you."

She, staring hard at him, suddenly turned on her heel and walked off through the doorway. Then, in a flash, she was back, holding one of his hands in both of hers, looking up into his face.

"Don't go down, John," she said. "I don't want you to see him. There's the devil in him this morning. I can see it in his eyes. Please, don't go down."

"You're young," said Pensteven. "You're so young that you don't matter. Go back and tell him that I'll be right down."

He was to regret that speech for a great part of his remaining life. He knew that he had gained something with her on the preceding day. He knew that he had thrown most of it away in that instant. But it hardly mattered. For Doc Shore was a part of the other thing, which occupied him more than all else; part of the trail that would lead, perhaps, eventually, to the avenging of his father's murder.

When he thought of him, waiting for death, laboring with all his might to make a fortune for the ones he loved, it mattered very little that the girl went from him with a white face.

He kicked off the carpet slippers as she left, went to a corner of the room, brought out the newly purchased riding boots and pulled them onto his bandaged feet. This hurt him, but, once they were on with the padding of the bandages, he became more comfortable.

He walked up and down in them, and then slung the clip holsters under his armpits and fitted the revolvers into them swiftly.

Finally, he went downstairs and met Mrs. Still, passing with a load of empty plates from the kitchen into the dining room.

She paused in the hall and her eyes filled with tears.

"Bobbie is in there crying," she said. "Why do you make her cry, John? She's no girl of mine, but she's the best girl in the world!"

"Hell, Mrs. Still," he said fiercely. "I've been trying to tell her that with all my might these last few days, but she thinks that I'm only flirting, like any other fool!"

Then he went out in front of the house, where he found Doc Shore balancing a chair back and forth on the front porch.

"Hello, Doc," he said. "What's the next murder?"

"Who said anything about murder?" Doc Shore replied

125

in an aggrieved tone. "What makes you bring up things like that?"

"You old innocent," the young man remarked.

"You young cutthroat," answered Shore.

He was making a cigarette; now he finished it, licked it into shape, sealed and lighted it.

He blew out a breath of smoke, then he said: "How's things?"

Young Pensteven was regarding the face of the other calmly. He recognized in Doc Shore more decision, more firmness, more intelligence than were present in the ordinary man, but also more cruelty, more casualness about matters that never should be regarded casually. Moreover, there was the stain of blood on his heart and soul. This was the man who was one of the trusted lieutenants, as he had reason to believe, of the great Jack Christmas.

"Things are pretty fair," said Pensteven. "You ought to be able to guess how fair they are."

"I don't waste my time guessing," said Doc Shore.

Then he added with a faint smile: "How d'you get on with the spitfire, the girl here, I mean to say?"

Pensteven sat on the porch railing and looked down at his visitor.

"I think you are now presuming slightly," he said.

"I can't see it," replied Doc Shore. He looked steadily at the young man. Then he added: "Her name is Bobbie St—" He was looking down the barrel of a steadily leveled Colt. 45. The words died upon his lips.

"I think you'd murder me," said Doc Shore.

"Murder isn't the name," replied Pensteven, "for executing the kind of a thing that you are, Doc."

Doc Shore took a breath, examined his cigarette, and breathed in a great whiff of smoke.

As he inhaled it, with smoke coming from nose and lips, he said:

"I know how it is. Women get to the head of a young fellow. Sometimes they get to the head of a grown man. It's worse, then. Kids are born with ideas about how other kids should be treated, male or female. But grown men forget almost as much as they learn. They forget more when it comes to the women."

"We were talking about something else," said Pensteven.

"We were talking of nothing else," said Doc Shore. "But

this here thing is worth a good deal to me. I get the low-down on what you think of me!"

"Yes. I think that you're low-down," observed the young man. "You know that now if it means anything."

"I'd pull a gun and blow your head off," said Doc Shore rather sadly, "except that there's no audience at all. Besides, I know that you're faster and straighter with a gun than I am. So I'll have to let that go for the moment, but I want to ask you why you call me low-down."

"I don't mind telling you," replied Pensteven, "that you sent me out to be killed. You thought that I couldn't live through Oñate and Al Speaker and the mountains. I don't mention Cracken and Jack Christmas."

The other sprang up and looked around him.

"You're crazy as a loon to mention those names," he muttered.

Then he sat down again abruptly and went on: "I sent you out to make a name for yourself. You'll see, if you think it over, that I wouldn't have sent you if I hadn't thought you'd work into the clear again. I sent you because I knew that you had the stuff in you. I hoped that you had still more than you had shown. That's why I sent you. I'm talking straight when I say these things. I mean 'em!"

The young man nodded.

"All right, Doc," he said. "Let the past die on its feet. Got any new little job to talk to me about?"

"I've got a bigger job still," replied Doc Shore.

"Then don't apply to me."

"Yes, I'll apply to you because I have to."

"What makes you?"

"Orders."

"From whom?"

"Jack Christmas."

Young Pensteven rose from the porch rail as Doc Shore continued: "He wants you to ride down the river and meet him at the Bluffs. You better start now. He's waiting for you by this time."

Chapter 25

He left Doc Shore behind him and saddled the beautiful Dainty, then rode her down the side of the canyon until its walls began to lift into cliffs of respectable dimensions. Now and then, the good mare picked her way along a mere ledge between the sheer wall on the one side and the rush of the water on the other. At other times the floor of the gulch widened; small groves, brush, even little meadows appeared again.

But it was not the difficulty of the terrain that made the man send the mare along so slowly. It was because he was turning a bitter problem in his mind. He might attack the great John Christmas at sight and kill or be killed, or both. He might wait until later on, when, riding perhaps on the same trail with the bandit, he could take him at a disadvantage. But that was dishonorable. If he took on himself the role of a friendly follower, he could not force himself to attack the criminal without giving him due warning. And John Christmas, forewarned, was more than forearmed.

What should he do?

He had no idea. He was simply drifting with time, once more, waiting for events to take him by the hand and lead him forward.

He was in this humor when a waspish sound hummed by his head, but far swifter than any wasp, even flying down a storm wind. He knew what it was before the small thunderclap of the rifle report rang down the ravine between the walls. As he pulled his own rifle out of its leather holster beneath his right knee, a second bullet struck the butt of the gun just as, in unsheathing it, he brought it up on a level with his head.

The impact of the lead jerked the stock against his forehead and knocked him out of the saddle and flat upon the ground. He was unhorsed as neatly as though a knight in the old days had picked him out of his stirrups on the point of a lance.

He would have been completely stunned had it not been that fear pricked like a needle at his brain and told him that he must move to shelter.

But he knew that it was too late. He felt that he was dead already for the marksman up in the ravine wall across from him was too accurate; he was shooting for the head and almost getting his target every time. The first bullet of all had been very close; only the stock of the rifle had turned away the second; and now a third struck the ground an inch from the face of Pensteven and threw up a shower of sand and stinging little gravel that cut against his skin.

The fourth bullet would end him, he knew.

He pushed himself up on his knees as a rifle spoke again, but this time the sound came from a tangle of trees just behind him. He thought that he was surrounded, hopelessly fenced in; and then, across the ravine, he heard a voice wailing.

From the upper ridge of the opposite wall of the valley, a man was plunging down, arms and legs sprawled out, a rifle clutched in his hand, the death scream on his lips.

He struck through a tangle of thick-growing brush that projected from the ravine, and the thorny branches took away the rifle and almost stripped the body of clothes. Out of the lowest brush, gradually, the body slid down with arms stretched up, and Pensteven saw the dead face of Dave Bell.

Then the fast current caught Bell by the heels and jerked him away downstream, the white face still turned up and the arms stretched above his head. Not far below a cataract was howling and rumbling and showing its white teeth.

Pentseven, as he got to his feet, was no longer dizzy. But he was cold at heart from what he had seen, for now the memory of the brisk and cheerful ways of the little man came back to him.

129

Then he turned and through the brush, he saw a big horse coming with a big man in the saddle. Then he made out the brown, handsome, smiling face of John Christmas. It was to him that he owed his safety; except for his intervention, he, not Dave Bell, would have died. Yet, Pensteven almost wished that he had died rather than come under such an obligation to the bandit.

As Christmas came up, he was waving a hand. "Hello, Stranger," he said. "That was a mean one. That fellow Bell was just getting the range."

"The next shot would sure have cracked my head open," said Pensteven. "Thank you, Christmas."

"That's nothing," said the big man. "I heard the beggar at first. Then I saw his body between a pair of rocks. He shoved out to get a clearer view of you after you fell off the horse."

"You've been a friend to me today, Christmas," said Pensteven solemnly, almost bitterly. "I'll not forget that."

"But I want you to forget it," insisted Christmas earnestly. "Unrepaid favors are like borrowed money. They spoil more friendships than they make. And I want your friendship, Stranger."

"Thank you," said the young man.

"That's why I sent for you today," went on the leader. "When Shore hired you at set wages, he didn't explain to you that you were working indirectly for me. And I want to find out if the idea's agreeable to you."

Pensteven hesitated a moment. There was nothing he detested more than to be in the employ of a dishonest man—a robber. There was not the slightest desire in him to go counter to the law. But now, for the moment at least, his hands were tied; the life which had been saved for him might be balanced against the murder of his father. Still, if the account could sometime be balanced, by working as an instrument in the hands of John Christmas, he might at last have his chance to get the long deferred revenge.

He was turning these thoughts over in his mind, frowning, when Christmas went on in his gentle voice: "I know why you're hesitating. You were given hard work in your first assignment. If you got a bonus for the thing, the bonus alone could hardly pay for the dangers in crossing those mountains. I would never have pressed you as Doc Shore did. But I'm afraid that Shore likes to surprise people and play the man of mystery. Al Speaker, too, when he found that you'd been intrusted with such a responsibility, simply forced you ahead, to test the steel in you, perhaps. I'm not quite sure. However, in one way or another, all the men who work for me have to undertake dangerous work. You can understand that."

"I understand that," said Pensteven. "You're not dealing in cattle or hay or grain."

Jack Christmas smiled.

"If you have had enough of my business," he went on, "I'll send word to Shore that you don't need to finish your month's work. You're free to go about your own business now. I want to leave this decision entirely to you; I don't want to drag you into crime, Stranger."

Pensteven hesitated no longer. "I've joined you already," he said. "And now I'll go with you. It may not be a long life, but it can't be a dull one."

"Of course, I'm glad to hear you say that," replied Jack Christmas. "You're ready to march now?"

"Ready," replied Pensteven, nodding in assent.

"Good!" said Christmas. "I have some work already lined out for tonight. It means riding till about dusk, then we'll have supper, and tonight we'll be at work. We ride up the ravine here and take the left fork."

And so Pensteven found himself riding peaceably on the trail with the man whom, sooner or later, he intended to slay! The strangeness of the thing took his breath.

Christmas did not hurry. He set a most leisurely pace and halted occasionally here and there, in places of interest, taking particular pains to point out matters that had to do with his own affairs.

About sunset, he came to a halt on the brow of a hill. At their feet, a great valley with a wide, even floor turned through a semicircle; in the midst of it a stream of water wavered; and beyond it the foothills climbed into the great mountains again. It was a pleasant country, partly grazing and partly plow lands; trees were scattered about, mostly in clumps around outlying ranch houses, sometimes in shadowy streaks beside the roads. A few real forests remained standing. Over the whole picture the sunset was flaring and smoking like the reek of a battle scene; but far away through the color and the mist, they could see the flashing windows of a town that spread out its arms wide.

"Lovely sight," murmured John Christmas, looking at it through half-closed eyes as a painter might have done. "Not many places in the world, you know, where one can get such a landscape effect. Not many places where the woods of the old forest have been cleared away and the rich loam of the forest is just beginning to be stirred with plows. This is the sort of a scene that I like to look at. Not one of your great cities, with railroads coming in on all sides, like the cables of a spider's web, and the smoke of factories going night and day! I hate a great city, don't you, Stranger?"

"Well, I like open country better," said the young man truthfully.

He was wondering how he would be able to understand the viewpoint of this poetically minded murderer.

The other went on: "I'm glad that you like the open country. I'm mighty glad. Because, you see, money in towns is not the same thing. A fellow may ride in and crack a safe in a city bank, take the lining out, and do all sorts of harm. Maybe he's snatching the money out of the hands of widows and orphans, and helpless people like that. Factory-made wealth is dirt stuff. It soils your hands even to steal it. But this is different."

"I don't exactly see what you mean by that," said Pensteven. "You're pulling my leg a little, aren't you, Christmas?"

John Christmas smiled at him. "It's rather hard to explain," he replied. "I don't think that I've ever tried to explain what I mean to any of the other people who work with me. They wouldn't understand. They couldn't. Their minds are too limited. They'd feel that I was just talking hypocritical cant, you know."

"Well, I'll try to understand your point of view," said the young man.

"It's this," went on Christmas. "That town over there, Riverdale, is not living on its factories. It hasn't any to amount to anything except a cannery. It's supported by the richness of the country 'round about it. When the ranchers get fat and lazy, they pack up and leave their big

132

houses in the country and move into smaller places in town. Their womenfolk join card clubs and such things. The youngsters can go to more dances. The callous spots begin to disappear from their hands. Their faces soften and fatten. They don't ride, but they drive around in buggies with rubber tires, and high-stepping horses of good trotting stock pull the rigs for them. They get servants, lots of 'em. They squander money. They begin to invest. They find out the meaning of stocks and bonds. You see?"

"Well, I can imagine that a good many of the ranchers move into town that way," said Pensteven and added: "That isn't why you like the look of things here, is it?"

"No," said the robber. "The point I make is this—a robber in a great city is a plain scoundrel; a robber in this sort of a country is a rascal, too, of course, but he's a little cleaner because he's not cutting throats."

"That's what I don't understand," said Pensteven.

"Well," said Christmas, "suppose that you look at it like this. Tonight, we're riding into Riverdale, and we'll put up somewhere in the town, where I'll see a few of my advance agents. Tomorrow is Saturday, and I think that on Saturday night, we'll begin to do a lot of work. Sometime on Sunday, I hope that that work leads up into the middle of the bank. Then what happens? Why, if we clean out that bank we're not really doing any great harm. It simply means that some of the ranchers will be cleaned out of their spare cash. Perhaps they'll be driven back to their ranches. All the better for the land and all the better for them. They'll have to repair fences, roofing, barns; they'll have to get out and windburn their faces at all seasons of the year. They'll have to work the cattle and live the way honest men ought to live, by hard work.

"And now, Stranger, I suppose that I talk to you as you expect to hear the worst sort of a hypocrite talk. Mind you, I don't pretend to virtue. But I'd rather work my schemes where they don't throttle babies in slums and starve sick men and women who can't work any more to help themselves. Out here in the West, in this sort of a valley, starvation isn't known; if a man is hungry, every man's door is open to him. Furthermore, every man in Riverdale could be fed by vegetables grown in their own backyards."

Pensteven listened in amazement. There was a certain

133

unction in the voice of Christmas; he really seemed to mean what he said. For the first time, Pensteven felt that he wanted to smile at the great robber.

Chapter 26

As they went down the slope of the hill, Christmas pointed out a small shack before them, with a number of trees huddled about it and smoke sagging on a long, lazy line down the wind.

"That's Pudge Murphy's house," said Christmas. "That's his land covering all the knolls around here. Pudge could make a good living for himself, but he's too lazy for that. He prefers to loll around. He keeps a vegetable garden, a berry patch, a few milk cows, some sheep and some pigs. He has plenty of pasture for them. In the early summer, he goes out and cuts down enough volunteer hay with his scythe to pack that little barn, yonder, full of it. His pork he cures in his own smokehouse in the autumn. In one of those trees, yonder, you'll generally find a small cask of whisky ripening—you know that motion makes whisky age more quickly, and the wind bends the trees enough to do the trick. So Pudge really takes life pretty easily. He never does real work; he never works for more than an hour at a time, I suppose."

"Where does he pick up money for tobacco, sugar, and coffee?" asked the young man.

"You see those six horses in the lower pasture there?" asked Christmas.

"I see them. Fine ones, too. He raises horses, does he?"

"No, but he keeps mine for me. I have to have reserves of horseflesh pooled here and there around the country that I operate in. Down the valley there, around the bend, I have another reserve, about fifteen miles from here; and over there across the valley, on the other side of the place where the river widens, there's still another pool of horses. That's about twelve miles away. Ordinarily, I don't have to keep the groups so close together, but if I'm chased over the flat, I have to move fast with my men and I need plenty of relays. Some people in my line of work depend on stealing horses as they go along. But that's no good. People don't like it when their horses are taken, even if better ones are left in exchange. It irritates them. They begin to talk about horse thieves, and all the bank robbers in the world are not as bad, in the eyes of the range, as one horse thief. It's very important to keep on the good side of the public."

Pensteven smiled.

"You ask their pardon after you've picked their pockets, eh?" he inquired.

"No," answered Christmas, smiling in his turn. "But I pay my way as I go. I never live off the country and I never let my men live off the country. No matter where they go, they pay, and they never argue about prices. Take a fellow like Oñate, with a real eye for values and a love of bargaining, for instance. It almost kills him to live up to the rule that I've established, which is, whatever is asked must be paid. I've paid as much as five dollars for a scrawny half-grown rooster. But it did me fifty dollars' worth of good. The price of that chicken was talked about through ten thousand square miles of range, and people said that Jack Christmas couldn't be such a bad fellow—that a thousand crimes were attributed to him that were really performed by other people. Yes, that chicken would have been cheap at a thousand dollars because the people all through that section are willing to help me now. I can leave a horse almost wherever I please, and it will be well cared for and the secret kept. You see, Stranger, that I have to have a policy and stick to it like a statesman."

The magniloquence of these words was lessened by the smile with which they were accompanied.

"It's mighty interesting to me," declared Pensteven, with truth. "I'd like to know more about it. I can understand how important it is for you to have friends scattered about through the country; but there's a huge price on your head, and you must be afraid that any one of your friends may sell you out."

"There was fear of that at one time," said the other,

nodding. "But I remedied the situation, took some radical measures, and got to the root of the trouble."

"How did you do that?" asked Pensteven.

"Three of my men, in the early years, were sold out," said the great Christmas. "And three times I escaped by the skin of my teeth from the same sort of a pinch. That made six cases when I or one of my men was sold. Three of my fellows were caught; two I got away from jail; one was hanged. That made one death against my account; on the other hand, eleven of the men who had a hand in selling us out were killed. Six of them I did in myself with my own guns. And the effect of that example is still a wonderful thing. It keeps me in security. The people feel, somehow, that I can never be caught but that, even if I am, my friends will round up the traitors and shoot them to death!"

"I understand," said Pensteven, nodding, full of thought. "And I suppose that you leave people on the range pretty well alone?"

"Never have touched calf, colt, lamb, or kid," said Christmas, turning his direct, fearless glance upon the face of the young man. "I've never taken a penny from anybody on the range. Except that I work the mining camps from time to time, but that's a very different matter. I've made some good hauls at mining camps, but I take it for granted that the whole lot are rascals, and nearly all of them are strangers."

The heart of Pensteven turned to stone; he looked down to the ground.

"But," went on John Christmas, "I confine myself to big jobs in the towns, as a rule; now and then I hear of a big shipment and hold up a train, but that's risky work which can only be done occasionally, when the conditions are perfect; sometimes I dip into Mexico to split up some of the melons that are down there; there's a good business in other odds and ends; but the banks in the towns are the chief source of revenue."

"And they're never used up?" asked Pensteven.

"No," replied the outlaw. "They grow faster than I trim them down. My territory is big, and I never overwork any part of it. A good forester simply thins out the woods and never destroys them. I'm covering as much ground as I want to now. I have good men working for me. They all get a big split of the profits. They're contented. This business is put on a sound basis all around."

Pensteven drew in his breath.

"Will you tell me one thing more?" said he.

"Yes."

"Do you paint the whole picture for every new man you take in?"

"No," answered the robber. "My system remains a mystery to nearly everyone, except a genius like Al Speaker."

"Then why have you told me so much?" asked Pensteven.

"Because," replied the other heartily, "I can't live forever, I know. I must have come close to the end of my days, considering the length of time I've been going. And it seems to me, Stranger, that you have the brain, the courage, and the way with people—you may become the heir to the throne!"

Chapter 27

Pensteven was still half stunned by this suggestion as they reached the open door of the Murphy shack. The fragrance of cookery came out to them on a warm breath of air, and then a hearty, deep voice called out:

"Hello, fellers! Hello! Put up your horses in the barn. You'll find some good, clean oats in the feed box. Fork down some hay. Got a lot of volunteer oats in it, and it's cured as sweet as sugar. It's candy and beefsteak for a hungry hoss. Then you come in here and I'm gonna surprise you. I must'a' knowed that you were coming along tonight!"

They put up their horses in the barn. All was clean and orderly. Well-oiled harness hung from several pegs on the wall. The mow was more than half full and the smell of the hay was clean and fresh. They unsaddled, groomed the horses thoroughly, and filled their mangers with hay. Then they came back to the house. It consisted of two rooms only, of which the most important one served as kitchen, dining room, and living room. But as in the barn, so all was neat and orderly here.

"Pudge" Murphy, a tubby barrel of a man, came to meet them and shook hands at the door. His face seemed white. But he was clean-shaven and clean washed. Much scrubbing had faded his overalls to a faint blue-gray, whitish about the knees; he wore loose slippers on bare feet; his belt disappeared under an overflow of paunch; his flannel shirt, time-dimmed from its once deep crimson, was open at the throat, and the sleeves were rolled over hairy, tattooed forearms to the elbows. On his chest was more tattooing; a pair of crossed flags was dimly visible, as through a deep twilight.

Pudge Murphy was all smiles and easy good nature. He showed Pensteven to a rocking-chair beside a table, which was piled with old newspapers, battered magazines, and a few books. That chair and table represented the reception hall of the house, as it were.

"The young man is the guest," said Pudge Murphy. "You're an old-timer, Jack. I tell you what I got. I got a venison roast in that there oven. I was gonna trim a coupla slices out of the heart of it all by myself, but there's gonna be enough for three. Yeah, even if you eat like men oughta eat. Jack, you step out there to the cooler, will you? And you'll find a dish of eggs. Bring 'em in. I'm gonna drop a dozen eggs in the pan to make an ornamental border, damn my eyes, around that venison.

"Hurry up, now! I got some honey here out of my own hives. You never tasted no honey like what I got, brother. Stir your stumps, Jack! You ain't eaten like I'm gonna let you eat, not for a year. And how about two chickens, that I could slice in half and roast them brown in a couple of shakes? There's some potatoes coming along with the venison. I put in a pile of 'em, because venison juice does something special to potatoes. It browns them right down to the marrow bones, what I mean."

He talked on in this manner, regardless of whether Christmas were in the room or out of it. His mellow voice boomed and rolled; he spoke as though there were a strong sea wind that had to be shouted down.

In the meantime, Pensteven took stock of the room in detail, the scrubbed floor with two or three goat skins spread out on it, the corner by the stove, where the wall was hung with well-scoured cooking utensils, the dining table laid out with knives and forks and tinware, and a picture on one side of the room of a clipper under topsails only, reeling through a heavy sea; and on the other wall, facing it, an enlarged photograph of a woman with a determined jaw and formidable spectacles resting on the bridge of her nose.

Then dinner was ready, a copious loading of the table, a silence broken now and then by the clinking of knives and forks. Moonshine whisky, wonderfully aged and mellowed, was poured forth liberally to accompany the venison. Pensteven felt as though he had never really eaten before in all his days.

Then they came to the last cup of coffee, after a dessert course of boiled dried apples, flavoured with honey, and still more honey poured on hot, soft pones. They drank their coffee now, lolling in their chairs, able to look the world in the eye with equanimity.

Pensteven asked polite questions.

"You've lived here quite a while?" he asked Murphy.

That turned on the tap of conversation.

"I been here altogether about fourteen years," replied Murphy, "but I only been living here for the last three."

He ponted to the picture on the wall.

"*She* was here with me the first eleven," Pudge continued. "I tell you what, you can't enjoy cold spring water unless you been hiking all day across the desert. And you can't enjoy your days unless you been and spent a big hunk of them with a wife. The best thing about a wife is being without her."

He speared on the platter a small fragment of venison, deposited it in his mouth, and considered the picture while he chewed. Then he pointed toward it with his unloaded fork.

"I'll tell you about that woman," said Pudge. "That nose of hers, like a cutwater, it was kind of a sign; and them jaws, like the quarters of a clipper that's built for the roaring '40s, they was another sign. Heavy weather was what she was made for, and heavy weather was what she could make out of the brightest, calmest day that you ever seen. There wasn't no let-up about her. They say that the devil would make a sailor, if he'd only keep looking aloft. And that wife of mine, she always had an eye-peeled for a squall. And if there wasn't a storm, she whistled, till she got one. I'm a patient man, ain't I, Jack?"

"You are, Pudge," said the outlaw, puffing contentedly at his cigarette.

"I'm a patient man," said Pudge Murphy, banging his fist on the table until the dishes jumped and jangled, "and I stood her for twelve years, and eleven of 'em right here in this spot. But pretty soon the time come when life wasn't worth while. Dawn was her time for getting up. There wasn't no sleeping past the gray of the morning for her, nor for nobody else. She was one of them that are busy all

141

the time making themselves plain miserable without company. Well, sir, finally I up and made her walk the plank. I told her that she was gonna leave, and she said that wild hosses couldn't, but Pudge Murphy, he could.

"I took and rolled all her stuff together into one big tarpaulin, and I dumped it into the back of the buckboard. And then I took and laid hold on Maria. I lost some hair, mind you, and a parcel of skin, but I knew that once around the Horn, I'd get fair weather. And I took and drove her to town, and she wouldn't budge out of her place. So I says that she can have the outfit, and I cut one hoss out of the harness and rode that plug back here. I left Maria setting there in the front seat of the buckboard, tellin' the crowd what kind of a hound I was. But I got home safe and, somehow or other, Maria, she never come back, and from that day to this I ain't heard sign or sound of her.

"You know how it is. Sometimes a good long day's work is pretty near worth while, because then you can loaf through the evening, letting the ache soak out of your bones, spreading your knees in front of the stove, pulling on a pipe, sipping a coupla glasses of moonshine, and spreading yourself gradual and lazy and easy. It's the same way with me and Maria. Sometimes I'm pretty near glad that she give me twelve years of her time, because now I'm gonna enjoy the rest of my life a whole lot more. I don't need no butter and jam on my bread. I don't need no company. Every morning I wake up and I say: 'I'm alone,' and the world seems like a pretty good place to me!"

He ended his recital concerning married life with a sigh of relief and poured himself another good swig of the white lightning.

Big John Christmas rose up from the table.

"You won't be missing a couple of horses for a day or two, will you, Pudge?"

"Never had a horse that I'd miss," replied the other. "Go out and help yourself. The deputy sheriff, a fellow by name of Easterling, he came by the other day and wanted to know where I'd picked up some of those horses out there in the pasture. I told him that mostly I growed them. He wanted to buy one, and I said that I growed for pleasure, not for profit. He went off, looking kind of sour, and maybe he suspects something."

142

"Let him go on suspecting," said the chief, "but the next time he wants to buy, let him have what he wants."

"How would I know what sort of a price to slap on?"

"There's nothing out there worth less than four or five hundred dollars," said the bandit. "And the gray gelding is good for a cold thousand, or I never saw a horse in my life."

"Did you pay that much?" asked Pudge, staring.

"I paid fifteen hundred," said the other, "but he's had something taken out of him since then."

"If he comes back again," nodded Pudge, "and I ask a thousand dollars for a hoss of mine, he'll go and arrest me on general suspicion of bein' a lunatic, or something like that."

Christmas and Pensteven went to the door.

"By the way," said Christmas, "I met a fellow in Denver a while back, and he said that he owed you ten dollars and gave it to me, to pay you. Here it is."

"Thanks," said Pudge. "So long, fellers. Drop in again soon. I ain't had a chance to talk about Maria for a long spell. Good luck."

They went off into the night.

"Many more like that scattered around?" asked Pensteven.

"Not many," said John Christmas, shaking his head in the dark. "Bachelors make the best bets. Old sourdoughs or young squatters, here and there, are my hotels and way stations. I avoid the married men, because if the husband knows better, sometimes a woman can't help talking for the sake of hearing herself rattle along. Here's the pasture. You take that gray I was speaking about. There's a low-geared bay in here that will do well enough for me."

Chapter 28

They got into Riverdale a little after midnight and found the town asleep. They went in by the river road, which wandered along, broad and leisurely, with big trees growing on either side of it, and some attempts at parking the bordering spaces. But the grass and the shrubbery had been allowed to go rather wild, and the result was something like a well-opened lane leading along the edge of a great forest.

They came to the bridge, crossed it and were on the main street of the town. It was macadamized, and the surface was so smoothly polished by wheels that the late-burning street lights streaked their dim reflections far away, as if in water. For three or four blocks the buildings rose to a solemn and important height of four and even five stories, and then they diminished again.

In the middle of one block there was one facade with four great Ionic pillars holding up a ponderous cornice, though this was not the top, and the building rose three stories above this classic effect.

"That's the bank," said the great Christmas. "That's where we'll be doing some work tomorrow. We've rented the adjoining house for a few weeks. You see the one with the little garden in front and the steps running up to the front porch? A crotchety old maid owns that house. Won't live in it; won't sell it and let a good business building be put up; just wants to spoil the looks of the business block. But how we should be able to get along without her, I don't know."

They went around the corner to a livery stable; a night

man with a pale, round, sleepless face came and took the two horses. He listened gravely, without comment, without reply, to the directions for grooming and feeding the pair; then he led them away.

"I'd rather not have seen that fellow," said Christmas quietly as they stepped out into the night again. "He knew me. Not exactly knew me, but he remembered that he had seen my face somewhere or heard my voice. I hope that he doesn't keep on remembering too clearly, or when we come to get our horses, they'll try to nab us."

He spoke with perfect good cheer, but Pensteven was not deceived. He realized, when John Christmas had spoken of being close to death, the man had not been assuming a tone or playing a part. He had merely been saying what he actually knew. He could not be lucky forever. There were beginning to be too many people on the range who knew him, and sooner or later he was sure to be betrayed into the hands of the law.

"Why don't you keep out of this entire range and go some place where your face would be brand-new?" asked Pensteven. "It is possible that you might last there for another twenty years."

"That's sensible advice, son," replied the other. "But after you've ridden with me for a time over my kingdom, you'll see why I won't change it for another. I love my country. The range I work in is my country. The people are my subjects, so to speak. They have to pay the taxes I levy, but, on the other hand, they have something to talk about. A good many people all over the world refer to this district as the Christmas country!"

Pensteven nodded. "I know."

He was greatly disturbed. This was not what he could call a real virtue in the outlaw, but at least it was a profound sentiment in Jack Christmas that made him prefer to die on his own range.

They came to the back gate, opening on the alley through which they were walking, and on this Christmas knocked softly. He was immediately hailed by a quiet voice that said: "Light a match close to your face, will you?" Christmas obeyed.

"Holy smoke," murmured the guard. "It's the chief."

He opened the gate at once. A narrow yard was before

145

the eye of Pensteven. Berry bushes grew high on wooden frames; there was a junk heap in a corner.

"Who's the gent with you?" asked the guard.

"Stranger," replied the chief.

"A stranger to you?" exclaimed the guard.

"No, John Stranger."

"Oh, him that crossed the range, eh?"

Apparently that first feat of Pensteven was now well known throughout the gang.

"Who's here?" asked Christmas.

"Everybody, now."

"You can come along in, too, Charley."

The three went in together, opened the rear cellar door, and Charley immediately flashed on a dark lantern; they went on into a room where wood and coal had once been stored. The smudge against the wall and on the floor on one side told one story, the splinters and bits of old bark on the other marked what had been the site of the wood-pile.

In that room were several stools and chairs, and occupying these were Oñate, Al Speaker and Red Turner. A single lantern burned on the floor. It showed several rolls of bedding made down, side by side.

"Did you rent the house, Red?" asked Christmas, as Pensteven waved to this group of acquaintances.

Red shook his head.

"The old woman was out of town visiting. I couldn't get to her," said Red.

"The devil you couldn't!" muttered the chief. "That may spoil everything."

"Yeah, it might," admitted Red. "But what could I do? Maybe it's better this way. If we tried to rent the place, there might've been too much publicity. Anyway, she almost never comes down here, and she's the only person that'll be likely to walk in. We can rest till tomorrow at noon. Then the bank closes. We dig through to the cellar of the bank by that time and then work up. Tomorrow night we ought to be at the safe. Anyway, we'll have Saturday afternoon and night, Sunday and Sunday night."

"How about the watchman?" asked Christmas.

"I saw him. You'd fixed him, all right. But he wants a bigger cut of the swag," said Red.

"How much?"

"He wants ten thousand flat, and five thousand in advance."

"Damn him!" said Oñate, puffing out his lips.

"I knew that he'd raise his rate," said Christmas. "Has he got any idea who's going to work the job?"

"He don't know that it's a Christmas job," replied Red. "But he might guess."

"When is he coming to get his coin?"

"I'm to meet him tomorrow afternoon."

"Anybody know you in this town, Red?"

"I think not."

"Very well," said Christmas. "All the risks are multiplied by three, because we haven't the house rented. But we're here and we've got to try to push the job through. I don't need to tell you fellows, if the pinch comes, the Riverdale men are going to lynch us before the law gets a chance to work on us. But now we need to sleep. There'll be plenty of work tomorrow. Let's turn in at once."

They followed that good suggestion. The floor was damp and cold. There was only one blanket apiece, but they wrapped themselves up and were presently asleep, each one, except Charley, who was on duty as the sentinel of the camp. He was a fellow with a long face that hung well forward at the end of his neck, and there was power in his rounded shoulders. He left the storeroom, and paced down the corridor. The soft pad of his footfall was the last thing that Pensteven heard.

When he awoke, light was sifting in through the small window, half of whose length was above the surface of the outside garden. Everyone else was already up, and sat still wrapped in blankets, quietly waiting for the right hour to come. Pensteven looked at his watch. It was nine in the morning.

He was glad that the dinner of the night before had been so ample; there was no sign of food for breakfast.

As soon as he joined the others, Christmas said: "It's exactly ten feet from the wall of this house to the wall of the bank. We ought to start cutting the tunnel now. There's a subcellar under this. We'll have to begin there."

The subcellar was totally unlighted except for the lanterns which they carried. It consisted of two small rooms;

the racks on the sides of the rooms told that this had once been a cellar for storing wines and liquors.

"Old Miller lived pretty high," said Al Speaker, looking at the racks. "Is this the wall, Jack?"

He tapped against the moldy outside wall of the cellar.

"That's the wall," replied Christmas, and nodded his head. "And here's the place to break through. You've got the tools, haven't you, Oñate?"

"Here," said Oñate.

And he undid a bulky tarpaulin, which he laid on the floor, filled with chisels, heavy wooden mallets, picks and shovels. Christmas picked up a mallet and a chisel and began on the bricks of the wall with energy and with the skill of a stone mason, cutting through the crumbling old cement, taking out the bricks one by one, then in large, heavy chunks. The others loaded old wood baskets with the refuse and carried it back into the second room of the subcellar.

Presently, a considerable archway through the wall had been opened, and the face of the earth beyond was revealed, roots tangled at the top and disappearing in clay, a deep and solid stratum, farther down.

Charley, armed with a pick, attacked the clay on one side; Red, from the other. When they had picked away a considerable heap, Pensteven and Oñate shoveled the debris into a pile farther back, and from this the baskets were loaded and again borne into the other room of the subcellar. They were cutting in steadily, removing about a foot and a half an hour. When they struck a streak of gravel, they went along much faster. The second room of the basement began to be filled!

Red went out in the late afternoon to see the watchman. He came back to announce that the man had been "fixed"; at the same time, Pensteven, now wielding a pick in his turn, sank the point through a thin screen of earth and drove it into a solid substance beyond. He broke out a chunk of cement. They had come to the foundation wall of the bank.

Chapter 29

They had run into bad luck, for it was one of the thick foundation piers that extended squarely across the middle of their passageway. They had to change their direction to the side and dig around it. Night was on them before they completed that side-step and reached a plain stone wall, not much more than a foot thick.

Red, as an expert miner, was left to moil and toil with mallet and chisel at this obstacle, while the others went back to the upper level of the cellar and there sat down for the first time in twenty-four hours, to food. The meal consisted of bread, raisins, and cheese.

"The less we eat, the clearer we'll keep our heads," said Christmas simply.

They ate, rested an hour, and went back to work, to find that Red already had cut through the wall, but instead of finding a room of the bank's cellar beyond, he found only more of the solid earth!

Christmas supplied the answer. "They sank their foundation wall a good bit lower than the level of their cellar," he said. "That must be it. Let me get in there, and I'll sink the shaft up."

"You sink the raise if you want," said Red. "My arms are tired."

Jack Christmas lay flat on his back in the excavation and began to strike upward with a shortened pick. He had a big handkerchief over his face to keep the showers of soil from blinding and choking him. He, by mere sense of touch, worked on like a mole in utter darkness, and there was a heap of debris almost covering his head, when his pick rang against stone.

Then he crawled out, sneezed and took breath.

"This is damned bad luck," he said. "We've got to cut up through the floor of the cellar. We ought to have stepped into the cellar of the bank hours ago. However, we still have time. Get a shovel in there, Speaker, and we'll clear out some elbow room. After that, we ought to be through pretty soon."

But they were not soon through. It was midnight before they had cut a hole big enough for a man's body to pass freely through the strong concrete flooring, and then Christmas dragged himself, a gun in one hand, a dark lantern in the other.

He turned and called to Pensteven to follow him, and the young fellow went up through the dark tunnel, stepping into the different atmosphere of the building, as a ray of light cut across his face.

"You're cool," said Christmas. "I knew that you would be, but it's pleasant to make sure. How do you feel, Stranger, now that you're about to put your hands on money that doesn't belong to you?"

"I feel tired, Jack," said Pensteven truthfully.

But for all that, his nerves were jumping. He heard a dull rumbling overhead as a dray or loaded ranch wagon moved through the street above them. It was late, but it seemed to him that the life of the world, which stirs night and day, was only waiting for the thieves to enter well into the trap. Then powerful hands would close upon them.

Jack Christmas now led the way through an unlocked door and up a narrow stairs. At the top, a strong lock and a steel door stopped them. A mallet and a cold chisel, in half an hour, cleared away the concrete from the socket of steel into which the bolt slid; they pulled the door open and walked into the street level of the bank itself.

Only a range of steel bars, passing from floor to ceiling, now shut them away from the big safe itself, the goal of all of this labor. But "tool-proof" is rather a term than a fact. Diamond-bitted saws, well oiled, began to eat patiently into the powerful rods. They worked at the saws by relays, and in the gray of the morning, they had cut their way to the face of the safe. Life was already beginning to stir through the streets of Riverdale, and John

Christmas, standing tall and gloomy before the safe, folded his arms and shook his head.

"It has to be blown, Al," he said to Speaker. "You can do that job, but we have to wait till tonight, when people are asleep. They'd be sure to hear the boom of the explosion, I think."

"They would," said Al Speaker. "It's going to take more than a thimbleful of soup to open that can. And we'll all need sleep."

They went back to their former quarters, lay down, and Pensteven was instantly asleep. He had only time, as he closed his eyes, to wonder at the grim silence in which the work had been performed.

Rarely had a word been spoken. Each man knew his task. As soon as the arms of a pick or mallet wielder were tired, he did not have to ask for relief. Willing hands took the tools from him, and hardly an instant was wasted.

As for his own part, was it not his duty to warn the town of the robbery that was approaching its culmination? No doubt that was his duty, but he never hesitated between that and what seemed to him a greater duty, the slaying of John Christmas. He could not kill the man while he owed him his life. That was all. He was simply entangled in a skein whose unraveling he could not foresee.

So he slept through the morning and into the afternoon, then he awoke with a hand on his shoulder, shaking him gently. It was Red, muttering: "Wake up; get a move on. Hell's to pay, and somebody's got into the house from the street! The chief is up there now!"

Pensteven was on his feet in an instant; in the corridor outside the room, he joined the others, standing with strained, set faces as they heard a door open above them.

The voice of John Christmas was heard, flowing along smoothly.

"No business of my choosing, ma'am," he was saying. "I'm only a plumber. I have to do what my boss tells me to do, and when he sent me down here to cut a tunnel out to the main sewer, I had to do it. I don't like this sort of thing. Neither do my men. We hate to work on Sundays, and we hate to burrow like gophers in a hole, Miss Miller. You can understand that!"

A sharply twanging nasal voice made answer: "This is invasion of the rights of a private citizen. I'm going to make things hum for this. I'm going to start a suit at law. I'll get hold of Henry Smith, too, and let him know how far he can get—daring to send a gang of his wretched men down here to tear my home to pieces. He may be your boss, but he's a scoundrel, too."

"I tried to get hold of him myself," said Christmas, "just a short time ago, but he's out of town."

"I'll find the mayor. That's what I'll do, and I'll have police put in here to stop this work!" cried Miss Miller.

"Well, ma'am," said Christmas, "I don't blame you for being pretty cross about it, but, just between you and me, I'll tell you what I'd do."

"I don't need telling," she replied.

"I'm no friend of Smith, even if he is my boss," said Christmas. "He's done these high-handed things too often. It's time that he was brought up short."

"If I don't fix him!" she exclaimed with a bitter passion. "Infringing on private rights!"

"If you want to fix him," said he, "wait till the job's farther along. By Monday, we'll have tunneled out to the sewer. Then, if you call in the police, you can show the whole world just what Smith dared to do, without any permission from you."

"I never heard of such a thing in my life!" said the woman. "Why didn't he dig down from the street level?"

"The sewer's laid deep," said the robber. "And if he opened up the street, the traffic would be blocked for a couple of weeks."

"Traffic!" she exclaimed. "What of it?"

"That's what I say," said John Christmas. "But if you want to get him into the fire, you just wait till Monday. You'll be able to find the people you want then. Everybody's likely to be out of town today."

"Yes," she said, "maurauding around and shooting at deer and ducks, the fools. I'm going down to see what's happening. I'm going to see what's happening in my own house!"

"All right, ma'am," said Christmas loudly. "You'll find my men down there, hard at work. I had orders from Smith; they have their orders from me. Don't blame them, ma'am."

"If you had half a brain in your head," cried she, "you wouldn't be a party to this sort of thing."

Her footfall was heard as she began to descend the stairs. In a whisper, Al Speaker warned the others: "Get to work. Dig like the devil. Be polite to the old lady. Damn Henry Smith and blame it all on him, whoever he may be."

Quickly they were at work in the tunnel, digging, shoveling, passing the soil back to the carriers. They could follow the approach of Miss Miller by the shrill exclamations which she poured out.

Now, as she came into the lantern light, Pensteven, carrying a basket of earth, saw a tall, thin woman, with white hair plastered down around her head, her face crimson with rage. She stood there with her black-gloved hands gripped into fists, shuddering with her fury as she eyed the mouth of the tunnel and saw the debris scattered.

"The worst outrage," she exclaimed, "that ever happened in Riverdale. I'm going to send Henry Smith to prison. It's burglary, that's what it is!"

And the smooth tongue of John Christmas agreed: "Yes, ma'am, that's exactly what it is. Forcing open a locked house and entering, what is it but burglary?"

"The scoundrel!" said she.

"Yes, he's a hard man," again agreed Christmas. "He leads us a dog's life."

"You poor fellows, I'm only sorry for you. Hard times make hard masters," said the spinster. "But I'm going to make an example of Henry Smith, the great, bloated, lying, smiling scoundrel! He sends me Christmas cards, does he? I'll Christmas card him. I'm going to get out of here before I choke."

Christmas went up the stairs with her and they could hear his voice softly soothing her, pointing out the strategic advantages of waiting until Monday.

A door closed, the voices ceased. Red Turner fell on the ground in a convulsion of silent laughter.

Chapter 30

They stood in grim silence when Christmas returned to them. He said nothing; his face was thoughtful as he joined the group, and Oñate broke out: "Why not catch her, gag her, keep her here? A woman like that should have her neck twisted like a chicken's!"

Christmas looked at the angry Mexican, saying:

"You're not south of the Rio Grande, Juan. Suppose that I locked her up here in the house, with her horse and rig standing in front for hours, for everybody to see. And what about the young fellow who was driving the buggy for her? No, no, Juan. I couldn't do that. I had to take another line. Tact, my old friend! Tact cuts through mountains."

"Will she wait till Monday?" said Oñate.

"She won't stop talking," said Christmas calmly. "She'll be sure to go to see some friends of hers and tell them the whole terrible story about the plumbers at work in her basement."

"The word will spread then?" suggested Al Speaker.

"It's sure to spread a good distance," answered Christmas.

"And suppose that it comes to this head plumber, Henry Smith?"

"Then," said Christmas, "we're done for. He'll know that there's something decidedly wrong, no matter how big a fool he may be. And we'll have police here in a jiffy."

Cold sweat stood out on the face of Pensteven; by the lantern light, he saw that every one of the others was glistening also!

"Well?" asked Oñate, the word bubbling up from his fat throat.

"Every man for himself," said Christmas. "At a time like this, every one of you can think for himself. But for my part, I intend to stay here and take my chances. The rest of you have helped cut into the bank. You'll all get just as big a split as though you remained. Why should you stay?"

Stoop-shouldered Charley swayed halfway around, hesitated, and then turned back again, shaking his head.

"I'm scared," he said, "but here I stay. I've been through as bad as this with you before, chief, and we always come out on top in the finish."

"If you're frightened, so am I," said the calm voice of Christmas. "All of us are. We're human. And any one of you or all of you are free to go."

"We'll stay," said Red, the only voice that answered. "One or two wouldn't have a chance, but if the police of this moldy town try to rush us, we'll shoot our way through the whole gang of 'em. When can we blow the safe?"

"Not till eleven tonight," said Christmas firmly.

"It's four now," said Oñate faintly. And faint was the heart of Pensteven also. Seven hours of deadly waiting!

He got a blanket, wrapped himself in it, sat down with his back to the wall, and strove to make himself forget. But he could not. Every now and then, in his imagination, he was seized, the irons clinked upon his wrists, the door of a cell crashed behind him; and then the charge in court, the twelve half straightened, half eager faces of the jurors, the grim judge who listened with head tilted to one side. Afterward, well, perhaps he would get no more than seven or eight years, considering that it was a first offense; perhaps the maximum, considering the gang with which he would be caught.

The frenzy would rise to a hysterical height and a cold hand would grip his throat. Then it would gradually ebb away, leaving him weak and uncertain. Seven eternities passed by him, and still he was sitting in that spot.

No, it was only ten thirty when the chief said: "We're going to win, friends. If the old lady hasn't got her chatter to the ears of that Henry Smith by this time, the plumber is probably now in bed.

"Al, you can start running your molds around the edge

of the safe door. Red, you get the rest of the horses and bring them into the back yard. We may have to get into the saddle and ride fast and hard. Stranger, you know where our two are. Will you get 'em and bring them to the back yard?"

Pensteven jumped up in willing haste. Anything, even facing the suspicious face of the night man at the livery stable, was better than this eternal waiting.

He and Red left by the back gate of the place, Red murmuring: "Another coupla hours of that in there, and I'd be a wreck. I'd bust down and start in crying. I ain't an iron man like you, Stranger. That was some lingo that the chief passed out to the old hen, wasn't it? Well, so long."

He went down the street in one direction, Pensteven in the other. He quickly came to the livery stable.

The night man was busy washing a little rubber-tired runabout, spinning a wheel, so that the spoke flashed in a solid disk of light under the dripping water from a sponge.

"I'll take that pair of horses," said Pensteven. "The gray and the bay. What's the charge?"

"Three and a half," said the livery-man.

It was a very large charge, indeed, for so short a time, and Pensteven was about to argue the point, when he remembered what John Christmas had said: no bills must be protested, not even five dollars for a half-grown chicken. So he paid over the money without a word.

The night shift looked at the coins, pocketed them, and disappeared among the shadows. He returned after a moment, leading the pair ready saddled, and with him came a second figure, a man broad, short, and stocky.

He came straight up to Pensteven and looked earnestly through the shadow cast by the brim of the wide Stetson.

"What's your name, son?" he asked.

"It's my own name," said Pensteven uneasily.

The other brushed open the lapel of his coat and gave a glimpse of a bright steel shield inside.

"I'm a deputy sheriff," he said. "What's your name, brother?"

"Wilbur Atkins," said Pensteven.

"Where you from?"

"Mill Hill."

"Where's that?"

"Across the range in the valley of the Mill River."

"Don't seem to recollect a town of that name," said the sheriff thoughtfully.

The night shift stood back, still holding the horses by their bridles; his white face was wrinkled in a suspicious sneer.

"It's not a big place," answered Pensteven.

"Humph," said the sheriff. Then he asked: "Who's your friend?"

"Doc Wiley."

"What's his front name?"

"Samuel, I think. I don't know. We generally call him Doc."

"Known him a long time?"

"Not very long."

"How long?"

"Well, about a year, perhaps."

"What does he do?"

"Buys cattle."

"Buys cattle, does he?"

"Yes."

"Represent a firm?"

"Yes."

"Who?"

"Reynolds and Young."

"Where are they?"

"In Chicago."

"I know a lot of the big Chicago houses. I never heard of one called Reynolds and Young," said the sheriff.

"Neither do I," broke in the dull, subdued voice of the night shift.

"No?" said Pensteven as in surprise. "They've been going for more than a year."

"Humph," said the sheriff. "What you and your friend doing in Riverdale?"

"We're bound for El Paso."

"That's a long ways. Why don't you go by train?"

"He's teaching me trailing, hunting, and all that."

"Oh, he is, is he?"

"Yes."

"No, Mr. William Atkins—that's your name, ain't it?"

"Yes," said Pensteven.

157

"He called himself Wilbur a minute back," said the night shift.

Pensteven glanced at the white face of the other and saw that it was distorted by a grin.

"How come that?" asked the sheriff. "Don't you know your own name, son?"

"It's this way," said Pensteven gently. "Everyone calls me Will. And about half the people think that Will is always short for William. Matter of fact, my name is Wilbur. But even the papers have called me William."

"What papers?"

"At home."

"Newspapers in Mill Hill, eh?"

"Yes."

"What did you get into the papers with?"

"When I was married."

"Oh, a married man, are you?"

"Yes."

"Any children?"

"No. My wife died three months ago."

"That's bad luck," said the sheriff, scowling darkly.

"My friend, Doc Wiley, thought that a cross-country trip like this might be good for me. Get some ideas into my head. That's why we're traveling south."

The sheriff stared, then he gradually shook his head.

"You may be honest. You may be just slick," he said. "But I'm gonna have a look through your pockets. I got an idea that you're just a nacherally smart liar. Shove up your hands, partner, while I see what you're made of!"

Chapter 31

It would have been a very rash man indeed who spoke to young Pensteven in such words without first having an advantage of position over him.

The deputy sheriff had a bull-nose revolver in his hand as he finished. He held it almost carelessly at his side, much as a man might hold a club in preparation for a fight against a man with bare hands.

Pensteven was not deceived, however. He knew that that gun was for instant use, and he exclaimed, in a tone of alarm: "Steady, there! You have the infernal thing pointing at me. Don't let it go off or—"

As he spoke, he raised his hands. His right hand went up honestly enough and stood high above his head, but his left hand, which started a fraction of a second later than the right, curved outward slightly and then turned into a fist which arched upward in that uppercut which Red had called long enough to kill flies on the ceiling and somewhat faster than thought.

The knuckles clipped the sheriff under the chin and he, with instinctive forefinger closing on the trigger, sent a bullet spinning right past the flank of the young fellow.

Then, as his head jerked suddenly and horribly back over one shoulder, as the head of a hanged man may do when the rope comes taut and the big knot throws the neck awry, the sheriff fell, his knees giving way first and his body bending outward like a bow in the middle. In this way he went down, a loosely piled body lying on the floor in a heap.

Pensteven knew by the shock of the weight against his

hand and the sound of his blow, that he had hit home. He did not wait for the other to drop, but went by him on the run, drawing his gun.

The white-faced night clerk was prepared.

He saw the punch and acted accordingly, dropping the reins of the two horses as he slipped to one knee and produced a long barreled Colt, which he leveled with both hands, as though it were a carbine.

He meant business. There was murder in his face. There was a certainty of success about him. But he made the mistake of delaying a fraction of a second too long. Pensteven fired as he ran, and he, also, shot to kill. There was something about the calm and acid savagery of the night shift in the livery stable that made him indifferent to the man's welfare. So he fired straight for the head, and his bullet, flying a trifle low, snatched the gun out of the grip of the fellow and hurled it spinning into his face.

He was not knocked flat. He was only sent staggering. His white face became a dripping, crimson face. He flung out his hands before him and fled at full speed, blindly, smashing into one of the wooden pillars that upheld the roof and spinning about, then madly running on again.

It was only as Pensteven got to the horses and whipped into the saddle on the gray that he became aware not of movements alone, but of sounds, also.

Then he heard the voice of the night shift shrieking out, "Murder!" and he saw the sheriff writhing on the floor, and groaning.

In the distance, men were answering with yells. Here and there, he heard the drumming of a galloping horse beginning, then rushing on toward the place.

Now he had his pair underway, their light, springing steps coming to a trot and to a canter as they were still on the big wooden floor of the livery-stable entrance, raising a hollow thunder underneath them and echoing overhead.

As he rushed the two into the street, he saw a man who was approaching on horseback sweep up, shouting: "Hands up, there!" He was pulling at a short-barreled rifle which was in the holster under his knee.

The gun stuck in its sheath. Pensteven did not have to shoot, but he blinded the fellow with a cutting quirt stroke across the face and eyes, just as he had sight of four more riders turning the next corner below him. They came, yelling, as cowpunchers have to whoop when they are excited.

Pensteven was going at full speed up the street, leaning well over in the saddle. Guns exploded behind him. Bullets sang briefly about him. He damned the bad fortune that had caused the alarm to be given just as he was about to make his escape. As he saw it, it could not possibly have come at a worse time. He rode three blocks, hearing windows go up and doors slam, along with the hoofbeats behind him, then he turned a corner sharp to the right, hurtled down the street; leaned back on the reins to bring his mounts to a halt, and entered the alley which led past the back yard of the bank and the house of Miss Miller.

At a walk he entered and pitched himself to the ground, bringing the pair on the lead as he took them behind the trees that lined this end of the alley.

He looked back, gun in hand. The roar of the galloping hoofs reached the mouth of the alley, and then went streaming past. He saw the riders using whip and spur, leaning forward to cut the wind of their own frantic gallop. As they galloped, they pursued the thin, hanging mist of dust which his own horses had kicked up. Before them lay the great shadows of the trees that fringed the river and the sheen of the river itself beyond the bank.

They took it for granted that the fugitive must have gone in that direction, and then, as it seemed, taken the road out from Riverdale, for without hesitation they took the way to the left!

Pensteven reached the back gate of the Miller place, entered, and found Red already there with his big string of horses. Oñate and Charley had run out into the yard with rifles. The starlight gleamed pale and dim on the long barrels as they came up.

All three converged on Pensteven.

"Did you see anything? What's gone and exploded in this damn town?" asked Charley.

"They spotted me in the livery stable. That's where the shooting began," answered Pensteven. "Then, as I got into the street, four bucks jumped me, besides one who met me at the stable door. I dodged them, and they went whooping up the river road just now. Why waste time chattering when there's still a job to be done?"

The "job," it seemed to Pensteven, now had to be accomplished. If he had felt hesitation before, it was removed from him now, with every scruple. He felt no fear, but only a wonderful alertness. There were eyes in him that looked from the back of his head. He was aware of everything around him and of every glassy black window that overlooked the yard where the horses were posted.

"You raised the devil, you young fool!" said Oñate through his teeth. "This is what comes of using brats instead of men, when there's man's work to be done."

"You fat-faced lump of tallow," said Pensteven. "I'll talk to you after the work's over." And he entered the house.

He heard Oñate puffing behind him and Charley. Red remained with the horses as the outer guard of the whole party.

So Pensteven went through the cellar and through the tunnel, up the stairs into the bank. He found Al Speaker and the great John Christmas at the safe. A dark lantern flashed in his face. Then there was a murmur from Christmas: "What's up?"

Oñate panted from the rear: "This brat, here, tried to raise the town and nearly did it."

"They've gone chasing dust ghosts," said Pensteven.

He added to Christmas: "It was the night man at the livery stable. He had you spotted. The horses were too good for ordinary people to be riding them. Anyway, they're in the back yard now. Go ahead with the game, Christmas."

"Good work," said the leader. "Go and lie on the floor in the corners, you. Al, touch it off."

As they got into places of safety and lay flat, Speaker lighted the end of the fuse and lay down close to Pensteven. The latter saw the powder of the fuse run crackling and dancing on its way. It reached the edge of the safe itself. There it clung, glowing; it seemed to have failed; and the instant Pensteven made sure that there would be no explosion, the floor quaked under him; a dull, muffled boom thudded against his ears; then a piece of plaster was loosened from the ceiling, fell down and struck the floor close to his face.

He felt sure that such a noise would certainly raise up every grown man in Riverdale and set him reaching for guns. But all that mattered to Pensteven was that the door of the safe now reeled outward and dropped with a thud upon the mass of sacking and tarpaulins which Speaker and Christmas had prepared upon the floor.

It was a neat job, the minimum of nitroglycerin for turning the trick, and so the least possible in the way of noise.

There was the dark lantern of Christmas already streaking in bright pencil strokes across the face of the interior, with its checking of steel-bright deposit drawers. There was still something between them and victory.

Now, Speaker, using a small, sharp-ended bar, inserted it in drawer after drawer, and with a sharp little snapping sound broke the locks open.

Charley and Oñate snatched out the drawers and threw the contents on a tarpaulin. Al Speaker, with lightning hands and cunning eyes of long experience, went through the papers as well as he could, and rapidly sorted out family documents, wills, and all manner of other things, from negotiable stocks and bonds.

There were any number of little chamois bags and other receptacles which were taken without examination; they were sure to contain family jewels at least of a sufficient value to need this safeguarding in the vault of the bank.

That work was interrupted by a sharp knocking at the door of the bank!

Chapter 32

They could see what was coming. Through the bars of the inner cages of the bank and through the big plate-glass window that looked upon the street, they could see in the ample light of the street lamps, half a dozen dark figures of men gathered.

It was these who had knocked upon the door.

Were they waiting for the night watchman to let them in? Well, they would not wait long!

Hastily, the last contents of the remaining deposit drawers were dumped into the tarpaulin, and the chief, gathering up the corners of this, tied them, whispering his orders.

They were to retreat at once, get to the horses, and ride like mad out of town and not down, but up the river road.

Fat Juan Oñate was now nimble enough to be first down through the tunnel. Behind him came Cherley and Al Speaker. Pensteven and Christmas were last.

They were already down in the basement, when there came a sudden, roaring clamor from upstairs; a gun exploded; they could hear furious shouting that spilled both forward and backward through the building. Then a door slammed above them. Footsteps came hurrying down the cellar stairs, and a jangle of voices. It was Pensteven who sprang back and locked the lower door. But bullets would soon smash it open again!

He turned to see that Christmas himself was now descending into the tunnel. He followed last, worked through the windings of the tunnel; and then heard loud voices calling behind him.

"They're down here!" called one voice. "We got 'em like gophers in a hole. We've got 'em!"

Pensteven heard that cry, and so did the others, but they in the meantime were issuing into the cellar of the Miller house.

Through the cellar rooms they raced to the upper level and so into the back yard. High above them, out of the blackness, a voice rang out from an open window.

"Who's there?" called the watcher, who had been dragged from his bed by the many noises in the middle of the night.

Pensteven sang out: "Deputy sheriff and posse. Who are you?"

"Deputy sheriff! Hell!" said the man overhead. "You ain't got the voice of the sheriff. Stand to, the whole lot of you, or I'll open with buckshot and blow you to—"

Al Speaker jerked a bullet almost carelessly up over his shoulder. There was a splintering of glass; the roar of a misfired gun; and then the howl of a man badly or, at least, painfully hurt.

Red had the back-yard gate open by this time and led the way through. One by one, the milling, impatient horses were allowed to bound out into the street. John Christmas went next to last, busily crowding bulky things into his saddlebags, riding his low-geared bay with the guidance of his knees alone, a masterly performance. Pensteven was the last to go through, as a charge of buckshot rattled against the gate and fence. One pellet of lead knocked the hat from his head. Another stung his shoulder.

Then they were in the open alley, racing. They had the town waking behind them, before them, and all about them with a roar. But Christmas led the way not straight up the river, but thundering across the bridge. By a miracle of horsemanship or sheer speed of his mount, he had managed to get into the lead, and now he guided the party across the bridge.

Half a dozen armed men ran out to meet them at the other end of the bridge.

"Straight down the river road, fellers!" shouted the bandit, with a voice like the deputy sheriff's. "Not this way, but straight along the river. Get your horses. They've robbed the First National!"

"Who robbed it?" yelled one of the pedestrians, a man half dressed, rifle in hand.

"John Christmas!" shouted the chief, truthfully enough.

Now they spurred to the right, doubled around the next corner to the left, and all in another minute they were streaming up the open road along the river, with the lights of alarmed Riverdale and all its voices behind them.

As the town dwindled, a sense of exultation and of guilt combined in the breast of young Pensteven.

The adventure was ended. He had borne no undistinguished part in it. Now they carried a fortune away with them, the peaceful stars were over their heads, and the security of the dark mountains was not far away!

The chief dropped back beside him.

"Were you hurt, Stranger, by that last discharge?" he asked above the noise of the creaking, beating gallop.

"Only grazed in the shoulder," said Pensteven. "It's nothing at all."

"Blood running?"

"I don't think so."

"Feel and make sure."

He felt under his coat. His whole side was sopping; his hand came away wet with blood.

"I'm bleeding a little," he confessed.

The chief shouted.

"Take the fellers straight on up the road. Follow the railroad where it leaves the river bank. Stranger is hurt! Take charge, Speaker."

The rest rushed on. The dust gathered in a veil behind them; the noise of the horses almost instantly died away. And there sat young Pensteven peeling off his coat, and listening to the mighty thumping of his heart.

Christmas, as soon as the coat was off, ripped the shirt and the undershirt away with magic hands.

He played the keen beam of a dark lantern on the hurt.

"It's deeper than I like," he said. "The hound was shooting from a high angle. Confound Al. He could have taken pains enough to kill that devil at the window. But wait a minute. Not so deep after all. It's down here, the slug, I think. Steady, Stranger!"

He had out his knife as he spoke. From a saddlebag he took a small case, instantly had it open, poured from a vial a few drops on the knife blade, and instantly cut a small cross in the front muscles of the shoulder of Pensteven.

A buckshot rolled out into the fingers of John Christmas.

"There's the beggar," said the bandit calmly. "Now we get this thing tied up."

He was working like lightning as he spoke. A roll of bandage was in his hands; he smeared a quantity of unguent that burned like fire over the two wounds and then wound the bandage dexterously into place.

"There we are," said he. "Tear away the bloody part of that shirt and undershirt. Put them on. That's it. Now the coat. That'll keep you from taking cold. In five days you won't know that a bullet ever struck you. You needn't have been the last man. I should have been the last through the gates, Stranger."

He was picking up his reins, as Pensteven answered: "You wouldn't have had as good a doctor to take care of you."

"I've learned how to take care of myself," replied the other. And led the way at a rapid gallop down the road. Still there was no sign of pursuit from the town.

"They've gone the other way," said John Christmas. "We're as safe as can be, I suppose, but we'd better keep on making good time. There's nothing better than miles between us and the last job we've done."

The band under the guidance of Al Speaker had gone on at a much more moderate pace, and not more than eight miles out from Riverdale the two overtook the rest.

They got, for a welcome, merely a wave of the hand, and the cavalcade went along at a brisk trot, Pensteven eased in the saddle by the matchless gait of the gray. Even Dainty had not a smoother trot.

They had gone perhaps another half mile when an engine followed by half a dozen box cars roared past them down the railroad tracks which they were now following. It rounded a bend, the noise of the locomotive ceased.

"That's a funny thing," said Al Speaker, with his handkerchief at his mouth, half stifling his words. "I'd say that that train had stopped around the bend."

"It's the wind," said Charley, "and that hill. It's covered up the noise."

For there was a small hill around which the track swerved, though the main chain of the foothills was still far away. As they rode up the slope of the hill, with Red well in the lead, he was suddenly seen to turn his horse and come flying back to them like mad.

"Twenty men on horses, riding like the devil this way!" he shouted. "They've come out of the box cars. The train's stopped over yonder. They've got runways down from the box cars. Ride like the devil!"

He set the example, leaning over his horse and streaking away for the wooded foothills, which lay a few miles off and to the right.

At the same time, as the rest of the party got under way, over the top of the hill swept a score of riders, and a volley of bullets boomed heavily on the air.

Chapter 33

The device of the men of Riverdale was simple enough. An engine, waiting with steam up in the switching yard of the town, had simply been commandeered and the pick of the mounted men and their horses had been placed in the box cars. Now they came freshly on the cavalcade of the robbers.

Well and nobly did the horses of the men of John Christmas repay their prices and the amount of tender care that had been lavished on them. They stretched away at fine speed and with wonderful endurance toward the safety of the hills.

But no matter what their breeding or their speed and their strength, they had to account for tough horses, handpicked from those of many volunteers in Riverdale, who were starting perfectly fresh, whereas the bandits already had put ten hot miles behind them.

From the first, there was little doubt as to the outcome. Al Speaker, light as a jockey, kept in the lead. Christmas, on the long-striding bay, did well, also, and the fine gray carried Pensteven like a feather. But even at their best, they could not more than match the first rush of the cow ponies out of Riverdale. And these already tired horses would soon be burned up. They could not continue that first rush for more than a mile at the most. No, some of them were already failing.

Charley, riding rather clumsily, and putting too much energy into the flogging of his horse rather than the handling of it, fell back with the taking of every stride.

Pensteven and Christmas, of one assent, dropped back

beside the laggard, unsheathed their rifles and answered the triumphant yells of the pursuers with some well-placed shoes.

No one fell; no one so much as reeled in the saddle, but the bullets, though fired from the uneven decks of galloping horses, came so close to the mark that the pack of the riders in the rear split to either side, and then came on again.

That momentary halt and the speed with which they came up again determined the leader. And he shouted to the rest of his men, in a voice that rang out over all the other noise; "Swing to the right. Make for the creek bottom, there, and take to the willows. Every man for himself!"

The moon was well up, and glinted on the tangle of the willows along the creek bottom. Down the slope turned the band of fugitive riders, and in another moment Pensteven was flinging himself out of the saddle.

He left the rifle behind him. Two revolvers were a sufficient burden to carry along with him.

Now he darted forward through the willows, until presently he found himself dashing in water and slime, knee-deep.

He put out his hand to rest it on a half-submerged branch, and the top surface of the bough came to life. A long snake opened at him a mouth white as cotton and glided off into the stagnant pool.

Pensteven, half sick, felt the sting of the fangs as they drove home through his clothes. It was a moment before he could go on again.

But, finally, he waded out of the muck and water to a strip of firmer land.

The foul odor of the marsh was in his nostrils now. And despair was in his heart, as he turned up the stream. There toward the hills the creek joined the foothills and, once there, the woods offered endless shelter, if only he could get to that spot.

He came to a higher spot, one of those places where spring floods pile up earth and the debris of decaying tree trunks, to make a bank between the main current and the back water.

From this spot, he looked across the heads of the trees and over the hill that lay between him and the railroad track. There he saw another stream of mounted men, their sweating horses agleam under the moonlight. There must have been forty. Riverdale was pouring in its plentiful reserves to seal the trap in which the bandits had been caught.

With a swoop and a rush, these riders disappeared behind the nearer trees. Cheering welcomed them. A little later, he saw half a dozen emerge and gallop down the course of the creek.

It was not hard to calculate the scheme of the men of Riverdale. They knew where the fugitives had been run to ground and now they would throw a cordon across the willows, well up and down the creek. Others would watch the sides of the strip. They had plenty of men for all purposes. More would come. Presently an army would gather and hem in the district like a wall of fire. That wall could contract, and so gradually press the outlaws together and scoop them up.

It was too horribly clear.

Upstream, therefore, was the only line of retreat, and Pensteven went onward as rapidly and silently as he could. The far side of the creek should offer the best possibilities.

He came to the edge of it and saw it shooting down a narrow channel, foaming white in the moonlight around the rocks that, like jagged teeth, waited for prey.

Those rocks had to be his stepping-stones. He knew that at any other time, by any other light, without death around him, he never would have dared the adventure. But now he stripped off his boots and boldly ventured, putting fear far behind him, and nerving himself to absolute steadiness.

He gained the center of the water. When he looked down, the world seemed to be leaping with one great flash beneath him. Then, stretching for a wide step to the next stone, he slipped in halfway to his knees. The force of the current tore at him. He staggered. Once down, he was lost. But somehow he managed to maintain his footing.

The rest of the way was comparatively simple, and he gained the other bank. There were two advantages. He was probably some distance from the other fugitives. It was not likely that many of them would get across this water on foot; Speaker and John Christmas, perhaps; hardly more.

Most of the posse were probably stopped on the near side of the creek, even though they had horses on which to ford the shallow, dangerous rush of the stream.

Furthermore, the ground was higher, drier, with strips of marsh glittering, here and there.

He moved straight across to the farther edge of the willows, without seeing or hearing a thing. From the trees, he looked out and saw that the way was barred. A half dozen men were riding up and down on the higher ground, with rifles or shotguns balanced across the pommel of their saddles. It would be an easy thing to empty one of those saddles, even with a revolver shot, but there remained the open stretch lighted by the moonlight, in crossing which he would call down the fire from five more, at least, who would be shooting with precision. There was no way out in that direction, therefore.

He turned up the stream. On the far side of the water, almost in line with his position, guns suddenly cracked, voices shouted, silence followed. Had some one of the fugitives striven to break through in that direction?

He went forward little by little, practically feeling his way, straining his eyes to pierce to the core every patch of shadow. He was moving with the utmost care, but just so would the men of Riverdale be moving. They were deer stalkers, every one of them, no doubt. They were armed and knew their weapons, and on such a night as this they would be shooting straight.

Then, as he stepped behind a broad-trunked tree, a gun boomed in his very face, as he thought. He saw the broad flash of the explosion and heard the rattling of buckshot through the branches of the willows.

"What was that, Mike?" asked a calm voice, a few scant feet away from him.

Another voice answered, to the side: "I thought I saw something move, there behind that tree."

"I didn't see a thing."

"You ain't got my angle on it. Whatever it is, it's dead. I put a whole load of buckshot right straight through it."

"We'll go look."

Pensteven, bearing a little to the right, glided back to the shelter of a shrub, dropped on hands and knees and wormed his way deeper among the trees.

Behind him he could hear the voices.

"Don't seem to be nothing here," said the man who had fired.

"I knew there was nothing," replied the other.

"Anyway, I'm gonna keep on shooting at every shadow. If we spray this here whole marsh with buckshot, we're sure to get 'em before long."

"Maybe," said the other. "But seeing things that ain't, that don't help much."

Pensteven, rising at last behind a group of trees, took thought.

There seemed no safety on the ground. Like a hunted cat, he looked up, and noticed the exceptional height and strength of the patch of trees that were just before him.

Three of them grew with almost interwoven trunks, and their boughs made a great tangle. It might be barely possible that the men of Riverdale, as they moved their lines gradually inwards, would pass under this tree. They might leave it unsearched. At least, that was the possibility.

At such slender hopes was he snatching, now, that he straightway climbed up into the interweaving branches. Well up, he found an easy place to stretch himself and to look down into the clearing beneath.

There he lay for a full hour, as it seemed to him. He saw nothing in the clearing near the tree. Now and then he heard voices, generally far away; several times guns fired a salvo or a single one exploded. Once, in the far away, he heard the roaring of a train coming out from Riverdale with fresh reinforcements, he had no doubt.

Then, disengaging themselves from the farther shadows, he saw half a dozen men stealthily leave the brush and creep downstream toward the tree.

Chapter 34

A gust of wind struck the trees among whose branches Pensteven was lying, and it seemed to him the direct intervention of a demon which wished to call attention to his hiding place. In fact, he saw two or three of the advancing party look straight up toward him.

They were all youngsters, looking as wild as hawks and as keen in the hunt.

"Coupla men could lie up there, Denny," said one.

"I'll go up and have a look," said another.

He was under the trees now and began to climb. Pensteven turned without sitting up and stealthily drew a revolver. But he did not think that he could fire; rather, it might be better to drop into the group below and take his chances of sprinting and dodging to shelter. He could not stretch out his arm and send a bullet into the heart of one of these young fellows, all of them his own age, all of them securely on the side of the law.

There was a sliding, scratching sound, then a solid thump, followed by laughter.

"That was on you, Denny!"

"I'll give those branches a searching without climbing again," said Denny, and promptly let off the barrels of a shotgun, one after the other. The shot roared and rattled through the willows, but though the branches on which Pensteven lay trembled a little under the impact of the charge, not a single leaden pellet scratched him.

"Well, I guess there's nothing alive up there," said the voice of Denny.

"That tree's searched. But you oughtn't to've made that

much noise," insisted another. "The sheriff wants us to still-hunt these beauties. You know what they are!"

"It's the Christmas gang, they say. Well, if it is, they're out of luck at last. They're going to be grabbed."

The group passed on, talking more softly, and soon they were lost. Pensteven, in the meantime, began to prepare to descend. He waited until the group was fairly lost to sight and sound, and then, as a big cloud obscured the moon for a moment, he sat up, ready to slide to the ground.

No sooner had he sat up, however, than he lay down again. For coming out of the shadows into which the six young men had disappeared, was another form, stalking softly across the clearing, sifting along smoothly from one shrub to another, bent far over to make himself as small as possible. He was a big man, with a flare of long hair and a beard which the moon lighted about the fringes; he was such a man as might come down from hunting and trapping in the higher mountains three or four times a year to turn in his pelts for provisions, ammunition, and a little hard cash.

One such pursuer, as Pensteven well knew, would be more formidable in the still-hunting of a man trail than twenty such reckless young fellows as had just passed.

Plainly, the big fellow had found his trail, but what could it be? Himself, perhaps, since it was straight toward his tree that the rifleman was walking?

The blood of Pensteven was flecked with nightmare cold. Slowly he turned himself until he was lying face downward, and from this position strove to trace the movements of the stalking hunter. Presently he saw the fellow come to a halt just under his twisted trees, almost directly below the place where Pensteven was stretched.

There he straightened and gradually brought the gun to his shoulder.

Straight before him and now in sight, must be the object of his trailing. And Pensteven, glancing in haste in that direction, now made out another big man gliding noiselessly toward the shadows on the farther side of the clearing. How he had been able to make the crossing to that point, undetected by the eye of Pensteven in the moonlight, the latter was unable to guess. But now the man turned his head, and Pensteven saw, with strange horror, the face of Christmas!

John Christmas about to die, not by the hand of the son of old Tom Pensteven, but brought down like a deer or a bear by this half wild hunter.

Pensteven glanced down and saw the rifle settling into the hollow of the hunter's shoulder, saw the head of the marksman twist a little to the right side. There was no need for haste. For John Christmas, unaware of the danger that had found him out, had been trying merely to move as noiselessly as possible.

Now, however, he turned his head against the slant light of the moon, and saw the rifleman about to shoot. His blood froze. Death was there before him!

What Pensteven did then he never could explain afterward—never very clearly. But he swung away from his secure place of hiding and hurled himself down through the branches.

The rifleman beneath heard that crashing through the branches and instinctively looked up, but only in time to receive the driving knees of Pensteven against his shoulders. They went down together with a crash; the rifle was not fired; and the man of the beard lay beneath Pensteven, stretched motionless, his arms flung out to the side.

His head had struck the knobby fist of a root that here twisted itself above the surface of the ground. There was a smearing of blood among the hair of the hunter; his eyes were closed; his heart scarcely beat.

He was not dead, but thoroughly knocked out, and Pensteven, getting to his feet, ran swiftly forward to that shadowy form which awaited him on the verge of the trees beyond.

The hand of John Christmas gripped his shoulder.

"That was my life, Stranger," said the outlaw. "That bearded fellow had it inside the crook of his trigger finger. They don't miss; sunlight or moonlight, they never miss!"

"That's only fair," said Pensteven. "D'you think that we're through the circle of the guards?"

"Nowhere near," replied the bandit. "They've sent some scouting parties to beat up the willows. But the main line is still ahead of us."

"We might rush them," said Pensteven.

"We might," agreed Christmas. Then he added: "Could

you shoot to kill—at men who've never done you harm, Stranger?"

"No," whispered Pensteven. "I couldn't do that!"

"I thought not," said Christmas. "But all of those men of Riverdale are ready to murder us; however, there's another way to break through. It's a chance in three, but it may work. Let's get to the edge of the creek."

They worked across to the side of the water, therefore, and above them they heard many voices, speaking quietly.

"There's the main cordon of the watchers," said John Christmas. "See the reflections of the man with the rifle in that bit of still water?"

"Yes," said Pensteven.

"They have us in the hollow of their hand; but we still have one chance. They're confident in their numbers. And no mob is very wide awake. They look at one another instead of at the danger that's coming. We might work past them here. You see how the roots and some of the lower branches thrust out from the side of the bank?"

"You mean," said Pensteven, "that we could crawl along under the roots and the hanging leaves?"

"We might," whispered the other. "It's my idea to try that."

He was interrupted by a sudden exchange of shots far behind them among the willows.

"Now," said John Christmas, and without further warning or discussion, he slipped down into the water, and Pensteven saw him half creeping, half swimming, sometimes pulling himself along by the trailing roots that extended from the shore.

Pensteven followed that example. It was a sort of skeleton tunnel in which he found himself. At hardly any moment was there perfect shelter from observation. As a rule, only scraggly roots and a few scattered branches formed the ribs that arched out into the water. It was simply that the observers would hardly be looking for human beings who adopted the tactics of water rats! That was the factor which the strategy of the great John Christmas had counted upon. Pensteven had not crawled and struggled and swum very far before he came to some rapids in the water where it closed over his head. He could float back down the stream, of course, until his head was free to rise to the air. But he preferred to struggle straight

177

ahead. His open, straining eyes saw several places where it seemed certain that he could lift up and breathe again, but always the intermeshed roots beat him down.

His lungs began to burst; fire lined them; darkness streaked across his bulging eyes; then he found a little embayment on the shore where he lay on his back, placid and still, fighting hard to control his breathing so that it should make no sound.

It seemed to him that he was two or three minutes there, only gradually recovering from strangling, because he dared not let the breath go wheezing out, to be drawn in again, while he gasped, to the bottom of the lungs.

At length he was easier. He started forward again, and now the icy water clogged his blood and sent a vital chill to his heart. It was as though the flame of life were being quenched.

He began to round the next bend, and he was halfway about it when something moved before him, dimly, and then thrust against his face and shoulders with a soft pressure. Fear made his heart leap. What water beast could it be?

Then he saw that it was simply the saddlebag into which the great John Christmas had thrust the booty stolen from the bank. Even Christmas had reached some obstacle that forced him to abandon the treasure! Pensteven gripped it, and went on.

Suddenly he found himself directly under the faces of men! Yes, the shore above him was occupied by half a dozen men who rested on their long rifles, and talked with one another. Moreover, where they stood, not a single root, not a trailing branch extended to make a shelter for the fugitive!

Chapter 35

That was the unforeseen contingency, no doubt, which had forced the bandit to let go his grip on the treasure sack. And what could Pensteven do?

He could not wait long for the group to disperse. He was getting numb from the icy water. He would hardly be able to move before many moments, and the group showed no signs of breaking up.

He determined that he would keep straight on. It was his one chance. If he were driven back down the stream, he could only expect to be taken when the rest of the bandits were gathered in by the law. Perhaps already several were gone.

Now he turned sidewise in the stream, fastened the thong of the saddlebag under the pit of his right arm and began to drag himself slowly forward. He was well over on his left side. Only his mouth and nostrils were exposed above the surface and he could simply hope that none of the keen-eyed men along the bank would glance down into the stream close to the shore.

He could praise fortune for one thing—the current, though comparatively mild here, had yet hollowed out the bank and made a deep enough bed of water to cover his body.

It was a matter of progressing inch by inch, and the inches were numberless.

Now, just above him, he looked up through the shadows which were thrown on the water by the bodies of his hunters. It struck him, frozen and terrified though he was, that a very odd freak of chance was giving him protection through the very corporal beings of his enemies! Thus he worked his way higher and higher up the current.

It seemed an hour before they were below his feet. He had a mad, a desperate desire to fling suddenly out of the water and rush off through the trees. But that desire he controlled. The cartridges that loaded his guns were soaking wet by this time. Besides, his body was so numb that he could not use his hands effectively.

He fought back that returning, persisting impulse, and little by little he rounded the terrible turn and felt the darkness of the trees close over him once more.

More than the blue of heaven to the blessed spirits was that darkness to the hammering heart and the aching brain of the young man.

But now he was through the line! His mind was a blur from the cold as he dragged himself, still cautious of making sounds, up the bank and almost crawled under the feet of twenty or thirty horses. They began to snort and stamp.

"Who's there?" called a man's voice.

Pensteven sank into the mud and lay dripping, freezing, on the verge of the brush.

Striding legs—he dared not turn his head to look up toward the man's head and shoulders—came straight toward him and paused, with the gleam of the spurs not a foot from his face.

"Thought that there was something over here," said the voice directly above Pensteven, seeming as loud as thunder in his ears. "Thought something went and moved. The horses begun to carry on."

"Coyote, most likely," said another.

"There ain't no smell of coyote."

The legs strode away from Pensteven.

Their voices went on, and Pensteven dragged himself little by little through the brush, until he was safely out of sight.

His fears were mostly gone from him now. Even the cold bothered him less because it began to seem that this was his fortunate evening.

When he had gone a little distance, he got to his feet, stepped into a clearing, and saw before him the silver ghost of a naked man; he started back.

"It's all right, Stranger!" came the whisper of John

Christmas. "It's only I. What have you got there with you? The saddlebag? Doggone, if you haven't got it!"

And he picked it up, weighed it, and laughed softly, a mere pulse of breath.

Pensteven was already stripping off his soaking clothes, and he began to wring them, as Christmas had done.

They made a four-handed job of it to squeeze the last drop of water out as far as possible. Then they rubbed down briskly. The blood began to leap through the body of Pensteven; hope returned; the world was again a simple, easy place for life.

Now they dragged the damp clothes back upon their bodies.

John Christmas was murmuring: "It was the closest call I was ever up against. I thought I was gone, Stranger. But the old luck still held; luck, and having you with me. The bag got away from me just as I was under the faces of those blind men on the creek bank. I was too frozen to go after it down the stream. Anyway, I couldn't have made speed enough to get to it without making a noise. I was bitter as the devil letting go of it, Stranger, but life was more than the coin in that saddlebag!"

When they were dressed, Christmas sketched briefly the plan he had in mind. He could talk freely now. That gust of wind which had struck Pensteven as he lay stretched on the twisting boughs of the willows had now freshened into a gale that grew with every movement, rushing hot out of the south and blowing down the course of the creek. A great thrashing was set up in the willows. Boughs groaned one against another; and the roaring of the wind in itself was enough to drown the voice of a man at any pitch lower than shouting.

The idea of Christmas was simply that they slip back to the horses which were held under guard among the willows—twenty or thirty of them—and there it would go hard if they were unable to take away a pair of mounts unseen by the two men who were guarding them. After that, they could head for the mountains. As for the rest of the gang, Al Speaker, as much spirit as man, would perhaps be able to fade through the line of the guards and get away. The others would probably be shot down or would surrender alive when day came and they found themselves still fenced in by a growing army of the men of Riverdale.

If they were thrown into prison, then they could be helped by hiring clever lawyers to fight for them; perhaps a jail break could be arranged.

So briefly, Christmas outlined the scheme. And Pensteven went back with him to the big herd of horses.

It was simple beyond belief, this part of the scheme which seemed dangerous. The two guards gave all their attention to the downstream side of their position, naturally. They could hardly expect that trouble would come from behind them. And so, without haste, the outlaw picked out two good animals, close at hand, and by degrees they were led back through the willows.

Twenty yards from the start, they mounted, and Pensteven felt the last chill of dread pass from his brain as the horse carried him swiftly on among the trees.

Not far from that starting point, they left the trees and came into the full blast of the wind, now a full gale in force. Before them was a half dried marsh, covered with gigantic tules, now mostly dead. Through this lowland they worked their way to what lay beyond—cleanly rolling hills, spotted with trees, covered with grass that made a perfect footing for the horses.

"Here we are," said John Christmas.

He turned in the saddle and looked back along the moonlit plain, now bright, now tarnished, as a great cloud swept up from the south across the face of the moon.

"And there they are behind us, the rest of the fellows," said Pensteven thoughtfully.

"The devil and all his fires could hardly help 'em," answered John Christmas. "I'd help them if I could. But in this business, Stranger, we all know that we take our chances. The stakes are high when we win. When we lose, it's a halter or a bullet through the head."

"Fire," murmured Pensteven. "There's something in that. Suppose we touch a match to the edge of those tules. In ten seconds there'd be a sheet of flame a hundred feet high running faster than a horse could gallop toward the willows. And when that flame hit the willows, they'd burn almost as fast as grass. Anything that's in earth or iron would have to burn with such a head start and such a

182

wind to fan it! In five minutes, Christmas, there would be nothing but fire and smoke down there."

"And the fellows could scurry out through the smoke clouds—out of the willows, Stranger?" exclaimed Christmas.

"That's the idea."

"A good idea. A grand idea!" said the outlaw.

They wadded together some bits of dead brush, lighted it, and in half a dozen places along the edge of the tules they started the fire. In every place it went out, except one. There the wind, instead of blowing it out, fanned it to a more intense heat, and suddenly a long streamer of smoke leaned to the north down the valley of the creek.

Widening as it rushed forward, that sweeping fire sent before it a dense fog of smoke, rolling as fast as the pouring wind. A great sheet of flame from the tules spanned the dried marsh, it struck the willows and suddenly diminished. Yet, though it progressed more slowly, it was consuming far more fuel, and the smoke turned from black to white, such immense volumes of steam were liberated by the heat. A vast smoke screen poured over all the lower valley, and out from the boiling fringes of that cloud, they could see men, tiny objects in the distance, rushing on foot or on horseback to gain the open air.

Chapter 36

The wind did not hang full in the south. It had begun to shift shortly after the fire started. Now it swung rapidly into the west and flung the smoke screen to the eastern side of the valley. "They can't help but get away, all of 'em," said John Christmas, exulting. "They can't help it unless some of them are flat on the ground with gunshot wounds. Those poor devils will be fried, of course; but better to burn than to hang! Stranger, the men are going to learn from me that it was your idea that saved the game for them; they'll learn that you brought the loot away also, after it had got away from me. I'm going to build you up until even Al Speaker will be willing to let you take the chief place after me when some day I strike a snag!"

He broke off to say: "How are your guns? Soaked, eh?"

"Soaked," said Pensteven. "Not a cartridge that will work, I suppose."

They sat their horses close to one another, and the animals bit at the grass that grew here as high as their knees.

Christmas had drawn his pair of Colts and examined them. Then he began to dump out the cartridges.

"All spoiled," he said. "It will be the first time in years that I've ridden without so much as a pocket knife on me, Stranger."

"Is that true?" asked Pensteven. "No weapon of any kind on you?"

"Not a thing of any kind. But we'll soon be back at the house of old Pudge Murphy. He has guns for us, and the sort of guns that I like to have! What's the matter, Stranger? You seem excited."

"I am," said Pensteven. "I've been wondering how I could do it. I've always known that I couldn't match you with guns. Hand to hand you're a bigger man than I am, Christmas, but I'll try to match you."

John Christmas looked at him with a frown of wonder which the moonshine blackened. The wind, still veering, was now driving smoke from the red-hot marshland in a sweeping cloud up the slope just below them, smoke and the ashes of the tules. But Pensteven paid no attention to that as he went on: "You've been fair with me, Christmas. You saved my life once. I saved yours once. That squares the account. You've been good to me, but I've also done some fair things for you."

"What in thunder are you driving at, old son?" asked the bandit, amazed.

"I want to point out that our accounts are squared for the present, but there's an old account in my blood, Christmas. Do you remember old Tom Pensteven, the consumptive, the miner whose claim you jumped?"

John Christmas said nothing, but his head lowered, and then thrust forward a little. His face altered suddenly, savagely. The nostrils flared, the eyes sank back under the shadow of the scowling brows. The handsome and easy gentleman disappeared, and the manslayer sat on that horse, staring at Pensteven.

"Damn all the fairy tales that ever were!" exclaimed John Christmas. "Are you going to tell me now that you're the brat of Tom Pensteven?"

"I am," replied Pensteven. "And God be good to one of us, because you or I will die here on this hill, Christmas."

"You treacherous rat!" exclaimed Christmas. "I'll show you what can be done with one pair of hands!"

As he spoke, he jerked the head of his horse around and buried the spurs in its tender flanks. The powerful mustang, with a squeal of pain, hurled forward. Its head thrown high in the pinch of agony, it struck the horse of Pensteven, sidelong with breast and shoulders, and knocked it flat.

By all the rules of chance, Pensteven should have been flung headlong to the ground, but if he had forgotten his horse he had not forgotten his hands. One of them caught the mane of the horse of Christmas. The other hand seized

Christmas himself by the throat, and as the horse fell from beneath him, Pensteven clung to his enemy.

The shock of the impact did not break his grip; instead he kept his hold, and Christmas sluiced sidewise from his saddle and fell.

He tried for a strangle hold while he was still lurching through the air. And though he missed it, he got an arm around the head of Pensteven and almost broke his neck with the twist he gave it.

Then they crashed against the ground, tumbled head over heels, and leaped up again from a fall that might have broken the bones of ordinary men. But these were whalebone and fire.

Thin streams of smoke were sweeping over the grass, knee-high, as Christmas stood braced and balanced, his long left arm extended; and Pensteven, eager as a terrier, silent with the battle frenzy, ran up the slope with the cuffing wind at his back and closed on the heavier man.

He paid for his eagerness. The left fist of Christmas found his head and stopped him as though he had struck a wall. And Christmas came rushing in to try for a wrestling hold. His convulsed face was new to Bob Pensteven. The mask was stripped off, and the devil looked out.

But if Pensteven were much lighter, he was by that much the swifter. His swerve to the side let Christmas pass him, and his iron-hard fists went home as the bandit halted, wheeled, and turned.

But that did not end the fight. Blows that would have felled powerful men like Vince Carter merely glanced from the iron of John Christmas. He was in again, wonderfully light and fast, and again Pensteven dodged and poured in a volley of terrible blows. The third charge found his foot slipping in the grass. The next moment Christmas had him down.

He was crushed as though by the falling of a tree. The trained strength of his athletic muscles became a feeble, useless thing now that he was in the arms of the outlaw. Such strength he had not imagined; he was in the hands of a gorilla.

Now the smoke that had been spreading rapidly covered them both with a thick blanket of white, a hot blanket that made breathing exquisite pain.

Pensteven saw the head of Christmas go back. He heard

the man gasp and choke, then curse savagely, for the changing wind had blown the glowing embers from the tule marsh into the tall, standing grass, and now it was aflame.

Humanity could not endure that burning mist even for a moment, and John Christmas, lurching to his feet, ran for his life.

Pensteven got up, stunned, bruised. The pain from his wounded left shoulder stabbed deep down into his body, but the entire surface of his body was scorched and seared with the rush of the fire. He saw the red rim of it gleaming through the smoke, and, turning, he fled also.

He stumbled over something and fell flat—it was the saddlebag. Hardly realizing what he did, his hands instinctively gripped it, and he raced on again.

Trees appeared before him, black, uncertain shapes, but the fire was close behind, pursuing with a roar.

He turned to the right, in fear of death, and ran with all his might until the smoke screen suddenly lifted and he blundered out into the open, gasping, choking, still blind and reeling.

Where was John Christmas? It was lucky for Pensteven that the outlaw was not in sight. Perhaps he had found his horse and fled straight ahead of the advancing fire that now rushed on with a widening front.

There, in the hollow below, was the mustang which Pensteven had ridden out from the willow. He went down to it, stumbling on the way.

His throat was bruised where the throttling grip of Christmas had seized on him. Fingers of steel had sunk into his flesh here and there. The pounding pistons of a great machine seemed to have beaten and bruised him to the bone. No man, but a terrible animal, had been revealed to him.

It was that memory which sickened him and made him dizzy as though he had seen a human being turned by some Circe's touch into a ravening beast.

He, Pensteven, had ridden far on the trail to come at this man. Yet now he felt like a foolish child rebuked by a master.

He got to the mustang, mounted it, and rode it at a slow trot down the slope, while the fire went on racing up the slope.

Now and then the flames struck a tree, or a group of trees, and flame burst upward as from a fountain, the sparks and the burning twigs flying high. He could hear the crackling wood even at a great distance.

Only rarely did he turn his head toward the inferno at his back. There was a goal ahead now for him and for the bag of loot which hung at the bow of his saddle.

He struck the lower valley road and followed it along its winding back toward the town of Riverdale. He was in no haste. The dawn came up; it turned red; it turned golden, and the sun lifted out of the east before Pensteven rode into the main street of the town along the river.

He went on until he came to the robbed bank. It was early enough in the day, but already scores of people had gathered, men with darkened faces, talking with mutterings to one another. Were they depositors in the bank, waiting to learn the full extent of the disaster?

He said to one of them: "I want to see the president of the bank."

The man looked at him gloomily.

"What about? Your deposits? Your checking account, son?"

He sneered as he spoke.

"Is he inside? Is the president of the bank inside?" asked Pensteven, his voice harsh with weariness, his eyes blurred with fatigue.

"Yeah, he's inside. Try to get in and see how fast you're thrown out again!"

Chapter 37

Distress commands as much respect, in a way, as guns on the one side and magnificence on the other.

Pensteven, at the door of the bank, found his way blocked by two burly guards, who carried rifles and wore revolvers and ammunition belts. But they gave way before him with only a few grumpy questions.

For the weary, sunken eyes of Pensteven commanded a way before him, and his bootless feet, his ragged clothes, the bloodstain which kept growing on his left shoulder, made him a power to be reckoned with, even in that town now filled with so many prosperous men of yesterday who were ruined men today.

He went on into the interior of the bank, one of the guards at his shoulder to show the way, and so they came toward the door which carried the legend "President's Office" inscribed upon the clouded glass. Out from that office a weary, monotonous, loud voice was carried dimly to them as the man inside was saying: "So the question that confronts us is not how we can continue in business, but how we may be able to meet the greatest part of our obligations. The surplus we have built up is wiped out; and such a great amount of money is lost to our depositors that when the doors of the bank open we are instantly bankrupt. Those doors must not be opened. We must make a settlement with our creditors. For myself, I have determined to contribute everything that I own, to the house in which I live, in order to help out the general situation. The sale of the bank building and the ground on which it stands should bring up the total amount we are able to repay to nearly ninety cents on the dollar. But the losses of over a million, falling upon the shoulders of no matter how prosperous an institution in a town of this size, cannot easily be recouped. The course of continuing in business in—"

"You see," muttered the guard at the ear of Pensteven, "they're winding things up. You can't see the old man now. Maybe you done some grand things out there in the willows to catch the damn gangsters, but now you better wait a few more minutes. It's gonna be over pretty soon, no matter how they groan."

The speech, in fact, had been interrupted by a murmur of many voices, hardly to be distinguished from groaning out of despairing throats.

Pensteven nodded, but, stepping quietly forward, he amazed the guard by suddenly throwing the door of the office open and stepping inside.

There he saw a long table with a dozen men gathered around it, some with chairs pushed far back, their bodies slumped down and resting on the small of the spine; some bolt erect, white-faced, taking lightning strokes with dull eyes; several had spilled forward, with their faces buried in their hands, while all listened to the speech of the president. He, an old man of seventy, erect as a soldier, gritted his teeth the harder, and was beginning his next sentence after the interruption of despair, when Pensteven opened the door and walked in.

The guard came after with a rush only to hear, as Pensteven threw his saddlebag on the floor, the most magic of sentences: "This is the whole of the stolen stuff, I think!"

It halted the guard. It brought every one of those despairing directors and chief stockholders out of their chairs; it caused the president silently, but with a sudden lighting of the eye, to stride forward and heave the damp, dirty saddlebag onto the table.

He opened it with trembling fingers, and then turned it upside down. Out fell a great mass of closely folded securities, jewelry, and a great, sliding, slippery mass of greenbacks. Some of them spilled off the table and slithered off into the air, gliding to far corners of the room. Much of the stuff was thoroughly soaked from the prolonged bath in the waters of the creek, but nothing was ruined. And a great deal in the middle of the well-compacted load remained untouched by moisture.

"All?" said one of the directors, making a crazy gesture with both hands and lifting a quantity of the paper up against his breast. "Did you say all, young man?"

"All," said Pensteven. "Every penny that was stolen is there."

He turned about and faced the door. As he did so, a wild voice cried out, and there was the white face of the night-shift man at the livery stable, set off by a big bandage around his head.

He was crying out: "That's the man! That's the man! Don't let him get away! He's poison! That's the man that shot me! That's the man that rode with John Christmas!"

The guard, who had seen the treasure that Pensteven returned, barred the entrance of the livery man with his rifle.

The president of the bank pushed out both the guard and the little man of the bandage.

He closed the door and put his back to it.

"We'll have to know more about this," he said. "What happened?"

Then he heard from the weary lips of Pensteven the shortest, strangest, and most compact statement that ever was made in the town of Riverdale.

"My name is Pensteven. Christmas murdered my father years ago. I came out here and joined the gang to kill Christmas. I worked with them through the robbery. Got through the willows with the loot. Fought Christmas until the fire separated us. Then I brought back the loot. That's all. I'm tired. I've got to sleep. I've told you all you need to know."

It was quite enough.

Drunk with joy, all their despair cast behind them, the word went swiftly through the town of Riverdale, and there was seen the odd picture of the venerable president of the bank, accompanied by several of the chief directors, accompanied by several of the chief directors, accompanying young Pensteven to the finest house in town, the house of President Drayton. A murmur, a hum, and then a shouting broke out from the townsmen, beating up against the gates that closed at the entrance to the driveway.

Once inside the house, Pensteven was tearing off his still sodden clothes and then falling utterly exhausted into

191

the best bed in the best room that the Draytons could offer him.

The doctor, afterward, came and dressed the wounded shoulder, but without rousing the tired young fellow. He slept, in fact, until the evening of that day; but it was two days before he could escape from Riverdale. The Draytons kept him a close prisoner. The next day the deputy sheriff, with a rather lopsided and swollen jaw, came to see him and grinned on one side of his bulldog face as he delivered his questions.

"What is it?" interrupted Pensteven, sitting in a big easy-chair, dressed in a suit of young Drayton's clothes. "D'you want to put me in jail, sheriff?"

"I wouldn't so much mind having you in jail for a while," said the deputy sheriff. "I've got a half-broken jaw that would like to see you in jail. But if I locked you up, the whole of Riverdale would come and break my doggone old jail to bits. No, brother, all I want to get out of you is some more information and descriptions of the looks of the gangsters, so's we can try to trail 'em down and jail 'em. I got a read-headed gent outside under guard, for instance. That's the only one we captured from the willows, and we can't quite make out whether he belongs to the John Christmas gang or is just a tramp that was loafing in the willows. Maybe you'd identify him for us?"

"Maybe I could do that," said Pensteven.

Then they brought in young Red, looking stolid and unconcerned. His eyes burned as they fell upon the face of the "traitor." Pensteven looked carefully back at him, and then said: "I never saw this man steal a penny for John Christmas or for any other gang."

Red blinked, bewildered; but, after all, there was strict truth in what Pensteven had said.

"All right then," sighed the deputy sheriff. "Turn him loose, boys. If he's just a tramp, he's had enough punishment. I kinder thought that he might be one of the real Christmas gang."

They took Red away, but he managed to give Pensteven one eloquent glance over his shoulder. By a single sentence, so carelessly spoken, he had been saved from the gallows that was his due.

But Pensteven cared nothing for that. It was John

Christmas that he wanted, and no other man. Even Oñate and Al Speaker could go free for all of him.

That evening, being the second day of his recuperation, he was walking about the room, gently exercising the sore shoulder, and finding that he could use it very well indeed, in spite of the inflammation around the surface wound. Old Drayton came in to see him and sat down for a serious conference.

"What you need, Pensteven, is a good long trip away from this part of the country," he said. "Europe, let's say. And the bank is eager to pay your way. You need to be away for a year, at least, or until we have managed to break up the Christmas gang. In the meantime, they're too powerful, and if you remain in this part of the country, I don't think that we can protect you. You've been too well advertised. The pictures that the newspaper reporter got of you, on your way from the bank to my house, have been published everywhere. The Eastern journals have run them with long stories, and the farther West, the longer the articles. They've made you a famous man because you've done a great, heroic, and honorable deed. You paid your blood for the sake of strangers, and the whole world loves an altruist. In the meantime, there's no doubt that the John Christmas people want your blood. They want to make an example of you, and sooner or later, unless you leave, they'll get you. What do you think of my idea?"

Pensteven answered: "I did over a thousand dollars' worth of work for Christmas, and I still have most of the money. I want to buy a horse and some guns and go back to Markham to wait for him. He killed my father, Mr. Drayton, and that score still isn't wiped out."

President Drayton began a solemn answer, but something in the face of the young man stopped him.

He merely said, "When do you want to start?"

"Now," said Pensteven.

"I'll telephone to Mr. Gregory, of the hardware store, and he'll open up his place to outfit you tonight," said Drayton.

193

Chapter 38

Pensteven arrived back in Markham early in the afternoon and went into town by a back alley that brought him abruptly to the Elbow Room Saloon.

He was riding the mare Dainty, which he had picked up on the return trip, and leading his newly bought Riverdale mustang.

In the Elbow Room he found Jerry, the bartender, and that formidable ruffian, Stew Carter. There were half a dozen others, too, but Stew was the one to be handled first. Going to the end of the bar, Pensteven ordered a glass of beer and began to drink it in small sips. A dangerous coldness had settled down upon him.

Jerry watched him with enchanted eyes. The other townsmen stepped back from the bar. But Stew Carter, now that his long desired opportunity was presented to him, could only hesitate. He felt that he might strike now for his own honor and for the sake of the John Christmas gang, but he was withheld by the dreadful knowledge that had gone abroad across the range; the John Stranger, that was Pensteven, had fought with the great John Christmas in person, and Pensteven was still alive!

What business had he, plain Stew Carter, gunman in ordinary, with a hero of such terrible repute as one able to measure weapons with that Achilles, John Christmas? The details were not familiar to anyone. No one could describe what had actually happened; because not even an Al Speaker or an Oñate dared to ask Christmas about the exact course of a battle, the total known result of which was that Pensteven, as it appeared, had taken the bank money away from the bandit.

Victory, therefore, must have been on the side of Pensteven! There were those who said that Christmas no longer led a charmed life, and that his downfall must be near at hand.

Stew Carter, considering these things, shifted uneasily to one side and then to the other. Finally he turned on his heel and strode from the saloon. He made his last step through the swinging doors a long jump for suddenly a chill had passed down his spine, and he felt a nightmare dread as though a bullet were about to crash through him.

When he was gone, the bystanders closed in around Pensteven. They had much to ask him; they wanted, above all, to know some of the details of the great fight. But he answered them with a shrug of the shoulders and a shake of the head.

They persisted. Then he said: "Here comes Sheriff Wace. Hello, sheriff!"

Wace came up and shook hands.

"I heard you were in here. I came to tell you that I was a fool, Pensteven."

"You don't need to say that," said Pensteven. "I want you to hear the yarn, and along with the rest of these fellows, you can put people right. They all seem to think that I shot it out with Christmas, or drove him off in some way. They're wrong. I didn't touch him with a bullet. Our ammunition was all wet. We went to it hand to hand. I got him off his horse; we fought toe to toe, and I held my own pretty well. But then he closed and put me down. He's all iron. Here's one place where he touched me!"

He pulled down the collar of his shirt a little and showed them a purple-green smudge. "He would have killed me in another thirty seconds," said Pensteven. "But the smoke of a grass fire choked us both. In the smoke I got away with the loot, and found a horse and went back to Riverdale."

He took breath while the men gaped at his calm and honest statement.

Said the sheriff: "If he beat you, Pensteven, then tell me what the devil you've come to this town for? To be killed?"

"I've come here for my second chance at him," replied Pensteven. "I can't stand to him hand to hand, if he manages to close on me. But perhaps the next time he won't be able to close. I know he's a better shot than I am, but the ammunition won't be wet, perhaps, the next time we meet, and I may have enough luck to set against his bull's-eyes. I'm telling you fellows this because I know that Christmas has to do something. The range knows that I came out here and hunted him down in his own place. Now, if his reputation is worth the flip of a penny, he's got to come here to Markham and hunt me out. I'm going to wait for him."

He finished his beer and went out of the saloon, leaving Jerry and all the rest amazed; a murmur of voices began behind him. That murmur, he knew, would never cease until it had spread, like oil over water, throughout the entire range. There was a spectacular element about this procedure that he hated, but, on the other hand, he knew of no other way to bring the great bandit out of the wilds to meet him. Hunt Christmas he could not, now that his face and purpose were both known. Therefore Christmas must come to hunt him!

Sheriff Wace followed him out to the sidewalk.

"You're a strange fellow, Pensteven," he said, "but I'll tell you what—I'm gonna give you as much protection as I can."

"Of course you will," replied Pensteven dryly. "You'll protect me to death. You'll keep a ring of deputies strung out around me, and the result is that Christmas will have to come down and shoot me by lamplight through the window of my room. Or at midday, through the back. If you want me to have a fair chance at him, Mr. Wace, just leave me alone, will you?"

The sheriff blinked.

"You sound like all steel, son," said he. "And maybe you're right. I dunno. Maybe you'll have a chance, too. Honest men are hard to kill, but liars die dead easy!"

Pensteven left him and rode out to the house of Mrs. Still. Tethering Dainty and the mustang in front, he went around to the back porch and wrapped on the screen door.

She was rolling out pie crust on the kitchen table, and came with her hands and the tip of her rosy nose powdered all in white. She held up those white hands and cried out when she saw him. She came running to the screen door.

"Come in, John Stranger, come in. Mr. Pensteven, I mean! Gracious me! To think of what you've been and done! Getting yourself all famous since I seen you, and famous enough before, for that matter. Reputation, it sure is an easy growin' plant in some folks, and no kind of fertilizin' or waterin' will make it sprout in the wrong sort of soil! Come in here and set yourself down and rest your poor feet. There, take this chair. That hoodlum of a Casey Walters, he went and broke the other chair, sitting there and yarning to me the other day. Have some coffee. This is fresh made and I roasted the beans myself. I got a good turn on 'em—just deep brown, and none of your black burn, that some folks want. They can want it, but they won't get it from me.

"Lemme look at you. You look pretty thin, poor fellow. You look real thin and bad. Wait till I go and call Barbara. Bobbie'll be all in a whirl when she sees you. We've talked ourselves to midnight every night since you been gone, wondering and wondering. Here's a piece of cold apple pie. It's a mite sour. I never can reckon on those apples with the russet skins. They look good and they taste good, but they don't always act the same way once they're in an oven. Sit down here and eat this, and try this coffee. If it ain't good, I'm a great big worthless liar. My, my, but this is a treat to see you. You sorter growed into a place in this house pretty quick, John."

She ran out into the hall, shouting: "Bobbie! Oh, Bobbie! Here's John come back, and looking just the same as ever, but thinner. Come down here and talk to him while I roll out the pie crust."

A rattle of footfalls swept down the back stairs, and Barbara Still swept into the room, her eyes dancing, her face flushed. She ran to Pensteven and caught his hands.

"Stand up and let me look at you!" said she. "Why, you look the same. Famous men aren't a whack different from ordinary punchers, I suppose. Come on outside and let me look at you closer. A kitchen is no place for a Pensteven, is it? Come out here in the open. That's better, isn't it, John? Or are you still to be called John? Or is it Robert, or Reginald, or Roxbury, or Riverton? Or Pensteven Pensteven, perhaps, and are you full of hyphens and everything like that?"

By this time he was with her by the chopping block and

seated on the fallen trunk. She was on the block itself, her bright, deep eyes consuming him.

"Bob's my name, but you can call me John if you want to. But don't badger me, Barbara," he said. "Sit still for a minute and let me look at you, will you? This is better than twenty-four hours' sleep and three square meals to me. Believe it?"

She merely smiled at him.

"And the great fight, John? You're going to tell me about that?"

"I've told about it once. I won't tell again," said he. "Except that Christmas beat me. A grass fire drove us both off, and I got away with the loot. The ammunition was wet. That's the only reason he didn't kill me. I'm waiting for him to come back now. There's the story. Don't ask me any more about it."

"I won't," said she.

"But tell me the news about yourself, Bobbie," said he. "Something's happened to you. You're so polished and bright that you shine, and you'd light your own way through the dark. What's happened to you?"

She examined him thoughtfully.

"Well," she said, "I have to tell you. You shoot straight from the shoulder, so I'll tell you the secret. I've found the big chief, and now I'm waiting for marching orders."

He lifted his head and looked. She was not smiling.

He remembered then what she had once told him: that on a day she knew she would meet with a man whom she would be willing to follow no matter into what, as a squaw follows her brave.

She had found that man. He did not doubt it. The blood of Pensteven was ice, and the rushing noise of the creek moved in upon him and seemed to carry him, like a wind, into some far-off obscurity. Life had gone flat, and the sky was dull.

Chapter 39

"That's a hard jolt," he told her. She frowned, and then made the frown go away.

"You mean that it wasn't just talk when you were here before?" she asked him.

"No, it was more than just talk. It was honest."

"I'm sorry," said Barbara Still. "I think that you waked me up, John. If you'd stayed on here, perhaps I would have begun to see in you what I see in this other man. At least, everybody was just the same until you happened along. But I couldn't pass you over the way I passed over the rest. There was something to you. That night the sheriff came, I stayed awake all that night, thinking about you. I suppose that if you hadn't gone away I would—well, I don't know. That's only supposing, and, of course, fame means more than a woman to any man."

She added: "Any man that's worth his salt, I mean to say."

"I'm not worth my salt then," said Pensteven. "Forget about me. Tell me about the other fellow."

"If you still feel a little homesick about me, John," said the girl, "I'd better talk about you, not the other fellow."

"Great Scott, Bobbie," said he, "when you're gentle this way, and considerate, I really see how much I care about you. I guessed it before. I know it now."

"Besides," she said, "when the hero comes home, the girl ought to fall into his arms when he gives the signal."

"Don't talk trash, Bobbie," said he. "I'm no hero. Christmas was killing me. That's the truth. Do you think that I'm lying about that?"

She shook her head.

"No, I don't think you're lying. And neither do I think you're lying when you say that you're waiting now for the man who beat you before so easily."

"Well, it wasn't exactly easily, Bobbie. He knew that he'd been in a fight. But I slipped, and so all at once he got in at me. He's as strong as a bear and as quick as a cat. But if I could have kept him at arm's length—" He stopped and shook his head. "I didn't though," he said disconsolately.

"Tell me, John," she said, her voice filled with this new gentleness, "did you really want to kill him? Would you have killed him—with your bare hands?'

He smiled at her. "Oh, I would have killed him, Bobbie, right enough. He killed my father, Tom Pensteven, you see. He was a consumptive, working to make his last stake for my sake, but for my mother's sake, chiefly. The news killed her. You understand?"

She drew a quick breath, like one who needed it.

"I understand," said she, and nodded. Her eyes had grown a little smaller as though she were studying him at a distance, or as though something about him overwhelmed her mind.

"Killing with bare hands, I mean. That's hard to understand," she murmured. "It's not what I'd expect from you somehow. But—well, there was over a million, I understand, in that saddlebag you took back to Riverdale?"

"So they say," he murmured absently.

"Didn't you look?"

"It wasn't mine, Bobbie. All it meant to me was the poundage. It was heavy enough, Heaven knows."

"The bank would have gone broke," she insisted. "That's what would have happened. Half the well-to-do people in Riverdale would have been ruined."

"Perhaps," he said indifferently. "I don't know. Except," he added with a sudden enthusiasm, "that the president of the bank was a grand old man. Seventy, and still able to carry his share and look the world in the eye. You would have liked him, Bobbie. There's a man you would have liked. No bunk about him. All clean-cut, and honest, and brave as the very devil."

"Like you, John," said she.

"Don't do that," protested Pensteven, frowning.

"All right, I won't," she replied. "Only it's true. And I can't help seeing what a fool I am."

"How?"

"Letting you really want me and deciding not to have you. I'm a silly fool, and that's all. But when John Christmas comes for you, if he ever dares—"

"Ah, he'll dare, well enough," said Pensteven. "He has to for the sake of his own reputation. He has to come for a fair fight, too. But he'll be glad to do that. He knows that he's got an edge on me."

"If he has any brains at all," said the girl solemnly, "he'll know that he might beat you once, but that beating you twice is a different matter. Even for a John Christmas."

"I wish that you'd stop talking about me and Christmas," he again protested. "I wish that you'd tell me about your man, Bobbie. He's a gorgeous person, of course."

"Yes. He's grand," said she. "You'd like him. He's worthless, but you'd love him."

"Worthless?" said Pensteven.

"Oh, you know," said she. "He'll never be worth a penny. He's just a big, brown, handsome, gentle-voiced, pleasant fellow. He's always smiling. But there's iron under the smile too. He's a man you'd like to see."

"What you say makes me almost think of—" began Pensteven, and then he stopped himself and shook his head.

"How long ago did you meet him?" he asked. "Is he an old friend?"

"No, only two days ago."

"Only two days!" exclaimed Pensteven.

"I told you it would be that way," said the girl. "When I saw my man, I'd know him by his face."

"You mean love at first sight, eh?" said he.

"D'you laugh at that?" asked the girl.

"No. I know all about it," said he gravely. "Go on, Bobbie."

"Well, it was this way. I was wandering through the woods down there. Oh, not very far from the house. I was thinking about you, as a matter of fact, wondering about you. Wondering, to be exact, why you didn't mean more to me, wondering if you didn't mean more than I guessed. You don't mind me talking like this?"

"It hurts a good bit," said Pensteven. "But it's pleasant,

too. Go on, Bobbie. You were wondering about me, and then you saw the real thing, and you knew the difference."

"Well," said she, "it was like running into a bright light. I simply blinked at him. I mean to say, he was so big and gentle, brown and smiling, and terribly handsome."

She added hastily: "That isn't all comparison, John."

He managed to grin at her. "Oh, go ahead," said he. "I know what my mug looks like. I'm not in for a beauty prize. Go right ahead. This big, fine-looking fellow, what is he, Bobbie?"

"I never asked him," she replied.

"Well, what was he doing when you met him?"

"Fishing," said she. "Fishing with dry flies. Down the creek, there."

"He's some bank president off on a vacation," said Pensteven. "That means the ruin of the country when the tenderfeet begin to come in. But go on, Bobbie. How old is he?"

"Thirty-five, forty, perhaps."

"As old as that?" exclaimed Pensteven.

She frowned.

"He's not a baby," she answered, "if that's what you're exclaiming about. No, he's a grown man. You can see that he's lived; even though his face is quite unmarked, except when he frowns. He's splendid when he frowns."

"All you know is that he's a good fisherman?" he asked.

"Yes, he knows how to cast flies. Oh, but it's the easy, grand, careless way about him that you'd love. He's as strong as a bear, too."

"Look here, Bobbie, does he like you as well as you like him?"

"Nowhere near," she answered readily. "You know, a fellow like that has been pestered by adoring women all his days. He likes me well enough though. I can tell by the way he looks at me. He likes me. He finds me a little different from the rest perhaps."

"Does he tell you that?"

"He doesn't tell me much of anything," said Barbara.

"Look here, Bobbie," said Pensteven, "does he even tell you whether he lives east or west?"

"No."

"Great Scott, my dear," said Pensteven, "tell me one thing."

"I don't seem to have much to tell," she admitted with a wry smile. "But what he is and does, where he lives, and all of that, doesn't matter. Not a bit."

"Well, has he told you whether or not he's a married man, or single?"

"No, he hasn't told me. I haven't asked."

The jaw of Pensteven slid gradually forward.

"What's his name?" he asked curtly.

"Mac."

"Mac what?"

"MacMurray."

"What's his front name?"

"John."

Pensteven sprang up.

"I want to see this John MacMurray," he said. "I've an idea that he's a Scotch swindler."

"Maybe he is," said the girl what astonishing frankness. "He might be anything, but he's the world to me. That's what really matters to me."

"I've got to see him," said Pensteven fiercely.

"You wouldn't fight him?"

"I hope not," said Pensteven. "You don't think that I'm simply a swaggering fool, do you, Bobbie?"

"No, of course I don't think that. And I want you to see him, too. Because I think that you'll like him almost as much as I do. He's a man's man. That's what he is, He's—"

"Oh, damn what he is," said Pensteven. "I'll find out what he is, right enough. I'll find out all about him, because it seems to me about time that you should know."

"You come with me tomorrow morning," said the girl. "I'm meeting him at sunup—yonder on the shoulder of the mountain. I'm going to show him where he can kill a deer."

"I'll come," said Pensteven.

Chapter 40

And he went. He was up in the gray of the morning without being called; for he had hardly closed his eyes during the entire night. But when he came downstairs the girl was already waiting, walking restlessly up and down.

She came to him at once with an anxious face.

"John," she said, "I've thought it over. You'd better not come with me."

"Why not?" he demanded.

"Well," she answered, "you want to ask a lot of questions, and something tells me that it might irritate him; and something else tells me that it would be dangerous if he lost his temper. You know, under all his smiling there's a sense of rather ugly temper. I've never seen it show through, but I never want to, either."

"You'd better let me come," urged Pensteven. "I can be discreet. I won't be a troublemaker."

"You promise?"

"Of course I do."

"Well, then come along. He'll be waiting by the time we get up the slope."

They started out, going down to the creek, fording it where a natural series of stepping-stones rose above the water, and then climbing up the small gorge that a runlet of water had cut in the side of the mountain, angling this way and that. It was slow work because there had been rain in the night which made the rocks and the clay soil very slippery. The sky was still threatening, for the western wind hurried great masses of clouds into the brilliance of the east.

Pensteven climbed as an athlete should, but the girl easily kept pace. She seemed to be as nimble and swift as a deer.

A rain shower whipped over them; but they marched on through it. A shower of hailstones a moment later made them take shelter under a big pine. While the stones crashed through the branches above them and rattled crisply on the ground, bouncing high up, like spume, she shook her head.

"I don't like it at all," she said slowly.

"Don't like what, Bobbie?" he asked.

"This whole business. Something in my bones is telling me that trouble's ahead."

"Stuff!" replied Pensteven. "I'll tell you what it is. You don't want the light turned on this friend of yours; you're afraid that there's something wrong about him."

"Well, maybe there is something wrong about him," said the girl. "I don't say that there isn't. He's the sort of a man—well, the sort who might be expected to do almost anything in a pinch. Anything violent, I mean. His big hands were made for action. You'll understand when you see him. Everyone knows what you are, and how fearless, John, but I think that even you may be a little afraid when you put eyes on him."

"Perhaps, perhaps," he snapped. "The hail's letting up. Shall we go on?"

They started forward again, over an easier slope, for they were now getting to the broad shoulder of the mountain, and the little stream they followed meandered more and no longer dashed itself to white spray. The morning had turned golden; and the eastern side of the trees glistened; to the west they were still shadowy and obscure.

The pines thickened, and then gave way suddenly in a natural clearing the floor of which was almost level. The grass was like a lawn, picked out with multitudes of flowers. As they came out from the trees, a big man started up from a stump, where he had been sitting, and came toward them.

It was John Christmas that Pensteven found himself facing. And the sight stunned his brain.

Why had he not guessed before when she spoke of a big, brown, handsome, smiling man, a careless figure, with an undefined sense of dangerous strength in him?

Now the brigand was coming toward him with the most

open and ingenuous smile, his right hand extended in greeting.

"Pensteven!" he exclaimed.

"John—MacMurray!" muttered Pensteven.

And he mustered a smile of his own and shook the hand of the outlaw.

Dangerous? Yes, John Christmas would be dangerous enough before this meeting had ended.

Barbara Still was dancing with excitement.

"You fellows knew each other before?" she exclaimed. "Why, I might have known that. The world couldn't hold two of you very long without making you rub shoulders. It's too small to have that much space in it. But are you really old friends?"

Bob Pensteven answered soberly: "Bobbie, you couldn't have given me a happier surprise in the world. Did you guess, Mac, that I was the fellow who lived down there in the Still house?"

"How could I guess it?" asked Christmas. "Wouldn't I have been down there rapping at the door the first moment that I guessed such a thing? John, I'm a happy man to see you here. And now, at last we have the chance that we need for talking together."

"We have," said Pensteven, readily following the hint. "But I don't think we can talk about that in front of Bobbie Still, do you?"

"No, we couldn't talk about that in front of anyone," said John Christmas. "Bobbie, will you give us five minutes, alone? Do you mind? Why, I've been praying that I could find Pensteven. We have to talk—about the most intimate thing that could be between two men!"

She looked at them half smiling, half in doubt.

"I'll scout up the mountain for fresh sign of deer. I know about where to look. But you know, the minute I leave, I have a picture of you two."

She paused.

"I'll go along," she said.

"Thanks, Bobbie," said Christmas, and laying his hand on the shoulder of Pensteven, he drew him closer and started walking slowly on with him, his head bowed, speaking in an intimate, subdued tone.

Barbara Still, at the sight of this, waved her hand and was instantly gone among the trees.

Then Christmas stepped back one pace and another. Pensteven withdrew a little also. He could not bear to be too near the other. The physical sense of the outlaw's superiority was too great to be endured when they were close.

It was better to stand back; the faint, contemptuous smile of Christmas was fixed upon him now as the outlaw said: "I knew that little fool would bring you to me sooner or later. But what a jackass you are, Pensteven, not to have suspected that I was the man!"

"I was a fool," said Pensteven, nodding.

As he talked, all the nerves in his body seemed concentrated in his right hand and right arm, ready to make the lightning move that would bring forth a revolver from beneath the pit of his left arm.

For suddenly he was sure Christmas would act, first throwing him off guard with conversation as much as possible.

Was it not better to snatch out his own gun and begin the battle at once? No, it would be better to let the girl get to a little distance up the mountain first.

"You came out to meet the wild man, the fisherman, the fellow who came from nowhere. Going to discipline him a little, were you, Pensteven? Discipline him for poaching on your preserves?"

He laughed softly.

"You're right," answered Pensteven. "I was a fool. All I guessed was that the girl was nothing to you."

"She? Bobbie? Oh, she's amusing enough," said Christmas. "I may take her. I may not. She's there for the taking. Nothing difficult about her."

He sneered as he spoke, and red rage flooded the brain of Pensteven, but by a supreme effort he became calm again.

"I see how it is, Christmas," he replied. "You want to madden me if you can. You want to make me blind. But you can't manage it this way. Not by talking about Barbara Still."

"No, she's not worth talking about," said Christmas.

The electric spark of rage again shot into the brain of Pensteven and had to be extinguished once more.

"She's one in a million, and you know it," he replied. "If she lost her heart to you, she lost it only for a moment.

207

You're big and handsome and enough of a sneaking liar to turn the head of any girl. But she would have recovered fast enough. Already she suspects that there is something wrong about you. She knows that there is a flaw somewhere. No, Christmas, don't think that I believe you when you talk down about her. But whether you do or not, she's a star. You can't smudge her."

"Why should we waste time talking about her?" asked Christmas. "We have something else to do, Pensteven. We might as well get down to it. Unless there's something I can do for you before I put a bullet through you. For instance, you may be curious to learn about your father."

"My father?" said Pensteven, emotion mastering his voice for a moment. "My father? Why, what can you tell me about him, except that you murdered him?"

"You might wish to know why I decided to get him out of the way."

"Well, what possible reason could there have been? My father never harmed a soul in the world except himself!"

"Tom Pensteven was a man I could have used," said the other. "He was a fellow with talents that would have been valuable to me. He knew how to talk and throw people off their guard. He would have been a perfect advance agent for me."

Sorrow, anger, and disgust were rising in Pensteven.

"You tried to get him to help you in your dirty work, and when he refused you murdered him. Is that it?" he asked.

"And why not?" asked the other. "I had to show him too much of my hand. I was sure that I could buy him in. But the fool held out. The more I told him, and the more I offered him, the more outrageous he became, and so the next day I simply went down and raided his claim. I killed the old fool. Besides, the mine was worth it."

Chapter 41

Suddenly Pensteven set his teeth and shook his head a little. Then an iron smile touched the corners of his mouth.

"I see how it is," said he. "You want to unnerve me, Christmas, by insulting Barbara and then sneering at my poor father. But I won't lose my temper. I need steady nerves if I'm to pull a gun against you, and steady nerves are what I intend to keep. I see how you've built up your reputation, Christmas. You use any method you can to put the other fellow at a disadvantage. You don't fight; you murder. But your reputation's gone now, you know. Everyone believes that you've been beaten. Everybody knows that the money from the Riverdale bank was taken away from you. The very fact that you didn't die fighting for the loot proves that you were simply kicked out of the way."

He saw a shudder pass through the body of Christmas. The big man's brown face was dusted over with gray. Was it possible that he had been able to turn the very weapons of the outlaw against him?

A tremor was in the very voice of the man as he answered: "Those lies will quiet down after the world knows that I've killed you, Pensteven."

"The world will never know that because it can't happen. I'm a better man than you are, Christmas, and in the bottom of your sneaking heart you know it."

"A better man?" said Christmas fiercely. "If the grass fire the other day hadn't driven me off, I would have throttled you then and there. Do you realize that?"

"You had that one chance, and you'll never have another," answered Pensteven, watching curiously, like a doctor noting the effect of a drug, the manner in which this badgering affected the other. "Opportunity doesn't knock twice at the same door, Christmas. The world knows that I'm the better man, but in case it should be in doubt, I'm going to leave the proof dead on the ground here today."

"I laugh at you," said Christmas.

But his lips were twitching with rage.

"Your own gang," Pensteven went on, hazarding a guess at things that he could not know, "has no more faith in you. They trusted you before. Now they've seen a million dollars and more slip through their hands. They wanted that money, Christmas. They're damning you because you let it go."

The gray face of Christmas turned suddenly crimson, and another tremor ran through his body.

"It was a clever move, that freeing of Red," he admitted. "You knew that he'd begin to make a saint and a hero out of you and a fool out of me. But his mouth will be shut for him. You guessed that Speaker would begin to scheme to get me out and himself in as the leader; but you first, then Speaker, and then Red—I have the guns that will stop you all. Fill your hand, you cur!"

He made his own move as he spoke, and the hand of Pensteven leaped at the same instant. Never had his touch been surer or swifter. Never had his draw been made with more lightning speed; but as the gun came out he saw that he was late—fatally late perhaps. As his long-barreled Colt flung forward, the weapon of Christmas was already exploding. The mouth of the gun jerked up; there was a violent blow against the side of Pensteven's head. But his eyes remained undazzled, and he dropped the hammer of the gun.

A second shot answered his; but it merely drove into the ground as Pensteven, the next bullet in readiness, held his fire. For he saw with unbelieving eyes that the revolver had slid out of the hand of the bandit, and that his right forearm was dripping with blood!

Blood was streaming down the side of Pensteven's face from the slash across his head, but what did that matter?

Yonder stood the murderer of Tom Pensteven with his gun arm useless, at the mercy of the leveled Colt in the hand of old Pensteven's son!

The miracle had happened! Not mere speed and skill had turned the trick, Pensteven knew, but the fury into which he had goaded the other had made that terrible hand waver for once.

With his left hand, Christmas grasped his wounded arm. His lips parted. Like a sleepwalker seeing incredible visions, he stared at Pensteven. It was not fury that now made his face pale as he muttered in a low voice:

"It's come at last; this is the day then!"

It had indeed come; that day which, as he had told Pensteven, could not be far away. Luck at last was gone from him!

Twice Pensteven told himself that this was not a crime, but a sacred duty. He called the image of his dead father into his mind. Still he could not force himself to shoot a helpless man.

At last he said: "The jail will hold you until you're hanged, Christmas. It's better that way. It's better to drive you down the street through Markham to the jail. People will remember that sight all right!"

"The rope was never made that will hang me," said Christmas. "I've lived by the gun, and I'll die by it. Shoot now and shoot straight, Pensteven, or I'll pick up the gun with my left hand and come after you. I can handle a Colt a little with the left hand, too."

Pensteven, again savagely alert, considered. Christmas must die. There was no doubt in his mind about that. No one in the world had so merited a bullet through the brain.

Yet Pensteven could not kill a disarmed man. There was one way left in which they could fight it out on level terms. He saw that way, and all his blood went hot at the thought.

"I've found the way out," he said. "I'll make a new fight, and an equal fight, out of it."

He went to the big man and looked at the wound. It had furrowed the forearm of Christmas to the bone, and the blood flowed in a stream. That bleeding had to be stopped first if the battle were even to seem equal.

First he found the second revolver of the outlaw and took it. Then he ripped away his own shirt, and, with strips of it, bound the torn flesh of that right arm until the bleeding had almost entirely stopped. After that he fixed his own right arm to his belt, tying it hard at the wrist.

Finally he stood close to John Christmas, saying: "We're both one-handed now. And this is the way we'll fight it out. You have no guns, and neither have I. But I know that one of us has to die, and I think that you're the man. Are you ready?"

"Ready?" said Christmas. "I'm going to smash your skull like an egg! Stand up to me, fellow. I've handled you once before. I'll handle you again."

As he spoke, he rushed straight in at Pensteven.

He had forgotten, perhaps, the first stages of his other battle with Pensteven. But he soon had cause to remember. To be sure, the man had his left hand only, but to a trained boxer the left alone can be sword and shield.

Lightly Pensteven avoided that rush and the next, and his own long, sharp-shooting left was ever in the face of the larger man. The strength of the great John Christmas was as iron, but even iron will yield to constant hammering. Like lead swinging in the supple heel of a blacksnake was the fist of Pensteven at the end of his long arm. So he swerved away from those rushes, and smote and smote with unwearying accuracy and force.

Again and again, as Christmas strove fiercely to close in, his hand clutched at the body of Pensteven. But with one hand he could not maintain the grip. The shirt and the undershirt of the young man were both gone. His body was red and bruised from the clawing fingers of Christmas, but still he avoided the wrestling hold that might be fatal.

Christmas, baffled and blinded by the steady rain of blows, at last stumbled over a rock on the ground. It was instantly in his hand. From under his bleeding brows he peered at Pensteven, red-eyed, and then rushed in again.

The rock, hard-flung, struck on the right shoulder of the young fellow and spun him around. He staggered back to the verge of the little stream, and there the rush of John Christmas at last overtook him; the grip of the big man closed in on his throat, and down they toppled into the shallow water and over the slippery, polished rocks of the runway.

Perhaps it was the water that saved Pensteven at that moment. It made his flesh slippery at least, and the terrible

212

grasp of Christmas slid from his throat as he writhed and twisted.

From the throat Christmas shifted his grasp to the hair of Pensteven, and attempted to batter out his brains against the rocks.

The water absorbed some of the shock, but Pensteven knew that he was only mortal seconds from death as he lay choking under the stream, held down with what seemed irresistible power, and with the contorted face of that human fiend snarling and gaping above him.

He struck feebly at the face of the monster. But the fist glanced helplessly off the battered jaw, and John Christmas laughed.

But now, with his fighting hand flung across his breast, Pensteven jabbed up and back with his elbow and caught the chin of Christmas with the point of it.

The giant toppled sidelong into the shallow water of the creek; and Pensteven, rising to his knees, picked up a five-pound stone from the bed of the stream, a great, water-smoothed rock, and poised it an instant before finally bringing it down between the dazed eyes of the other.

The stroke would have fallen surely had not the wild voice of Barbara Still pierced like lightning through the black mist of his brain and showed him what he was actually doing.

He dropped the stone. With a sort of savage contempt for all that might happen now, he grasped Christmas brutally by the hair of the head and so dragged him to his knees and then helped him to his feet.

Chapter 42

Into the dazed brain of Christmas, sense was returning, but the will to battle was gone. Sagging lines of weakness formed in his face. The fury had left his eyes, perhaps forever. With his pride his strength departed, and his knees sagged beneath his weight. He staggered, not toward Pensteven, but away from him.

A sort of horror passed coldly over the young fellow as he saw the work of his hands, this subtraction of an unconquerable soul from the mighty form of John Christmas. As he stared, it seemed to him that his labor was done, and that the thing which had made the man great was gone forever, the cruel cunning from his mind, the power from his will.

He did not close on the big fellow again, because there seemed nothing left to fight. That was the chief reason, and the other was the voice of Barbara Still, crying out as she came running through the trees: "John Pensteven, what have you done?"

He pointed. "Go take your man," he said. "You're welcome to him if he wants you. Go follow your brave like a squaw. John Christmas is his name!"

She had started toward Christmas with her hands held out to him, but the name stopped her like a bullet through the brain. Balanced against his pitiable state, murder, treason, a thousand tales of cruelty and devilish cunning came pouring in upon her as she stood there aghast. Then a voice came with a strange, half-stifled utterance from across the little stream, saying: "Bad luck, Jack. This ends your day!"

The three of them turned and saw a small man with a great brow and luminous eyes beneath it, but almost no chin. It was Al Speaker who stood there, calmly looking on; and it was plain that he would not use the big revolver that weighed down his hand and stretched the arm at his side.

As for Christmas, when he saw the three of them before him and understood the meaning of this moment to which he had come, far worse than the death which he expected, he turned and flung his left arm before his face and fled staggering away among the trees.

Al Speaker crossed the stream daintily, picking his way from stone to stone. He came up to them, dabbing his handkerchief against his lips.

"Miss Still," he said with that obscure, sibilant enunciation, "I'm Alfred Speaker. You know what I am. But there's nothing to fear from me today. Nothing to fear from me ever, I hope. Pensteven, I saw the whole fight, from beginning to end. I saw you master him with your wits, and then with your gun, and then with your hands. I've seen all sorts of battles. But I never saw a finer thing done than you've done today. I suppose, in the long run, that honesty can't be beaten. It has an iron hand.

"Sit down here on the stump," he continued. "I want to dress that wound where the bullet clipped against your head. You're losing more blood than you think."

So Pensteven sat down on the stump, and his wound was dressed. Then Speaker helped him down the hill carefully, supporting him under the pit of his right arm, while the girl walked on his left. She also aided, for the dizziness remained in the head of Pensteven and his feet moved crazily, out of his control. Twice, in spite of them, he stumbled to his knees, but at last they came to the edge of the trees and looked out on the old house by the creek.

There Speaker said: "I'm leaving you here. You have boarders who would be too interested if they saw my face, Miss Still. I hope that you two have found one another for good. Pensteven, I think you were right to let Christmas go. He's a broken man now. He'll never be a leader again, and because of what he's done before this, he'll be hounded to death by creatures whom he has kicked out of his way in the time of his strength. He has tasted worse than death, and death itself won't be postponed long."

And he went swiftly back among the trees. The girl went on slowly with Pensteven; they reached the house, and her call brought her stepmother out.

She gave one horrified exclamation when she saw the blood. Then she set her lips firmly together and rose to the occasion. Together they got Pensteven up to his room and stretched out on his bed. Barbara hurried down to ride for a doctor, and Mrs. Still remained with the young man.

As Speaker had said, he had lost more blood than he had suspected. The battle fury had filled him for a time, but now he was very weak indeed, and blackness whirled before his eyes.

He was aware of little until the doctor came. He took six stitches in the scalp of Pensteven, but the prescription which he left behind him was a simple one.

"He needs rest, and this is a peaceful house. He needs good food, and is there any food better than your cooking, Mrs. Still? I hope that he'll spend most of the next two or three days sleeping. That will be best for him."

The very name of sleep was enough to seal the eyes of Pensteven. Afterward he dreamed his way through several days. It was simply eating, sleeping, eating and sleeping again. But strength came swiftly back to him, running like sap in the first hot days of the early spring.

On the third day he was up, sitting in the afternoon sun on the back porch of the house, which faced to the south. Mrs. Still, busily at work in her kitchen, chatted with him through the screen door.

"Now I can let people be coming in to see you, John?" she asked.

"What people?" he asked.

"Why the whole town. It ain't any use to set down and use names. The whole town wants to see you, John."

"The town can go to the devil," said he.

"John, you don't mean that," said she. "After you've gone and made Markham famous like you've done. You have a kindly feeling about the folks, I know."

"I have," said he. "But I don't want to see any one, Mrs. Still."

"Well," said she, the hinges of the oven door grating as she opened it, "Bobbie said that you'd be this way. Bobbie is an understanding sort of a girl, I must say. If I was you, John, I'd be sitting down in the middle of town, on the

216

front veranda of the hotel, just sort of taking the air and letting the folks look at me. I'd have strength enough to let 'em shake my famous hand, too. But Bobbie said that there wouldn't be any foolishness in you about that sort of thing, and I can see that Bobbie was right. It's a terrible thing, in a way, to have a bright girl like that around the house. A mighty terrible thing. She always makes an older person seem just about half-witted, and no more. By the way, how you coming along with Bobbie?"

"Coming along?"

At this she crossed the floor and stood at the screen door with her fists firmly planted on her hips. "I ain't supposed to know, am I, that you're a little fond of Bobbie?" she asked.

"What makes you think that I am?" he asked.

"Well," said she, "maybe I'm wrong, but I just sort of thought that I seen signs of it."

"What signs, if you please?" he asked with some irritation.

"Well," said Mrs. Still, "signs like turning red, sometimes, when you hear her coming, and turning pale when she's finally got in the room. Then I've seen a calf look in your eyes, too, following her around and just dwelling on her face and haunting her."

"Humph!" said Pensteven.

"But I'm wrong," said Mrs. Still. "You ain't interested in her, are you, John?"

"I love the ground she walks on," he said tersely. "But it's no good."

"What's no good?"

"You know, Mrs. Still. Bobbie isn't interested. It's a bore to her."

"What's a bore?" she demanded, with a certain amount of heat.

"All that business—love and such stuff. Just a bore to Bobbie. She prefers freedom, or a better man than I'll ever be."

"Love and such stuff?" quoted Mrs. Still. "It's a bore to her, is it?"

She stamped to the inner door and bawled loudly: "Bobbie! Bobbie Still! Come down this minute."

"Great Scott, Mrs. Still," said he. "You won't bring her down here and talk about it. Will you?"

Instead of answering him, she muttered: "It's a great bore, is it? A great bore, indeed!"

The light, quick step of Bobbie came into the kitchen. "March out here on the porch with me, you young hussy," said her stepmother.

And she took Barbara by the arm and kicked open the screen door and planted her firmly before Pensteven. The latter, crimson of face, with agony in his eyes, entreated: "Please don't! Please don't say a word, Mrs. Still."

"Not say a word? I'll say a thousand words. What's this, you minx? Love is a bore, I hear, to you. You can't be bothered with it. Stuff and nonsense! Did you ever say such silly things in your life?"

"Let me alone," said Barbara Still, shrugging her shoulders and pulling away. "Of course I said them. What about it? Why can't I say that?"

"Of course, you can, Bobbie," said Pensteven. "Don't pay any attention. I'm horribly mortified. I wouldn't have had such a thing happen."

"Keep still, John, if you can't say anything more sensible than that. I don't want to hear a word from you. Not a single word. I'll do the talking and get the truth out. You're too bored, are you, you silly little rattlehead, to pay any attention when a man like Mr. Pensteven puts his heart on the ground in front of you?"

"He doesn't put his heart on the ground in front of me," said Barbara. "Take your hand off my arm, mother. I won't stand here and be made a fool of."

"Won't you? But you will, though," declared Mrs. Still. "Right here is where you'll stand, too. Life is all stuff and nonsense in your eyes, is it? Bless my soul and body, it drives me out of all patience. Tell me this instant, did this young man ever say that he was fond of you, you little idiot?"

Barbara flushed to the roots of her hair. Pensteven, purple with confusion himself, was amazed at this sight.

"I'm not going to talk," said she. "What if he did? Are you trying to make a fool of me?"

"I don't have to try. You made one of yourself," said her stepmother. "Out with it. Did he say that he loved you, Bobbie?"

"Mrs. Still, will you please—," cried Pensteven.

"Not one word from you, young man," said Mrs. Still.

218

"Bobbie, did Mr. Pensteven let you guess that he loved you?"

"What if he did? Yes, he did; and what then? Was I to throw myself on his neck?"

"Yes," said Mrs. Still. "If he would so much as hold out a hand to catch you. Mr. Pensteven wants to marry you, you silly little thing, and you haven't wit enough to take him! No, loves bores you, and you can't be bothered with such stuff. Indeed!"

"I'll have to say enough to stop this horrible scene," said Barbara to Pensteven.

Facing her stepmother, she went on: "He knew that I made a fool of myself. I fell in love with another man. And he knew it. I fell in love with John Christmas! There, you had to have the whole story; and I hope," she added in a voice that suddenly quavered, "that you're satisfied!"

"You fell in love with John Christmas? And why not?" said the amazing Mrs. Still.

"You mean to say that you're not shocked?" cried the girl.

"Stuff and nonsense," said Mrs. Still. "What difference does it make to a woman whether a man's good or bad, so long as he's a man? The worse he is, the more we're apt to think of 'em. Many a scoundrel gave my silly heart the jumps and the fidgets before I met your poor dear father. And what was he but a rascal who spent everything at faro and poker, poor darling? What if you fell in love with John Christmas? It showed you were a girl of spirit, that's all. But I'll wager that you fell out again when you stood by and saw this man give him a solid, fine thrashing! Tell me, didn't you?"

"I won't say another word," said Barbara faintly.

She was vigorously shaken by the shoulder.

"D'you dare to tell me that you still love John Christmas?" demanded Mrs. Still.

"No. I don't," said the girl.

"D'you dare to tell me that you don't love Pensteven till your heart fairly aches to have him?"

"Mother," moaned Barbara, "will you please let me be?"

"I won't let you be, you rattlebrained little fool!" said Mrs. Still. "I don't know what he sees in you, but there he is. He's asked you once if you'll have him. Go and ask him

219

now yourself. Go this minute. Get down on your knees, too. Get right down on your knees."

And she forced, or seemed to force, Barbara down on her knees before Pensteven. The young man groaned: "Mrs. Still, in Heaven's name!"

But he stopped. For he saw bright tears running down the face of Barbara, and he heard a tremulous voice say: "I was a fool; and I don't amount to much; but tell me, John, if you will have any use for me?"

Mrs. Still jerked open the screen door and went inside, letting it slam loudly behind her.

"And high time that she should show a bit of sense, the proud little minx. I don't know what you see in her, John. But she's a darling good girl, too, bless her soul. She couldn't be bothered with love and such stuff, eh? Well, she'll be plenty bothered from now on, I guess. I hope she'll be bothered nearly to death. But for Heaven's sake, don't be a fool over her. She's pretty enough, but there's nothing that you hold in your arms that is worth loving; it's only the soul inside a woman that counts, and when you find that, hold it with an iron hand, John, and keep it forever!"

Chapter 43

It was six weeks after this that Young Bob Pensteven and his wife sat together on the front veranda of their new little shack near Markham. They had not much of a house, not many acres of land, nor many cattle grazing on it; but there was not a man on the range who would have exchanged what the two of them possessed for millions and palaces. For they knew Pensteven and they knew his wife. As for the fewness of the acres, they would grow as the man grew; time cannot deal harshly with such a pair.

Now, through the gloom of the dusk, when the stars were beginning to burn through the twilight, a horseman loped up the hill toward the house.

"Somebody in a hurry," said Barbara Pensteven, "to go and burn his horse out uphill that way."

The rider came to a halt and dismounted.

"Pensteven?" he said.

"Great Scott, Red, is it you?" said Pensteven. "Do you want something?"

He hurried down the steps.

"Is it all right, John?" asked his wife anxiously. She still called him by that name.

"Of course, it's all right. Red's a good friend of mine," replied Bob Pensteven.

"Ma'am," said Red placatingly, "I know him from his left uppercut to his right cross. And he's the reason that my neck wasn't broken by a hangman's knot."

He drew Pensteven farther away into the gloom.

"Al Speaker sent me," he said.

"I know, Red," said Pensteven hastily. "I wish you weren't in that business."

"I'm stuck in it for good," said Red. "What's more, I wouldn't change it. But Al sent me down here with a message for you. Al thinks a lot of you."

"Thanks," said Pensteven.

"Al," continued the messenger, "is always talking about you, and he's always saying that honesty has the iron hand that wins in the end. Al's kind of a pessimist. He talks that way about honesty to us thugs every now and then."

"What was his message?" asked Pensteven.

"Well, it's like this. There was a couple of our fellows riding up a draw toward a railroad bridge, and they pulled up to see a long freight train go by. They was all empties, and the sliding door on the side of one of them freight cars —a box car—was wide open. Then they made out that some gents were having a fight inside the car, and pretty soon one of the men, he staggered back and stood on the edge of the door, waving his hands to catch his balance, but he couldn't get it, and he fell out.

"He come down and wrapped himself around an iron stringer, and he unwound from that like a loose rope end and fell down the rest of the way to the bottom of the canyon.

"The fellows rode up and took a look, and they was able to recognize the face, all right. You'd be interested to know who it was."

Pensteven shuddered.

"Was it Christmas?" he asked solemnly.

"It was him all right. Al thought you'd sleep better if you knew."

And Pensteven said slowly: "God help him. He was meant for better things."

THE UNSHAKABLE, UNSTOPPABLE, UNKILLABLE CAPTAIN GRINGO IS BACK IN:

RENEGADE #2, BLOOD RUNNER
by Ramsay Thorne   *(98-160, $1.50)*

They're waiting for a man like Captain Gringo in Panama! In this soggy, green hell where the French have lost a fortune in lives and francs trying to build a canal, the scum of the earth — and their scams — flourish. Every adventurer with a scheme, every rebel with a cause wants a man like Captain Gringo — running guns, unloosing a rain of death from his Maxim, fighting Yellow Jack, Indians, army ants, even the Devil himself if he stands in the way!